Books by Philip Ross

BLUE HERON
A GOOD DEATH
HOVEY'S DECEPTION
THE KREUZECK COORDINATES

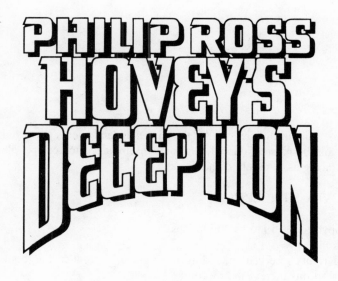

PHILIP ROSS
HOVEY'S
DECEPTION

TOR

A TOM DOHERTY ASSOCIATES BOOK

HOVEY'S DECEPTION

First printing: June 1986

A TOR Book

Published by Tom Doherty Associates
49 West 24 Street
New York, N.Y. 10010

ISBN: 0-312-93318-5

Library of Congress Catalog Card Number: 85-52256

Printed in the United States

0 9 8 7 6 5 4 3 2 1

CHAPTER 1

Mixed applause greeted the end of Professor Lawrence Hovey's presentation. Janos Czerny, with more than one motivation, clapped vigorously, leading his fellow advocates of interpretive revision. Leonid Leonidovitch Bondarchuk merely tapped right fingers against left palm, and most of the other scholars and purists followed his example. Since they, among the seminar participants, outnumbered the theater artists, the overall reception of Professor Hovey's paper might have been embarrassing, but there were students in the audience eager to endorse any break with orthodoxy, and the final volume of approval was provided by the secret police.

"Professor Hovey . . ." Bondarchuk waited until the clapping ended, and through the throat-clearing, shuffling, and murmur that always followed. He rose slowly from his place in the third row, looking at some papers, not looking left or right to see if anyone else might be seeking the floor, but taking it as his by right. Though not a professional practitioner of theater, he knew all he needed to about dramatic timing. Everyone expected he would lead the attack, and they were waiting for it. He made them wait. He stared at Professor Hovey as though searching through all the words he knew in twelve languages to find some equal to his incredulity. With a shrug he acknowledged that there were none; that meaning would have to be understood behind the simple ones he had to use.

"Professor Hovey, do you truly believe that Anton Chekhov wrote *Uncle Vanya* to advance the cause of feminism?"

Professor Hovey had known it would come. He leaned back in his chair behind the reading desk up on the dais, removed his glasses, dangled them from one hand just below his lips, and looked at Bondarchuk with the expression he used to assure students that they should never fear to question him, however uninformed, wrongheaded, and callow their biases might be. Professor Hovey welcomed the debate, which would be vicious. He would have enjoyed it at any time, but now it would distract him from the anxiety growing in him at each moment closer to the one when he would meet Janos Czerny personally, and carry out his mission as a secret agent.

•

"Thomas Talley took an ax, gave Westmoreland forty whacks; and when he saw what he had done, he gave Bill Colby forty-one."

"Hello, Walt."

"Hello, Tom. Do I dare get out of the car?"

"I'll put it away."

"What kind of an ax is that?"

"It's not an ax; it's a splitting maul." Talley went around the car and put the maul into a front corner of the nearly full woodshed adjoining his house. Walter Simson got out, but remained on the far side of the car, looking over the hood.

Although Talley wore a checked shirt and corduroy trousers, and handled the tool like a person accustomed to it, Simson had the sense that he would never pass successfully as a country man. Out of constant habit he tried to analyze why that was. Not because of Talley's professorial eyeglasses, nor the neat haircut; not because he was used to seeing Talley in other clothes and surroundings, and knew these were recent. He decided he would have to study country people more closely before knowing how Talley differed, but there was something about him, his manner, that was different.

Simson let the line of thought pass quickly. He had to concentrate on sensing and responding to Talley's mood at the moment, not on his general character. That mood, he could feel, was ambivalent. Talley seemed glad to see him, and yet cool as well. As a way of starting conversation, Simson glanced up at the bright, warm, mid-May sky. "I'd think you could take a break from your wood-chopping for a while, Tom. I think it's really going to be spring."

"Up here you learn it's best to be prepared."

"You split all that with that thing?"

"I do most of it with a power splitter. I just save out a cord to do by hand from time to time. It works out aggressions."

Simson looked at the panorama of fields, woods, and mountains beyond Talley's snug cottage. "I wouldn't think you'd have many aggressions in a place like this."

"I don't. One cord usually lasts me a whole year."

"How come you're working on it today?"

"How come you're here?"

Simson smiled his good-fellow smile. Talley recognized it; he had worked for Simson before, with men who had looked like the patchy academics they otherwise would have been. And Simson, with that smile, had always looked like a college president. Even fifteen years ago his hair had been thin and silvery, his glasses gold-rimmed, his suits three-piece and pin-striped but a little loose, and he seemed to be able to bland his way through any unpleasantness. President of a good school, but not one of the best, probably in the Middle West. He never offended anyone, but you had to know him well to like him.

"I guess I couldn't get away with saying I was just passing through this way."

"No, Walt. I pass through Washington sometimes, and you pass through Boston sometimes. Only migrating geese pass through northern New Hampshire."

"Okay, but how do you know it's bad news? I just said I wanted to talk with you."

"Maybe I'm still drawing unwarranted conclusions. You want to come in?"

"Thanks." Simson joined Talley, and they strolled up the path of large flat stones set into the lawn. "You're still enjoying country life?"

"Oh, yes. Wouldn't live anywhere else."

"Have you made many friends? I should think it would be lonely."

"I have. Some. But it is."

"I was awfully sorry to hear about your divorce."

"So was I."

"Do you think you'll marry again?"

Talley held open the screen door. "Yeah, I think about it." He smiled ruefully. "I'd say I think about it . . . oh . . . about sixteen thousand times a day."

"I'm sorry."

They went down the hallway and into the tidy kitchen. Talley paused.

"Can I get you something? I've got some decaffeinated instant."

"No, thanks. I've decided that if I can't have the real thing, the hell with it."

"It's a little early for a drink. Will you stay to lunch? We could call it a drink before lunch."

"Yeah, I'd like to stay for lunch. But it is a little early. Why don't we just get to it, Tom?"

"Good."

They went into the living room and sat in two Eames chairs that faced each other in front of the now cold wood stove. Simson glanced around, taking in the house, still trying to judge how his friend fit into this world. He did fit somehow with the house. It was an old country house, but Simson decided the match was not in any particularly rural quality; it was in the straight lines of the uncarpeted wideboard floor, the exposed posts and beams, the straightforwardness—the revealed structure.

Simson had not removed his jacket or loosened his tie. Talley offered the use of the ottoman between them, but Simson sat with his feet on the floor. Talley knew, then, that the forthcoming conversation would be formal and unpleasant. He slouched into his chair, with his own legs up, out of perversity.

Talley's attitude was the one Walter Simson had expected. He had thought of several approaches he might use in overcoming it, and had decided to begin with the story. That would be straightforward and open, and would minimize his own sense of manipulating a friend. Of course it would be a manipulation, too: if he could interest Talley in the story, in the problem, he'd have him. Simson had long ago decided that all human relationships involved manipulations; the only distinctions to be made were in purpose and method.

He began, "Okay, Tom. You undoubtedly know everything that's been in the media for the past two weeks about Janos Czerny—the arrest, the trial."

"Yeah. It looks like the agency really screwed up again." Talley tried to sound neutral, but he couldn't hide completely his satisfaction.

"Yes. It does look that way."

"Ah. I see. And what would make any of us think that's not what happened?"

"The clincher in the trial—what seemed to prove the Czechs hadn't just set Czerny up themselves with faked documents—was Professor Hovey's confession. There is no doubt—no one at the trial doubted: none of the press, none of our embassy people—that the confession was genuine. He says he was sent to contact Czerny by the agency. Well, he wasn't."

"You say so."

"I know so."

"But does the right hand know?"

"It wouldn't have been done; it wasn't. Take my word for it now. I'll tell you in a minute why we can be sure, why Hovey's story makes no sense. What does make sense is that the Czechs set him up themselves, as a way of setting up Czerny.

"Look at it, Tom—from their perspective: it's beautiful. I mean, if they'd tried seriously to shut up Czerny when he was just criticizing them, condemning Afghanistan, supporting Solidarity, they'd have made him a martyr. If they'd done it by proving he was the one who got out the Kropotkin manifesto, or Pawel's plays—they'd have made him a hero.

But to catch him red-handed trying to give military secrets to the CIA—then he's a traitor, threatening the lives of his own countrymen. He's nothing but a tool of American imperialism. And by extension backward, everything that he'd said and done—all his so-called 'human rights advocacy'—is discredited as the same thing.

"And as for Lawrence Hovey, here's the CIA infiltrating the academic community, polluting cultural exchanges, cynically deceiving and manipulating scholars, and then cold-heartedly abandoning them."

Talley raised his eyebrows in mock horror. "Golly, Walt! How could anyone believe we'd do things like that?"

"Okay, Tom—but we didn't. Not this time. Now I'm going to give you some highly classified information."

"I'm not under the contract now."

Simson touched the breast of his jacket. "I've got a new paper. Just for today."

"I won't sign it. I don't want to receive any information."

"Tom . . . please."

"Don't put it that way, Walt."

Simson took the folded sheet of paper from his pocket, opened it, extended it. "Tom, I'd like to talk to you. I know I can trust you, but *you* know it's my ass if anybody ever found I'd told you things without having you sign. It's bad enough I haven't had your clearance updated. So, please."

Arousing Talley's interest would be the best way to get him. There were two other approaches, though. Simson went on to the second. "*I'm* asking you to. I need your help." He brought out a ball-point pen, clicked the point down. "Just listen."

Talley finally leaned forward and took the paper and pen. He scanned the brief statement to be sure. It was the standard acknowledgment that he had received classified information

and agreed not to divulge . . . under penalties . . . article
. . . section number. . . . He rested the page against his
thigh and scrawled his signature.

"Thank you, Tom." Simson took back the paper and pen,
returned them to his pocket. "All right. First, Czerny *was* in
contact with us—with the agency. He was passing military
material."

"Jesus Christ! Military?"

"Evidently he had come to feel that, failing disarmament,
the cause of peace would be best served by keeping the arms
race even. At least, he didn't want the Russians to get ahead.
So, he put out the word through his net of artists and intellec-
tuals that he would receive material relating to arms matters.
And since that kind of stuff isn't like what he used to just slip
to a journalist or publisher, he made contact with us."

Talley straightened from his slouch. "And he thought he'd
get away with it? He must have known they'd be watching
him because of everything else."

"I've seen the profile on him, done when we were deciding whether to take him up. What people say about him as a
director must apply generally: vanity even bigger than his
talent. Either he thought he *would* get away with it, or if they
caught him he'd rise again on the third day.

"But now we're going to get to the main point, Tom.
Czerny almost always carried out his material himself—
especially the military material. He never handed that over in
his own country. Well, a big-time international celebrity—he
was always going in and out—how could we do better?"

Talley shook his head. "Except that he would have been
watched, and probably searched. Wouldn't he?"

"Up to a point. As long as they were going to let him go
out at all, they couldn't hassle him past a point."

"But they'd get to his baggage, any papers."

"Sure. And that's part of it. We had . . . let's say we had given him a very good invisible ink.

"Okay, so he was supposed to be going to Vienna for conferences on a new production of *Figaro* he was going to do there next year. That was to be at the end of February, two weeks before the Chekhov seminar. Then, after the seminar, toward the end of March, he was supposed to go to Paris and do *Hamlet*. Suddenly he was told that the Ministry of Culture wanted him to give three lectures in the Soviet Union before the seminar, and delay going to Paris so he could do something at the State Theater in Prague afterward. They didn't ask him.

"I guess he didn't know what to do. He had just gotten word that he would be passed some really hot material. So he—"

"Don't tell me."

"You got it. The stuff they caught him with. So, the only chance he was going to have to pass it on soon would be at the Chekhov seminar. Now, it just so happened that the designer for *Hamlet* was in Prague conferring with him when he got the orders from the Ministry of Culture. When the designer gets home to Paris he brings word to us that the material is coming—that it has to be passed at the seminar, and he has a protocol from Czerny to be used so he'll recognize whoever we send as contact."

"Oh, boy."

"Right. This makes the Frenchman look bad—part of the setup. But the point is this: two weeks after Czerny was arrested, someone—a prominent international artist who is a defector, okay?—made contact with one of our embassies and asked to see the military attaché. Not someone on the attaché's staff—*the* attaché. He delivered some material that had come to him through a contact he wouldn't identify except to say that it had come from the Soviet Union. The message with the material was that it had been left in safe-keeping, to be passed along only if something happened to Janos Czerny, in which case it was to be given to someone who would get it to a high level of *military* intelligence before it was seen by the CIA.''

"No shit.''

"And the material is good, it's valuable, and of course we have to presume it's what Czerny was going to pass at the seminar.''

Facts. What relationships could be made among them, what conclusions drawn? Simson sat back and let Talley run it for himself, knowing he would.

"Okay,'' Talley said after only a moment. "That's a setup too. They feed you some genuine product, expendable, so that it looks like Czerny thought he might be betrayed from within the agency.''

"That's what we all believe, Tom. Except General Cartwright at DIA, but that's to be expected. But we also agree that though it's all probably just a really neat ploy by the opposition, we do have to look into it. I mean, we can't just ignore the possibility of a leak, or a penetration. There's one more point.''

"What?''

"We did have a contact for Czerny at the seminar. A civilian, a guy named MacDonald—professor out at Indiana. And he was blocked. *He* was, not Czerny, not anyone else with access to Czerny. Just our man.''

At the farm down the hill beyond Talley's property a tractor drove around a field. Birdsong filled the air. All the sounds came clearly through the open windows, yet both men had a sense of profound silence as they considered the implications of Simson's story.

Finally Talley spoke. "All right, Walt. Why are you telling me this?"

"Well, as I said, everybody believes this is all just a setup, primarily to get Czerny, but doing us some damage on the side. But it does have to be looked into. So, who's going to do the looking? We—the agency—feel we should handle it ourselves, as an internal matter."

"Naturally."

"Naturally. However . . . You know enough about how HUMINT works. Normally the identity of a source would be known by only a few people: control, case officer, the people who were actually dealing with him. People above wouldn't know it unless there was a special need to know. Well, Czerny being who he is, there was thought to be a need. Chief HUMINT knew. The director and Operations knew. And some deputies and assistants. Just a few, but . . ."

"Strategically placed."

"Yes."

"So, here's the problem, Tom. If we handle the investigation internally, and we find that—as we believe—there is no leak, no penetration, who's going to believe it? Who's going to believe it wasn't a coverup? On the other hand, if we let the FBI do it, or DIA—Cartwright is more than willing—they're going to want to get their hands into everything. The more they don't find, the more they're going to want to look. Wouldn't they love to get on to our sources? And dig dirt? They might not find anything wrong about this Czerny thing, but you can just bet they'd find all kinds of things the oversight committees, or even Jack Anderson—I wouldn't put it past them—ought to be let know about. The director isn't going to stand for that, and he's got his friends on the committees, too."

"So what are they doing about it?"

"What else? A committee has been formed. Representatives from DIA, FBI, President's oversight, House and Senate committees, NSA, the National Security Advisor's staff, and the agency: everybody. With someone from the agency as chairman, to confirm we're not being examined from outside as though we were presumed guilty. Me."

"Oh, hell, Walt, why *you?*"

"They wanted someone from the analysis side, since Operations might be tainted; I'm about the highest ranking person who didn't know about Czerny; and—best of all— I've got just two more years until I retire. I don't have to worry about my career. No matter how this turns out, I'll still get my gold watch."

"You poor son of a bitch." Talley's sympathy was genuine, but then he shook his head. "Walt, I don't know what you want me to do to help you on this, but I'm not going to do it."

"I thought you would."

"No. I'm sorry. We're friends, and I might do a lot of things for you, personally . . . but not for the agency."

Simson started his third approach. "I thought you'd want to."

"What would make you think that?"

"I would think you'd find it very satisfying. This is serious, Tom. You can appreciate that, even if you are enjoying it. The kind of suspicion that's been raised here would be devastating if—to be safe—a major section of the agency's leadership is taken out. But how could they be left in under suspicion? It could ruin the careers, maybe the lives of half a dozen people, all of them probably innocent, all but one certainly so. You aren't vindictive enough to want that, are you?"

Talley raised his eyebrows and smiled slightly.

"No, you're not, Tom. If you were that kind of guy you'd never have quit the way you did. Now, I need someone as a personal assistant, to help me go over the lines in this, to help think up new lines, to look at all the pieces very carefully and find how they go together. There's been a once-over already: the FBI has already talked to people at Hovey's college and so forth, but it was just routine, can't be considered any more than preliminary. Everything needs to be looked over and maybe done again by someone who really knows how to get into things."

"You mean in the field?"

"If necessary."

"I don't do that. I just look at product. You want somebody from Operations who—"

"I want you. I can get all the regular staff I need, and obviously those people will do the internal work, in the agency. But I need someone who can look at the data and see the animals hiding where everyone else just sees the bushes. And also, I would like to contract someone from outside, someone who can't be suspected of wanting to cover up, and I want it to be someone I know, someone I trust, someone whose work I know is good."

"You can find other people—"

"Sure. I'm not going to try to persuade you that the fate of Western civilization is on your shoulders, and no one else can carry it. If you won't do it, I'll find someone else. But I want you, because I think you're the best. And I would think the idea of the agency coming to *you* for help would give you a lot of satisfaction; would be a kind of vindication."

Talley looked to the side, through the window at the green lawn and budding lilac bush. "Yeah. Yeah, Walt. Even after all these years . . . yes, it would still give me some satisfaction to rub some noses in it. But how would you get away with it? They'd never accept your using me."

"Then I'll threaten to resign from the committee."

"Will you?" Talley tried to keep it flat, but the edge was there.

"Yes, because they couldn't accept it. It would look too bad. I have that power now, Tom; I didn't have it fifteen years ago."

The men looked at each other levelly. Finally Simson said, "I'm asking you, Tom. I'm appealing to you. For patriotism. Because this is important, this can hurt us—the country—and you can see that. Or just for yourself. Settle the account. I offer you the gift of revenge."

Talley sat still for several moments. "If I do it," he said, "do I have to tell you which?"

•

It all happened quickly, at the end.

The chairman had finally signaled to the technician to give his microphone more volume, and calmly kept thundering, "Thank you, Herr Scheel; thank you, Doktor Krantz; thank you, gentlemen; this session is ended, thank you. Thank you, Professor Hovey. This session is ended." He continued until enough people had risen so that Scheel and Krantz could no longer see to shout at one another. It was five minutes past the hour, and the chairman saw no need to allow the discussion further overtime, especially since it had so degenerated.

The end was slow in coming, though. Debate continued. Smashing its focus, which had been held by the men from the two Germanys, merely scattered it throughout the room.

(Professor Hovey's paper had certainly made the seminar exciting, and that was justification enough for inviting him, if that was what the ministry wanted. The chairman had yet to comprehend any other reason.) Knots and blocs of people stood arguing with one another, everyone speaking at once, of course; their intellectual passions had been aroused so highly that it took some time before they began to realize they could be eating hors d'oeuvres and drinking champagne, without having to stop talking, if they would but pass into the next room. A group blocking the door seemed to be the last to achieve this enlightenment.

The room into which they all finally went spread across an acre of gardenlike Oriental carpet to walls forested in green damask, and up those to a high heaven where plaster cherubs dangled crystal chandeliers. In contrast to the meeting chamber, which had been quite cool (possibly to keep the audience alert), this grand salon was a balmy oasis within the mid-March cold that still claimed Prague for winter. Perhaps the heat, the sense of space, or the food and drink altered the mood of the seminar participants enough that confrontations of antagonists dispersed, and the discussion went on more among groups of the like-minded.

Professor Hovey found himself the center of a large one. Half a dozen people were trying to tell him all at once how brilliant they thought he was for having formulated so forcefully ideas that agreed with theirs, and pointing out implications of his philosophy that might not have come to his attention. There were more than those six people around him, but Professor Hovey thought the two silent ones were merely other scholars uncharacteristically listening. He had no realization that they were police.

He was worried, of course. He tried to focus his worry on how he would meet and manage to be alone with Janos

Czerny so that he could deliver his message, rather than about the possibility of arrest. He had, after all, been assured that there was no possibility of arrest. His mission required him merely to speak to Czerny, to say a sentence that would have meaning to that hero of the universal struggle for intellectual freedom even though it had none for him who delivered it, and to receive a similar reply. Unconsciously he fingered the red and white striped necktie he had been given to wear, making sure that it showed prominently.

The problem that worried him solved itself. All at once some of the crowd fell back. The man who had been telling Hovey as rapidly as possible why Shakespeare should be totally rewritten in prose looked up and stopped mid-word. Czerny himself towered next to him, looking (as some admiring film columnist had put it) like a great, angry white eagle.

"Professor Hovey," he said, tipping his head forward a degree in a gesture of imperial graciousness. "Czerny," he said.

"Mr. Czerny, ah, what a pleasure. How do you do?"

Those who had been pressing close to Hovey, positioning themselves to speak, drew away slightly in deference to the great man, but they remained close enough to listen, in hope of hearing an artistic insight or at least a quotable cut at Bondarchuk and his school. They were disappointed. Czerny congratulated Hovey effusively on his paper. In fact, he said, he had found it so provocative that he would like to pursue a point or two in greater depth if Professor Hovey would grant him a moment away from his other admirers.

Hovey said of course he would, how honored he would be, in a voice so loud and eager that it might have made the onlookers wonder what emotions it was meant to mask. They didn't wonder, though. Most thought Hovey's excitement a natural reaction to praise from Janos Czerny.

The policemen stepped back with the rest, allowing Czerny to steer Hovey (by a hand on his elbow) out of the group and across the room. They couldn't, without being noticed, follow closely enough to see if something were handed over, but one caught the eye of an attentive waiter.

The room was full but not crowded. The two men made an easy, winding way past groups of talkers. For Hovey the passage was like a dream in delirium. Sweat ran down his neck and soaked his back. Glints from the chandeliers hurt his eyes; the light seemed intense, glaring, as inescapably revealing as a tropical sun at noon. People they passed materialized suddenly and vanished just as fast before any impression of their features could be formed. The din of conversation was ringing in his ears.

Czerny, leaning slightly toward the shorter man, murmured words incomprehensible to him until they reached one side of the room where a couch sat flanked by potted palms.

"Shall we sit here?"

That, Hovey understood. "Yes. Fine. Thank you."

Czerny had on the pleasant face he could assume if convinced an occasion required it. He presented it to Hovey.

Hovey smiled back, though his eyes looked as though he were about to be ill.

After a moment of waiting Czerny said, "That is a very nice necktie you are wearing."

"Ah, thank you." Regaining awareness, Hovey blurted, "Oh! I should like to see the Moldau sometime. I hear it's very beautiful."

Czerny nodded, looking even more pleasant. "It is. It runs through Prague, but it is more beautiful in the countryside. Perhaps you will be able to see it someday."

And that's all there is to it! Hovey thought. He heard Czerny's words again and again in his mind so that he would be able to repeat them exactly. But that was easy to do, because they were so simple, so innocent! Relief swept over him like a cool breeze. He could say those words to anyone. No one could suspect, could accuse him because of those words. His head began to clear and his smile became genuine.

The party was at an early stage. Still slaking themselves, greeting friends, most of the guests stayed on their feet, congregating toward the center of the room. Only a few had moved to sit on the couches around the sides as Czerny and Hovey had done.

From many places, even within the crowd, those two could easily be seen chatting in their isolation. When Czerny, having praised Professor Hovey extensively, asked if he might have as a souvenir the copy of Hovey's paper that had been read from in his presentation, autographed, Hovey could easily be seen responding with delight; he could be seen drawing the folded sheets from his jacket, taking his pen, laying the pages on his knee, signing, handing them over. And then when Czerny, in return, offered a paper of his own, Hovey could be seen at first still delighted, then having one moment of awful apprehension.

And then the end happened very quickly.

CHAPTER 2

Evidently the concierge, if that was the correct word for him, was accustomed to dealing with foreigners. He held an expression of pain endured in good humor while Talley explained in his execrable French that he had come to see Monsieur D'Avignon, who was expecting him. Talley could never decide which was the greater embarrassment—using that language so badly or seeming to require people to speak a foreign tongue in their own country.

The man nodded as he said *"Oui, monsieur"* so that Talley would be sure to understand the answer as affirmative. *"Prenez l'ascenseur, s'il vous plaît. L'a-scen-seur."* He raised and lowered his hand, palm up, several times. *"Là,"* he pointed. *"Le deuxième étage."* He held up two fingers.

Talley knew his ears were red. He thanked him, and went along what was the building's entrance corridor, although it looked like a steam tunnel. The walls were of pitted concrete, and pipes and cable raceways ran exposed. He went up in an elevator whose walls looked and smelled as though they had been made of reprocessed automobile tires.

19

When he got out, he found himself in what was essentially a single huge, long room under a sloping glass roof. For some reason that must have seemed good to the architect, the roof was hung from steel girderwork rather than being supported by it. Pigeons in multitudes had found the design good too; their droppings spattered and streaked the glass, following the pattern of the structure above, unaffected by the steady spring rain.

Movable partitions cut the room into separate work spaces. A man stood out from one of them, clearly waiting for Talley. He wore black trousers and a black turtleneck, a small man, thin, with a dark beard that did not conceal or strengthen his receding chin.

"Monsieur D'Avignon?"

The man smiled, extending his hand, and said, "Meestair Tal-LEE?"

Talley knew he was being slashed for his own mispronunciation, since from then on D'Avignon spoke very good English, only slightly accented, but the blade was so finely honed, the cut so swift, that he'd never prove it.

D'Avignon gestured Talley into the cubicle and to a chrome and black plastic chair at one side. A goggle-eyed mask glared like a gargoyle down at them; sketches, drawings on flimsy yellow paper, and swatches of fabric carnavalled the walls.

As though he were Mephistopheles among his visions, the designer perched on a high stool at the drafting table where, evidently, he had been working. Though he looked at Talley pleasantly, he projected the sense of having been interrupted and wanting to get back to his mysteries.

"Thank you for seeing me," Talley said. "I'm sure you're very busy."

D'Avignon shrugged. "One of the rules of the theater is that there is never enough time."

"I won't take much of it, then. I'm sure whoever called you from the embassy told you I'm trying to find out some things about the Janos Czerny business."

"Yes." It seemed more of an effort for D'Avignon to maintain his pleasantness, but he managed. "I take it that you are from the CIA."

"No, I'm not."

D'Avignon rocked his head to the side in an expression of not believing but not arguing.

"It doesn't really matter to me whether you believe me. If it's important to you, then I'll tell you again: while obviously I am working for the United States government in trying to find out some things, I'm not with the CIA."

"I don't think it really matters to me, either, Mr. Talley. What is it you wish to know from me?"

"You were in Prague in early January, conferring with Czerny about a production he was going to do here this fall, correct?"

"Yes."

"And he asked you to get a message to someone here in Paris."

"Yes."

"Did he tell you why he wanted you to do this?"

"Yes. He said he would be receiving something that he wanted to bring out of Czechoslovakia but that unexpected obligations placed upon him would make it impossible for him to carry it out himself until he came here in July, and it was important that whatever it was should come out sooner. I—"

D'Avignon clamped his lips for a moment, then went on. "I had no idea. . . . Janos Czerny is a great man. A great, great artist, and a great, brave man. I considered myself honored to be asked to help him, because I thought this whatever-it-was he wanted to get out would be something like Bronek Pawel's plays, or some document dealing with matters of human rights. I had no idea . . . I can only believe that someone, some *agency*"—D'Avignon looked narrowly at Talley—"deluded him, misled him into thinking that he could serve the cause of peace—one of his greatest concerns— by becoming involved in espionage."

"You had no idea the person you were to contact here was CIA?"

"If I had known that, Mr. Talley, I would have refused to carry the message for Janos. I must tell you that I feel he deceived me. This does to me—this *causes* me much pain, because I thought we were friends."

"I see. What, exactly, was the message?"

"What I have told the person who came here previously: that he would be receiving material that must be transmitted as soon as possible. That Czerny could not bring it out himself until July. That, therefore, someone should be sent to the seminar on Chekhov which would be held in March. That the person should identify himself by wearing a certain color *cravate*—necktie—one having stripes, red and white—and then, when Janos and he were able to speak, that he should say something about the Moldau."

"That was all?"

"That was all."

"Did you speak to anyone else—anyone besides Mr. Hendricks here in Paris—about this matter?"

D'Avignon looked steadily at Talley, looked as though anger were rising and he were struggling to control it. "No," he said at last in a tight voice. "No, I did not speak to anyone else about this matter."

"Mr. D'Avignon, I'm not implying anything. My questions

are purely routine. For all I know, you and Mr. Czerny may have close friends in common with whom it would have been perfectly natural for you to have discussed this matter."

"I am more discreet."

"When Czerny made his request, were the circumstances— do you believe it possible you might have been overheard?"

"No. We were walking by the river. It was a cold, gray day, a light snow was beginning to fall, and Janos wanted me to feel that atmosphere and capture it in my design. (We have worked together often—for films as well as for the theater.) We often worked in that way: he would suggest a place, a time of day, and we would go there, and he would say, 'So.' And I would capture it for him."

Talley pictured for an instant this small, dark man and the huge white-haired Czerny strolling beside a gray river. He suddenly realized the picture came easily because he had already seen one like it, probably in a magazine article on Czerny, the genius instructing his minions, and D'Avignon had been one of them.

"Really? I've seen most of Czerny's films, of course. And of course everyone says how wonderful he is in getting an atmosphere. *The Wild Swan, Autumn Dreams.* Did you do the design for those?"

"Yes."

"I never realized that. Well, thank you, Mr. D'Avignon. It was very good of you to see me." Talley stood.

D'Avignon slid off his stool and offered his hand. "Good-bye, Mr. Talley."

"Good-bye." Talley started to turn away, then paused. "If you had known what kind of material Czerny was trying to pass, would you have tried to stop him?"

"Yes. By trying to persuade him. Because I would have felt that if he continued, I would lose a dear friend and the theater would lose one of its greatest artists. The people who are responsible for involving Janos in espionage have done a harm to the world—have caused a great loss. But then, they are the same people who would incinerate us all to save us, no?''

•

Narrow nameplates set at right angles to the doors identified faculty offices. Talley came to that of Professor Boudreau before reaching the departmental office, so he didn't have himself announced.

The door stood open. Professor Boudreau sat writing. Her desk faced a side wall; the window was in the end one beyond her. Sunlight struck the thick white wooden window-casing, reflecting into the room. She was turned away from Talley, toward the window, to write; her head tipped in a way that suggested to him a detachment from the words appearing on the yellow pad, even a skepticism about them. Something in the Vermeer-like pose kept him standing in the corridor, silent, watching her.

She paused, raised her eyes from the page to the wall before her, then swiveled and saw him standing in the open doorway.

''Professor Boudreau? May I speak with you for a few moments?''

''Certainly.''

He took the chair next to the end of the desk. ''My name is Thomas Talley.''

''Jane Boudreau.'' She had pushed back, rolling herself a

little away from the desk. She leaned forward again and shook his hand.

Talley sat erect and kept his stomach pulled in. Meeting such an attractive woman always did wonders for his posture. He knew she might be hostile when he told her his business, so he used the salesman's trick of establishing a friendly relationship before getting down to it.

"This is a very pleasant office," he said.

"Thank you," she said. "It seems only fitting that history should be in the oldest building on campus, so we get these lovely big old rooms: cool in the summer, freezing all winter."

"Your plants seem to like it. Does your Christmas cactus bloom?"

"Oh, yes."

"I can't get mine to. It's growing just fine, puts out new leaves. But I couldn't get it to set any buds last fall."

"Did you put it in a closet? You know, if they get too much light . . ."

"It wasn't that, I'm sure. It's in my bedroom. It gets hardly any artificial light."

"Even a streetlight outside . . ."

"I live in the country."

"Perhaps too much water. They have to dry between waterings in order to set. If it's not light, it's likely to be that."

"Could be. I'll try giving it a little less."

"Do you have many plants?" she asked seriously, as though it were important to know about his possessions, his interests. She didn't seem to be talking superficially. He had the feeling that nothing about her would be superficial. Maybe that was because she wore glasses, the cinema symbol for intellectuality. Talley thought Professor Boudreau probably looked better with glasses. Without them her nose might seem a little large, and . . .

Suddenly he was aware of the appraisal in *her* eyes as she looked at *him*. "No, they were left by my former wife."

"Ah. I have a lot of plants. I have them all over my house, too. I suppose they're a substitute for children."

He smiled. Her self-revelation seemed an acceptance and an exchange for his. He felt that she might be as interested as he in their getting to know each other. That surprised him, because of her relationship with Professor Hovey.

"Well," he said. He nodded abruptly and Professor Boudreau nodded once too: the official conversation would begin.

Talley started in the roundabout way he'd planned. "I make a living as a consultant, a sort of analyst, mostly for companies that do business in Southeast Asia. I prepare reports, projections on whatever they need to know: local politics, economics, whatever. I imagine that my work is actually a lot like yours, only reversed. Your book on Carrie Nation—brilliant, if I may say so—was done by finding all the things in her life that made her what she was, the facts about the people who supported her, opposed her. You put her in a context. Well, I start with all sorts of facts, try to form a context out of them, and project what *will* happen. A very similar process, I would think."

Professor Boudreau put her elbows on the arms of her chair, steepled her fingers against her chin.

Talley went on. "As I said, I'm self-employed now— working for commercial corporations. But I used to work for the government, doing—"

Professor Boudreau lowered her hands to her lap. Her shoulders came up, and a wall came down between her and Talley.

"You work for the CIA."

"No, I don't. I did once, but now I'm—"

"You were indirect because you thought that if you told me the truth, I would refuse to speak with you."

"Yes, but I don't—"

"You were right. Good-bye, Mr. Talley."

"Professor Boudreau—"

"Good-bye."

"Professor Boudreau, you're a scholar. It's not scholarly—"

"Mr. Talley!" she almost shouted.

Talley kept his seat but let his voice rise above hers: "—to refuse even to listen—"

She shot to her feet. The swivel chair snapped upright behind her. She did shout: "Get out of this office at once or I will—"

Talley jabbed one forefinger up at her. "Refuse to *listen*! Blind prejudice! Know-nothing! Closed-minded!"

Professor Boudreau stood wavering.

Another voice came from the doorway: "Is everything all right, Jane?" A short bald man with a beard stood there.

Talley kept his eyes on Professor Boudreau.

"Yes, Peter. Thank you."

"You're sure?"

"I'm quite sure, Peter. Thank you."

Reluctantly, Peter went away, an unemployed knight-errant.

Professor Boudreau hesitated, standing, for another moment, then sat again abruptly. "Well?"

"My employment with the Central Intelligence Agency terminated in 1971. Officially, I terminated it, but there was pretty extreme prejudice on both sides."

"Why?"

"There was . . . what you might call a scholarly dispute, a dispute about what certain facts meant. Or should mean. Or whether, if the facts didn't meant what certain powers thought they should mean, the problem was with the facts, and therefore they should be ignored or changed.''

"And why are you telling me this?''

"To remind you that you shouldn't make absolute judgments based on partial data.'' He chanced saying that, and for an instant it did make her more angry. But his own quick judgment had been correct: she was a person who listened. She nodded, accepting the rebuke and letting him go on.

"And because once again there's a question about the facts and what they mean. I've been persuaded that the question is important enough that I should help look for some answers. I've told you about myself to try to convince you that if *I* can be persuaded of that, you ought at least to listen and to help me if you can.''

"Who persuaded you?''

"An old friend—a former colleague. He's still with the agency. I'm sort of under contract, just like with any other client. I don't like this one, but I don't have to like my clients. And I have been persuaded of the importance of the job. And I think doing it is of importance to Lawrence Hovey—may be of help to him. And I need your help.''

•

The boy crept a step closer. He held his hands up in front of himself, palms stiffened, the way he'd seen them held in the movies. Chip Bolander watched him, waited for him, standing on guard, slightly crouched, weight balanced, his own hands at waist level.

The boy had seen a lot of those movies; he thought he

knew a trick or two. He faked a jab with his left hand, then kicked upward at Bolander.

With the grace of a bullfighter, Bolander pivoted backward, grabbed the boy's ankle and twisted, shoved against his buttock, and then, clutching his trouser seat, eased the boy—rather than slamming him—facedown on the mat. He stepped back, waited until the boy had gotten himself up, then bowed.

Most of the other kids standing around the mat laughed, and several of them tried to ask questions at once. Bolander recognized one of the youngest.

"Mr. Bolander, what would you do if somebody had a knife?"

"Try it and see." From his gear at one side he took a foot-long rubber Bowie knife and extended it handle first, smiling and nodding to encourage the lad.

Apprehensively, the boy turned the knife from hand to hand, eyeing Bolander, who (still smiling) had stepped back to await his attack.

"Go on, Mikey! Go on, try it!"

Mikey suddenly flung his fist above his head and ran to strike at Bolander's chest.

It was no trick to parry him, and because the boy was so small, and because Chip Bolander liked to give a good show, instead of tripping or knocking him aside, he grabbed the boy's arm and belt, swung him high overhead, and laid him back-down on the mat. The crowd laughed and clapped and cheered, but Bolander kept his face neutral and bowed respectfully to his vanquished opponent.

For another fifteen minutes Bolander took on all comers, four of them at once for his grand finale. Then, as the boys sat and sprawled around him, he gave his summation.

"Now, of course if somebody has a gun and stands ten feet away from you and pulls the trigger, you've had it. Bought the farm, as they used to say. But what I've tried to show you tonight is that in any kind of a close encounter, if a man knows how to use his hands and his body, he's got nothing to worry about.

"And—even if it's out of style to think so these days—I happen to think it's important for a man to have that feeling. I think that if a man has that feeling, that confidence . . . well, it's a funny thing: he's probably never going to have to use what he knows. The men who try to push other men around, the bullies, they're usually the ones who're worried about themselves. So they pick on some guy they think is weaker, to prove something to themselves. But the man who can take care of himself—he doesn't need to pick on anybody. And if he has that confidence, and other people know he can take care of himself, then nobody is going to pick on him. And you can apply that philosophy to politics and international relations, too, if you want to. That's not what I'm here to talk about tonight, so I won't say any more, but you can just think about it if you want to.

"Anyway, I hope you all have enjoyed this demonstration. It's been a real pleasure for me to be here and to meet all you guys. And, of course, if any of you want to take up a serious study of the martial arts, I'd be happy to see you down at the school. Thanks again for inviting me."

While the Boy Scouts were having their closing ceremonies and their cookies and punch, Bolander showered and dressed in the locker room. He knotted his knit tie carefully, and buffed away a blemish on his spit-shined cordovans. He didn't have to comb his hair: what was left he kept buzzed down. He'd always worn it that way, and though he didn't try to hide the baldness on top, he thought it better not to make a point of it in contrast to long sides. His mustache had grown back fully; he was pleased to be past that dirty-lip stage while it came in.

Before picking up his canvas bag and leaving, he checked his appearance carefully in the full-length mirror. He had nothing else planned for that evening, was only going home to watch TV, but he always tried to look good. Charles Patrick "Chip" Bolander believed a man should always take care of himself.

•

"You're going to record this?"

"I don't have to"—Talley paused, holding the little tape machine above the corner of Professor Boudreau's desk—"I can take notes. But I find—in going over things—that even just the way someone says something, a pause, can suggest a new idea to me. Do you mind?"

"I guess not, really. It somehow seems to add a more . . . inquisitorial tone. Everything I say really is being taken down and may be used against me."

"It's not going to be used against anyone. But if you'd really prefer . . ." He hesitated, but didn't move to put the machine back into his case.

"No. It's all right."

She seemed to be a person who followed through with decisions once made. She had agreed to an interview, asking Talley to return at four, after she had finished giving an exam.

A typewriter crackled in the departmental office down the

hall, but it could barely be heard after Talley closed Professor Boudreau's door. Few of the faculty seemed to be in their offices, and there had been no students in the corridor. It was easy to believe that everyone in the college had gone out to bask by the blossoming trees. The springtime sun, high even in late afternoon, shone brightly on the lawn, but its light entered the office now in reflection. Professor Boudreau had not turned on the overhead fluorescent fixture, nor did Talley, so they sat in a sort of comfortable twilight.

Talley liked that mood, liked to work in that kind of light. It reminded him of great old libraries; it was vellum-colored, soft as ancient leather bindings.

Professor Boudreau liked it too. It knew no rush. It was a time to speculate, and to be meticulous. Under its influence she settled back in her chair, prepared to answer his questions. She could not deny that her interest in Talley had grown during the afternoon as she had thought about seeing him again. Was it the light, she wondered, that now made his features seem both sharper and less threatening? Why did she suddenly feel so at ease with him?

"Well, to begin somewhere," Talley said, "what do you know of how Professor Hovey came to go to the Chekhov seminar? Did he apply? Was he invited? How did it happen?"

"He was invited to apply. Back in February—this all happened very quickly—he got a letter from some foundation suggesting that he apply to the Czech government, to submit a paper for the seminar that was going to be held just six weeks later, in March. They said that if he were accepted they would sponsor him."

"Why did this foundation choose him for a grant? Had he contacted them?"

"No. The whole thing came as a complete surprise to him. He was very pleased, of course."

"Had he applied for any grants at all for anything—from any source?"

"No. He was going to apply. He was getting together material for an application to NEA or NEH for a grant to work on adaptations of four of the full-length plays. But he hadn't made it yet."

"Did anybody know he was preparing it?"

"Of course. Everybody. I mean, everyone on the faculty is strongly encouraged to apply for grants."

Talley nodded. "Whether they have a suitable project or not."

"Any project that is worth doing is worth seeking a grant for. Conversely, any project not grantable . . ."

"Yes. I taught for two years myself. Why did this foundation say they had chosen Professor Hovey?" Talley had seen the letter, but he wanted to know her understanding of what was in it.

"They said Larry's work had been called to their attention. They mentioned the article he had published in *Players* about his adaptation and production of *The Boor*, and the one in *The Educational Theatre Journal*."

" 'Chekhov, Our Contemporary'?"

"Yes. Have you read it?"

"Yes."

"You're very thorough. Did you really read my book?"

"Yes."

"Would you have read it if you hadn't been going to ask for my help?"

"Probably not. But I'm glad I did. It really is very good."

"Did you read it all?"

"Yes."

"Because you liked it, or because you're thorough?"

"Both. The foundation said that Professor Hovey's work 'had been called to their attention.' Did he have any idea by whom?"

"No. That was something of a mystery. However, Larry was pleased simply to think that his renown was spreading so that people anywhere, all over, might be recommending him."

"Ah. Who knew that he'd gotten the letter?"

"Everyone." Her emphasis on the first syllable was slight, but that and her manner in answering the previous question were enough that Talley almost changed his line of questioning. He disciplined himself away from pursuing that personal interest.

"Did he try to find out anything about the foundation?"

"No. It was credential enough for Larry that they wanted to support him." Then she caught her tone herself and hurried on, trying to change it. "He was tremendously excited. It seemed such an honor, and if he got to go to the seminar and give a paper, it virtually guaranteed his getting tenure. He was up this year."

"And so he just accepted the award without question."

"Well, he was surprised, of course. I think he would have been more so if he had known it was really coming from the government."

"Assuming it did come from the government."

"Didn't it?"

"Why would he have been more surprised if it had come from the government?"

"Why are you asking me things you already know?"

"I'm not. I don't know Professor Hovey, so I don't know how *he* would have felt about anything. I'm trying to get a sense of that, instead of substituting my own idea of how he would have felt."

Professor Boudreau stared at him for a moment. "You're right. I'm sorry."

A surge of sexual excitement shot through Talley. He knew where it came from: the flash of conflict and its resolution; her conceding through persuasion, not through weakness. He had thought her good-looking when he met her. He had appreciated her slimness, the length of her fingers, the lean line of her thigh revealed beneath her skirt when she crossed her legs. But what had made him most eager to see her again was his sense of a congruence of mind, of spirit. They were like members of a tribe who know each other by signs that strangers never notice.

"As you must know," she began, "Larry was very anti-Vietnam as a student. Sit-ins, protests, burned his draft card. They were going to prosecute him for that—that's a federal crime, as you know. They might have sent him to prison, but then the war ended, so I guess neither side saw any point in it. Larry applied for a new card, and the government dropped the case. But he always assumed they had a file on him, and that he'd never get any grants."

"You said he was going to apply for a NEA."

"Well, that was a no-lose proposition for him. In the first place, he was satisfying our administration by applying. Secondly, he might get it. And then if he didn't, he could scream about being blacklisted—and get the college behind him—and get mileage out of that."

"So he applied to the Chekhov seminar."

"Yes. I'm sure it was like any international conference. It must have been announced in the appropriate journals, and papers were invited. Larry sent a reprint of the *ETJ* article, which he was going to use as a basis and supplement with a description of his production of *Uncle Vanya* last fall."

"When did he hear that he was accepted by the Czechs?"

"About . . . Let me think. It must have been about three weeks later."

"Then what happened? Did he notify the foundation?"

"No. They called. It all happened the same day. He was notified of his acceptance by telegram. It came in the morning. He called me from his office to tell me. And when I got home, he was really flying. He said that the foundation had called that afternoon and confirmed their support."

"How did the foundation know he'd been accepted?"

"He didn't say."

"Did he ever write to this foundation, or call?"

"Not that I know of. What would have happened if he had? They say there's no record that the foundation ever really existed, isn't that right?"

"Right. No trace beyond a post office box and an answering service. If he had tried to contact them, he'd have gotten a reply. So, he never contacted them?"

"No."

"All right. They were sponsoring him. How did he get his money?"

"They—I've already told this to the FBI—they never sent him any money. A plane reservation was made for him. The ticket was waiting there, already paid for. He was to keep a record of other expenses, and be reimbursed when he got back—up to some limit, I think."

A new thought struck her. "I wonder if he'd ever have gotten anything if he did get back, since there wasn't really any—"

She stopped speaking suddenly, and Talley could see her eyes go wide behind her glasses.

"They must have known he wasn't coming back!"

"Okay, I'd like to ask you next—"

"They must have *known!* I don't understand. . . . How could the CIA know. . . . *Why would the CIA want Larry to be arrested as a spy?*"

"I really can't . . ." Talley paused. Screw it! he thought. I'm not with them anymore. I'll tell what I want to, and if they don't like it, they can get somebody else! "Our primary hypothesis is that the CIA didn't want that, and didn't know, and that when the agency denied any knowledge of Professor Hovey they were—for once—telling the truth."

"But then . . . how . . . who . . . ?"

"That is what we are trying to find out."

"Do you mean . . . ? Then it was some kind of plot by the Czechs? My God!"

"Professor, you're very astute. That's a possibility. One possibility. But we don't know, and we're keeping an open mind until we find out."

"My God. But I should keep an open mind, too, shouldn't I. I did refuse to talk to you earlier because I had closed it, hadn't I? What do you want to know now?"

"The next thing that happened, I'm told, was when a man who identified himself as being with the CIA came to talk with him. Is that correct? Was there any other contact from the 'foundation' or anyone else?"

"Well, there was a letter from Czechoslovakia, a confirmation. And I think a confirmation from the foundation about the travel arrangements. Nothing else that I know of."

"Okay. About this man who came to talk. You saw him."

"Yes. He came to the house. In the evening. I gave a description to the FBI."

"Yes. Now would you describe him for me?"

"About five feet nine inches, medium weight—"

"Just a minute. You're repeating the description you gave the FBI. Don't remember your description—remember the man. Did you like him?"

"No."

"Why?"

"I don't . . . He was nice enough. We didn't really speak. He asked if he could speak with Larry privately, so I went up to my study. But . . . He was very polite, he knew who I was—addressed me as 'Professor' and 'ma'am'—but he was one of those men . . . I could tell he thought a woman should be kept in her place, and her place—to be frank about it—was on the bottom, being screwed by him."

"What about him made you feel that?"

"I don't know. The way he looked at me."

"How did he look at you? I mean, you seem very sensitive to expressions. Was there something about his eyes? An expression around the mouth?"

"I see." Professor Boudreau leaned against the chair back, tipped back her head, closed her eyes. She let her feelings about the man bring his face, his presence, to her. She concentrated on that image for the moment, ignoring her appreciation of Talley's method. "His eyes were rather round. His face was round—not fat, just not long or lean. When he was being friendly, introducing himself, he made his eyes big, as one does to show how open one is. But when he looked at me he narrowed them—sizing me up. The left one more than the right. One thing that may have made me aware of his eyes is that the eyebrows were very dark."

"Heavy?"

"No. Just dark."

"What color was his hair?"

"Brown. Light brown! That must have been why his eyebrows seemed particularly dark."

"How did he wear his hair? Full? Short?"

"Full. Not long. Neat, but full."

"Are you recalling his face clearly now?"

"Yes."

"Well, I won't ask you more about it right now, then. But I will ask you to work with someone from the FBI as soon as you can to make an identikit picture. You know what they are?"

"Yes. Why didn't they do that before?"

"I don't know. What else can you tell me about his appearance?"

"He stood up very straight. I could believe he was athletic. He was wearing a sport jacket—or a suit—I don't remember. I'm afraid I don't pay that much attention to men's clothes. He was nicely dressed."

Talley took up his attaché case and sorted through the papers inside. "Would you look at these?" He showed her two fashion plates cut from magazine advertisements. In one the model wore a dark, banker's suit; in the other, a jacket and slacks. "Does either of these look like whatever mental picture you can form of him?"

"That one." She pointed to the second.

Talley shifted the papers, spread two new ones beside the one she had indicated, and offered her a choice of different jacket types.

"Well, not that one. He wasn't wearing anything that loud. But I really couldn't say about the others."

From other pictures she decided that the man had been wearing a long necktie, not a bow-tie, but she couldn't describe more about him. She found herself, though, looking more and more carefully at Talley as her admiration for his preparation and thoroughness grew.

"Okay. Think about him talking. What did his voice sound like?"

Talley needed forty-five minutes to go over to his satisfaction her remembrances of the three-minute meeting.

"All right. After the man left, did you and Professor Hovey talk about him? Did Professor Hovey tell you what he had asked him to do?"

"No. Larry was very tense. Naturally I asked him what was going on, but he wouldn't tell me. We . . ."

"Yes?"

"Larry tends to be short with people when he's upset. We had some words about that, since I was only being curious about what was bothering him and . . . We didn't talk about it anymore."

Finally Talley came to the end of his list of questions and of the new ones her answers had suggested. The interview had ended. By then the secretary had closed her office down the hall and gone; all of the other faculty had gone. The soft, pale light had mellowed more, to rose.

"Well," Talley said. He shut off the tape machine and brought his case up to his lap. "I want to thank you for your help, Professor."

"I hope I've been of help."

"You certainly have. I'll probably want to talk to you again, after I've gone over all this."

"Certainly."

"Well." Talley opened the case and put away the machine, deliberately, without dispatch. He closed the lid. He snapped the latches. "Well," he said.

Professor Boudreau had leaned back in her chair, watching him, apparently waiting for him to leave so she could go too. But she hadn't gathered her own papers, or fidgeted, or looked at her calendar. She had continued to look at him steadily throughout the interview, as he had at her, each with a sense that there was an entirely different list of questions to be asked. She still waited for them, afraid he would ask them, afraid he wouldn't, confused by that ambivalence and by another: a feeling of guilt contradicted by one of emancipation.

"I really do appreciate your help," Talley said. "I was wondering . . . ah . . . would you let me take you to dinner?"

She looked away from him. "Thank you. I . . ."

He felt that she was embarrassed, perhaps offended, but didn't want to be rude, didn't know how to tell him. "Of course, if you have other plans . . ."

"No, I'd like to have dinner with you. It's just that—"

"I'm sorry. Obviously I know about you and Hovey. Maybe I shouldn't have—"

"No, it's not—"

"I didn't mean—"

"Stop." She put her hand on his forearm. "There's a roadhouse out in the country I've been meaning to try—if you'll risk getting poisoned with me."

•

The roadhouse had a neon sign flashing outside, and plastic flowers by its entrance. Inside, only three other tables were taken.

"Good evening, folks," the waitress said as she cleared the extra paper placemats and stainless from the cigarette-burned table of the booth they took. "How's everybody tonight?"

"Fine," Talley said, looking at the menu printed on a single sheet. The choices were roast beef, charbroiled steak, or chicken. There was no choice offered about the country and western music.

"Would you like anything from the bar?"

Talley deferred to Professor Boudreau.

"I don't usually. But you go ahead."

He didn't want to drink alone, or seem to need a drink that badly. "Do you have a wine list?"

"It's on the back. We just have wine by the glass. Red, white, and rosé."

"I'll have a martini. Straight up. No olive or lemon."

"And one for me. On ice. With a twist."

By the time Professor Boudreau returned from the ladies room, the drinks had come and Talley had reminded himself of the reason for meeting her: she was living—had been living—with Hovey. One of Talley's rules was that you don't break up a happy family no matter how attractive the woman is. That he had allowed himself to think seriously about trying to develop something was a triumph of emotion over mind. He was now determined simply to have a pleasant evening with an interesting person. He had thought of four topics on which they might intelligently converse, to get it started.

Professor Boudreau had smoothed her hair, removed the shine from her face, and put lipstick on, and she smelled of fresh cologne. She slipped again into the booth opposite Talley and said, "Hi."

"Hi. That's a great trick."

"What?"

"To go into the ladies room at the end of a long day and come out five minutes later looking like the Birth of Venus. I wish I could do that."

"If you could do that, it really would be a great trick."

"Cheers."

"Cheers. I'm sorry about the music."

"Ah, well. Mozart all the time gets so dull."

"I'm sorry about this place. I hadn't been here before."

"Never going to learn unless you try things. Win some, lose some. What are you working on now, after Carrie Nation?"

"I've been doing some work on the suffrage movement. On the antisuffrage movement, really—on the women who were against it. I mean, the parallels with what's going on now—Phyllis Schlafly—straight down the line, the arguments are exactly the same!"

When the waitress brought their dinners Talley asked if there could be some other music. She didn't seem at all offended by his peculiar tastes and said, "Sure," and went off and changed to a station offering music that was soft and rich and equally easy to listen to or not. And since it was growing dark outside she lit the candle inside the red glass shade on their table before she went away again. The room was dimly lit, the other diners quiet, so Talley and Professor Boudreau sat in an island of warm light.

"How's your steak?" she asked.

"It's all right."

"That bad?"

"It's okay. How's your roast beef?"

"That bad. Anyway, what seems to be going on is this strange intertwining of feelings of inferiority and superiority. Women can't handle the vote because they can't deal with the nitty-gritty of the real world, and if they get it they'll lose their superior moral position on the basis of which they already run the country."

Talley never got to introduce the other topics. Discussion of Professor Boudreau's work led to talk about contemporary politics, about social revolutions throughout history, about whether principles could be drawn from their study. She refused dessert, so did he, but they had some brandy.

"Would you like another?"

"No, thank you. God, this is wicked enough to last all week. I've got to read finals in the morning. What time is it?"

"Almost ten."

"Oh, I'd better get home. Thank you, Tom. This has been very nice. Despite everything."

"My pleasure, Jane."

•

They were quiet in the car, except as she gave him directions, but it was a quiet of shared contentment.

He pulled up at the house she indicated. He turned off the engine but kept his hands on the wheel as he looked at her sideways. He wondered if she'd ask him in for a drink. He wondered if he wanted her to.

She smiled. "Thank you again. I'm glad you asked me out."

"Thank you for going. I had a very good time."

"I'm sorry it was such a terrible place. I . . ." She turned to look forward again. Shadows from the leaves of the fine old trees along the street veiled her like dark lace. He could see her cheek and mouth. One corner of the frame of her glasses gleamed, but her eyes were masked. "I didn't want

to go to the inn in the village. I was afraid someone might
see us.''

''Ah.''

''No . . . I . . . Goddamnit! How can I be a widow when
I've never been married! It's worse. If Larry had died in a car
accident or something, everyone would be telling me I had to
go on living, that I'd get over it, that he'd want me to.
They'd be throwing all their eligible friends at me. But now
. . . everybody's solicitous. They're always inviting me to
dinner, but I'm either the odd one at the table, or they've got
old Dean Lassiter. And the single faculty . . . Torey Walsh
used to try to score me right in front of Larry. Now I'm
supposed to keep the flame—keep the home fires burning. If
anything happens to him, I think they'll expect me to commit
suttee!

''And I don't even like Larry anymore! I was going to
leave him—one of us was going to have to move out. I was
going to tell him when he got back. I didn't want to upset
him before he went—although half the time the month before
we were hardly speaking.

''But now everyone assumes I should be loyal, that I
should support him in his hour of need, that I owe it to him
for all he's gone through!''

She wiped the corners of her eyes, then set her glasses
straight again. ''I'm sorry.''

''Do you care what they think?''

''No! Well, of course I care. They're my friends, my
colleagues. If I had to, I could go somewhere else. I get
offers all the time. I mean, I don't have to care what they
think. But . . .''

''But you think they're right.''

''How can I write to him when he's in that prison? How
can I write to him when he feels he's been betrayed by his

country, by everybody, and tell him . . . ? I loved him. I did love him, once. I lived with him for nearly three years. How can I do that to him? How can I?''

Talley had leaned back into shadow himself. He didn't know what she might see in his face. ''I don't know. He was sentenced to five years. Are you going to wait that long to tell him?''

''I don't know. What do you think I should do?''

''I don't know. I can't tell you a thing like that. And . . . I don't think I'm disinterested.''

She stared at him. Her face now was turned away from the streetlamp altogether, but he didn't think he'd see any expression if it had been daylight. She had the academic's way, as he did, of being blank-faced while analyzing what she'd heard.

After several moments she said only, ''Thank you,'' and ''Good night,'' and got out of the car. He waited until she had gone up on her porch, then drove away, not sure whether she hadn't reached a conclusion yet, or had and had given it to him.

CHAPTER 3

Chip Bolander still had his trousers and shirt on when the phone rang. He liked to get the girl naked first before taking off his own clothes.

He rolled away from her, grabbed the receiver, and almost shouted "Yeah?" furious both at the caller and at himself for not having pulled out the phone when he got her home.

"Could I speak with Mr. Clarence Brown, please?"

Bolander froze for an instant, then in a voice that by its tightness conveyed a sense of outrage that had to be strictly controlled said, "You've got the wrong number. If you aren't sure about a number, you shouldn't call people before morning." He slammed down the receiver. For a moment, though, he stared at it, wondering, uneasy.

"Hey, tiger, don't lose your train of thought."

"Don't worry, baby!" Quickly he disconnected the phone, then spun back to her, his mouth down hard on hers, one hand mauling her breasts.

She twisted her head away. "Easy! Not so hard!"

He relented. He could be easy with a woman, too. He knew what they liked. He could drive them crazy.

"Oh, yeah!" she gasped. "Oh, that's nice! Oh, tiger!" She twisted her hips, starting to push down her panties with one hand.

But he grabbed her wrist, forcing her hand away. When *he* was ready, he pulled them off her himself.

•

After he had dropped the girl at her place the next morning, Bolander drove to a pay phone at a gas station, one he hadn't used before.

"This is Clarence Brown."

"Couldn't you call back last night?"

"No. You didn't say it was urgent, and I was busy."

"Ah. I am sorry to have disturbed you."

"What's up?"

"They are investigating. It is important for us to know what progress they make."

"Yeah. So? What do you want me to do?"

"They have brought in someone from outside. His name is Thomas Talley. He also worked for them at one time. It might be a good idea for you to locate him and keep track of him."

The man gave Bolander Talley's address and business number. "It would probably be best for you to keep back, but to let us know—if you can—where he is and what he is doing."

"How long do you think this is likely to go on?"

"Difficult to say. You will be on your usual per diem, of course. Is this good?"

"Sure thing. It'll be a pleasure."

•

As soon as he awoke, Talley thought about calling her. He thought about it all the time he was showering and dressing.

She had told him she didn't love Hovey anymore. Didn't even like him. She was going to leave him anyway.

But she hadn't left, hadn't broken with him, hadn't decided. Did he have the right to influence her? Talley's wife had left him for another man; or, at least, the other man had been part of it. Talley had strong feelings about "other men."

Of course, Jane and Hovey weren't actually married. Did that make any difference?

He sat on the edge of the bed, staring at the phone. He reached toward it, pulled back his hand.

It rang.

"Hello?"

"Hello, Tom? It's Jane. Jane Boudreau."

"Good morning." He made his voice calm to cover the thrill that shot through him.

"Good morning. I hope I haven't called too early or anything. I—"

"No, no. I was up."

"Good. I was afraid I might . . ." She spoke in bursts of words with momentary pauses between them. "But I have to get off for my office, and then I'll be tied up. I wanted to thank you again for last night. For dinner. I'm sorry it was such a terrible place.''

"It was fine. I had a good time.''

"I did too. But . . . I thought . . . Are you finished with what you're doing here? Or are you going to be . . .'' Then she rushed on through it all. "I thought if you were still going to be in town this evening you'd let me make it up to you for that awful dinner last night, and let me cook dinner for you at my place. I'm really a pretty good cook, and if you are going to be staying . . . ah . . . .'' She faltered again.

"I'd like that very much, Jane. Very much.''

"Good. About six-thirty?''

"Yes.''

"Do you think you can find the place again?''

"Yes.''

"Well. About six-thirty?''

"Six-thirty. See you then. Thanks.''

"Well. Good-bye.''

"Good-bye.'' Talley replaced the receiver slowly, and a great smile spread through him.

•

He had managed to catch five minutes of the dean of the faculty's time the day before, between the interviews with Professor Boudreau. At first the dean had divided his attention in three by giving instructions to his secretary and scanning a letter while saying "Hello" to Talley and inviting him into his corner office and offering a chair. Then he had sat himself in another, almost too close for Talley's comfort, and with a visible effort of concentration focused on him fiercely.

The dean hadn't remembered much about the "FBI agent" who had come to make a routine check on Hovey. Talley played his game with the fashion plates, and with some similar cutouts of men's faces. All they established was that the man the dean recollected hadn't looked like a banker, been bald, or had a beard.

"Oh, yes—perhaps one thing. I remember him as being extremely polite, almost obsequious. Perhaps that's putting it too strongly, but I remember that he kept calling me 'sir.' No one calls a dean 'sir' these days."

Talley went next to meet Hovey's departmental chairman. The man came from behind his desk, gave Talley a seat on a couch, and took a captain's chair nearby.

"Oh, yes. I remember him clearly. Having someone from the FBI come asking questions about one of my faculty is an unusual event. And frankly, when he said he'd come to ask me some questions about Larry, I was a little worried."

"Why?"

"Well, you must know about Larry's background. I mean, I guess he was something of a radical when he was a student. And he's still . . . well, I don't mean to suggest anything about his political views. I wouldn't think it was any of my business or yours whatever his views might be. But Larry's a very forceful young man. He forms strong opinions about things, and he . . . advocates . . . them strongly. The one criticism that's been raised about his teaching—he's a brilliant teacher, a fine mind—is that sometimes he can seem a bit intolerant of other people's views."

"Ah. He was up for tenure this year?"

"Yes. Actually, it's been awarded in his absence. There may have been a degree of sentiment in that—a sort of gesture. But he deserved it. I took his side wholeheartedly."

"Why did you have to take his side? What objections were raised?"

"Well, the tenure process is supposed to be confidential."

"I appreciate that. Please don't tell me anything you think you shouldn't. But if you can tell me anything you feel is proper that would help me to understand what he's like . . ."

The chairman took breath for speech and released it in a sigh twice before deciding how to put it. Finally he said, "As I've said, Larry is brilliant, dynamic, and forceful. He has new ideas, and people tend to agree or disagree sharply with him. And that sometimes seems to lead him into kind of 'us and them' or '*me* and them' feelings. Not that this was a serious problem. I've talked with him several times about it, and I think he was watching himself and developing a more . . . mature . . . attitude."

"I see. Thank you. That's helpful. Now, to return to the man who came to see you about Professor Hovey . . ."

The chairman began repeating the description he had given when the real FBI men came, and Talley stopped him as he had stopped Professor Boudreau.

"No," the chairman answered, "I can't say that I liked or disliked or had any particular feeling about him. He was here only for about five minutes. Very polite, businesslike." And then the chairman proved to be a gold mine. "But let's see what I can tell you about him. To begin with, he was wearing a hairpiece."

"How do you know?"

"Oh, well, I've worn them myself. Here, in this department, we believe in studying theater by doing it. Faculty and students alike. I direct, mostly, but I act in some of the productions, too. Character parts, usually. So I've worn hairpieces, wigs, beards, false noses, all the tricks of the trade.

So I notice those things. The one this man had was very good. I almost asked him where he'd gotten it."

The chairman went on to describe in detail the man's face and clothes. "Glasses with very dark rims. Gray suit—three-piece, blue shirt, knit tie. And his shoes—brown cordovans, highly polished. I'd say spit-shined."

"You have an incredible memory for detail, Professor."

"Well, being in the theater . . . I guess you just learn to notice things automatically. I mean, if I ever were doing a play with an FBI man in it—I don't offhand know of one, but if there isn't, somebody may write one and we might do it—well, then it would be useful to know what a real one looks like."

•

Talley finished his interviews by noon. He ate lunch at his inn. He had planned to go up to his room afterward and look over his notes carefully, but while waiting for his sandwich to come, he had let his mind move as it would over the material he'd gathered. All at once, like the cacophony of a tuning orchestra resolved into a single A, isolated bits of description came together. He almost jumped up to call Walter Simson.

He restrained himself. The idea he'd had might not be true; even if true, it might be of minor importance. And he wasn't going to let himself get caught up in this thing. He had agreed to work for Walter for the sake of friendship, and . . . for various reasons. He'd try to do a good job because he always did. But he wasn't going to give them any enthusiasm, any commitment; he wasn't going to care.

He ate his sandwich, and then ordered cherry pie and ice cream before he called Walter Simson.

"This may not amount to anything, Walt, but I think I've got one line. I'm pretty sure the guy who came here to do the 'FBI security check,' and the one from 'the CIA' the week after, who talked to Hovey, were the same man using simple disguises. Obviously, if whoever is behind this had more than one person available for those contacts, it would have made sense to use them. I don't know what—if anything— knowing that gets us, but maybe it will help somewhere. A couple people remember the guy's face—the version they saw—pretty well, and I'm getting them to do identikits, and I'll bet with a little pushing around of hair styles and color, and so forth, we'll get a good idea of what he looks like. The general height-weight-age descriptions they all gave before still hold.

"And there's more. The guy knew what he was doing—I mean, how to do a check. I believe he may have been someone who is, or was, in the FBI or security somewhere."

"Or in the agency."

"Well, that is one of the hypotheses, Walt. Now, another lead: I think also he's been in the military."

"Why?"

"Says 'sir' a lot, spit-shined shoes, stands up straight."

"Oh, sweet Jesus. Do you suppose, Tom—do you suppose God is going to be good to us and give us General Cartwright's ass? Do you suppose this whole thing could be coming out of DIA?"

"I wouldn't know, Walt, and frankly, old buddy, I don't give a damn. A plague on both your houses. Anyway, can you run the personnel files for those variables?"

"You mean for the agency, FBI, military intelligence, all branches—"

"Secret Service; Alcohol, Tobacco, and Firearms . . ."
"Former and current."
"Sure."
"Sure. That should narrow it down to about five thousand people."
"Okay, don't."
"Okay, okay. Listen, I ran the Frenchman again. Left-wing causes, cultural exchange work in the East, but signed petitions against Afghanistan, for Sakharov, close to some of the émigrés. Nothing conclusive either way. Why didn't you like him?"
"I don't know. Maybe just because he didn't like me."
"Well, there's nothing against him. And he and Czerny go back for at least ten years. We're keeping on him, of course."
"Just wanted to check it again."
"What are you going to do next?"
"I've got some details to clean up here. Tomorrow I'll go to Indiana to see MacDonald. I'll call you afterward."

•

At 6:25 Talley pulled past Jane Boudreau's house. He turned at the corner, went down a block and on around as slowly as he could without making anyone who saw him wonder what he was doing. It was still only 6:29 when he got there again. She answered within five seconds of his pushing the bell.
"Hi," he said. "I hope I'm not too early."
"Oh, no! Just on time." She was grinning broadly, nodding. "Hi!" She backed in, let him enter. He brought up into

sight and extended the bunch of daffodils he'd bought for her at the supermarket.

"Oh, Tom! Oh, they're lovely. I love daffodils. Thank you! Come on in."

The frame house was not distinguished but was old enough to have large, open rooms. She showed him into the living room. It was pleasantly furnished, some old pieces, some new. There were bookshelves, and (as she had told him) plants everywhere.

"What a nice house."

"Oh, it's nothing special. We bought it two years ago, mostly as an investment. Sit down." She indicated the Victorian couch upholstered in lime-green velour and set perpendicular to the fireplace. "Can I get you a drink? We're having wine, but I have some gin . . ."

"Sure. A small one."

She went to a marble-topped washstand, took ice from a wooden bucket, and poured from a full, obviously newly purchased bottle. "Oh, I don't have vermouth! Oh, how stupid of me!"

"It's all right. I can drink it that way."

She came over and extended the glass to him. Her hand quivered slightly. "Cheers."

"Cheers."

"We can eat anytime. Tell me about your work. Oh! Let me get you a napkin."

She went back to the washstand, brought small paper napkins for them, and sat on the edge of an ottoman facing him. "Now."

Talley began to describe his business.

"Oh! I forgot the peanuts. I didn't have time to make hors d'oeuvres." She sprang up, dashed to the kitchen, and came back with a bowl of peanuts.

"Thanks." He took a handful.

She perched again, leaning toward him, her napkin wadded in one fist. "Do you travel much?"

"I make a swing through Southeast Asia about once a year—what I can still get to: Thailand, Malaysia. I got to Japan first. The Japanese are doing a lot in Southeast Asia now, and I have quite a few clients there. And then I stop over in Taiwan, Indonesia, or the Philippines while I'm going that way."

"That must be fascinating."

"Yes."

"What's wrong?"

"Nothing. Why?"

"You keep looking at me."

"I was thinking how attractive you are tonight."

"Oh. Thank you." She flushed even pinker than she had been. "Have some more peanuts. Keep the bowl over there. I shouldn't eat them anyway." She leaned toward him, then stretched as he half rose and caught hold of the bowl.

She quickly sat back, smoothing her skirt, embarrassed at the awkwardness of the maneuver.

Talley kept looking at her. She seemed even more attractive tonight—smart and sophisticated in a fuschia silk blouse that flattered her long waist, and a tight white skirt. She had used more makeup than on the previous night, and wore a necklace of ornate gold chain, and gold bracelets.

He, of course, was limited to the chino slacks and tweed jacket he'd worn the day before. He only had that outfit, because he'd expected to have done his business and gone back home by now. But he had bought a new shirt at a mall, a button-down with narrow brown stripes that might make him look trimmer.

The ice in her glass rattled whenever she lifted it to drink.

Talley was keyed-up himself yet felt his assurance growing. To take command of the situation and relieve them both, he set a slower pace to his speech. They seemed to be more relaxed by the time they went in to dinner.

She had put a yellow cloth on the round table, and had yellow candles at either side of the daffodils.

She brought an iron pot, served the *boeuf bourgignon* that was one of her specialties, and tried not to look too eager to see his reaction.

His exclamations made her blush with pleasure. Tasting carefully, he named the seasonings.

"You must be something of a cook yourself."

"Well, I enjoy it."

"Do you cook a lot?"

"When I'm at home. And I cooked about half the time even when I was married."

She sipped her wine. "How long have you been divorced?"

"A little over two years."

"Do you mind my asking about it?"

"No. I don't mind talking about it. I don't feel any compulsion to talk about it, but I don't mind."

They were silent for a moment. She had left it to Talley to choose a record to play during dinner. He had put on a Brahms piano quartet.

"This is very nice wine," he said. "You like wine?"

"Yes. We always drank it at home." She sipped again, then put her glass down and turned it, watching the candle reflecting in the bowl. "It got to annoy Larry that I knew more about wine than he did."

Twilight faded slowly as they ate, until they were left again on a cozy raft of candlelight. He didn't put on another record after the Brahms ended. If any car passed by on the tree-lined street, they never heard it.

They didn't talk so much this time of ideas in abstract terms as about themselves: their backgrounds, their memories, what they thought and felt because of the lives they'd led. Sometimes, for several moments, they didn't talk at all. The sense, then, of feelings, of meanings beyond words, that they wanted to communicate and yet already knew and shared, was as heady and full of promise as the scent of blossoms on the balmy air.

"How long were you married?"

"Almost seventeen years."

"That's a long time."

"Yes."

"I wonder about that, about whether I'll ever have a relationship that will last like that. I lived with another man while I was in graduate school. And with a boy—I shouldn't call him a boy—in my senior year at college. Does that bother you?"

"What?"

"That I've lived with three men, and never been married?"

"Why should it?"

"Well, I don't mean I think you're a prude, but with a marriage like yours, that lasted so long . . . that's why I wondered what you might think of me."

"I don't think a relationship is wrong or sex has to be legalized, and I don't think it has to be for forever. It's a matter of whatever you've agreed to commit yourselves to."

She was staring into her now empty glass again. They had finished the bottle. The candles had burned down to two-inch stubs.

"Well," he said. "I should go. You've probably got to be in early again."

"No. What time is it?"

"Ten-fifteen."

"Already? No. Don't rush. I don't have to be in until my meeting at one o'clock. Would you like some brandy?"

"Sure. Thanks."

She brought two small snifters and a new bottle of Courvoisier.

"You went to a lot of expense for this evening," he said.

"Oh, all we had was some old Drambuie that Larry got last Christmas."

Talley heard tightness coming back into her voice. Her hand trembled again as she poured.

She sat again. "Do you want to put another record on?"

"Sure. What would you like?"

"You choose."

Talley surveyed the shelf of records, chose one of Chopin nocturnes. He didn't like the change in her mood, hoped he could make it mellow and romantic again.

"Tell me more about your house," she said.

Talley did, and she seemed genuinely interested, but her uneasiness seemed to be growing. As he talked about the peacefulness of hills and woods, he was ever more, himself, on edge. He admired her, he liked her, he lusted for her. They had eaten well, drunk good wine; the warm night's air wafted through the open windows, stirring the candle flames; Chopin poured his heart out. Talley talked about the brook at the edge of his property, and watched for something from her.

Draining his last sip of brandy, finally, he again made ready to leave. "Well, I really should be going. This has been wonderful."

She nodded, not speaking. She didn't look at him. They rose.

He stood there, not sure of what to do. He started to turn to move toward the living room, the hall, the door.

"Tom . . ." Still she looked down at the table. Her arms were stiff at her sides, her hands clenched. "You can stay here. If you want to."

He turned back, stepped to embrace her, but as his hand came toward her she gripped it in her own fingers, hard.

She leaned and quickly blew out the candles. At once they were in a forest jungle of shadows from trees outside and her plants. She walked past him, leading him through it, then dropping his hand as they reached the hallway. She went up the stairs, not looking back at him as he followed. They went into one of the upstairs rooms. She turned on a lamp on a table next to the bed.

Again he moved to take her in his arms; again she evaded him. "I'll just be a minute." She took a robe from the closet and left him.

Talley looked around the room. The bed had magnificent head- and footboards of brass. A table and lamp stood on each side of it. There were two chests of drawers. The walls were covered in flowered wallpaper.

He folded down the bedspread, turned down the sheet and blanket. He didn't know what to do. He looked back and forth, caught his image in a mirror over a dresser. His hair had gotten a little disarranged; it stuck out at one side. He brushed it back with the heel of his hand. He stood up straighter, smoothed his necktie, started to tuck his shirt tighter into his waistband, stopped. He shrugged his shoulders at himself in the mirror and then undressed. He got into the bed and pulled the sheet up to his waist.

In a few minutes Jane returned. She didn't have her glasses on. He was amazed to see how large her eyes appeared.

She came around to the other side of the bed. She stood, not facing him, not with her back to him, either. Without looking at him at all, as though he weren't there, she untied the belt and took off the robe.

He caught his breath.

She laid the robe over the chair on her side, moving matter-of-factly. Then she turned, and in one smooth movement raised the sheet and slid into the bed and over against him, her arm coming across, her hand on the back of his neck.

They kissed, holding the kiss for a long time, with their bodies together full length, yet almost chastely. Then she parted her lips, and her tongue touched his.

He pulled away. "Wait. Let me see you." He sat up, pushing the sheet away from them. They explored each other with their eyes, with fingertips.

Gradually, as they learned each other, their explorations became caresses. Her eyelids closed and she rolled her head back. "Oh, that's so nice."

And gradually their gentle fondling aroused them past restraint. He held himself back until sure of her, then entered her, and she held him to her, her arms around him, her fingers in his hair, urging him, exciting his two years' desire, his need for love, his need to love. Her gasps rose in pitch, at last catching and then releasing in a long, high moan, freeing from him all that desire, need, loneliness, pain.

For some moments she held him and he lay upon her, conscious of nothing but joy and wonder. Then, when he could think again, he raised himself to look at her face.

Suddenly she flung her hands up over her eyes and burst into sobs.

"What's the matter?"

"I don't . . . I don't . . ."

She twisted away, and he pulled back from her.

"Jane, what is it? What's wrong?"

"I don't know."

He tried to take her shoulders. She rolled to him, her head against his chest, still sobbing convulsively.

He held her, trying to still her, stroking her hair. "I'm sorry. Did I hurt you? I'm sorry."

"No. It wasn't you. . . . It was wonderful. I . . ."

He held her to him, trying to comfort her, until her sobs subsided.

She pulled away from him at last. "I'm sorry." She turned, went to her dresser for tissues, and sat on the bed again blowing her nose.

"I'm sorry. It wasn't you, Tom. You were wonderful. Something just came over me. It was . . ."

"It was Larry, wasn't it?"

"Yes."

"Well."

"What are you doing?"

"I guess I'd better go."

"No!" Up on her knees, she reached to hold his arm. "No. I decided . . . I decided to leave Larry. I decided I couldn't . . . It didn't matter. That's what this meant. I . . . but I guess you can't just decide in your head . . . I guess I had mixed feelings about . . . I guess I felt guilty. I didn't expect to cry over it, or for him, or whatever it was. But I feel better now. It's done. It's over. Now, it is."

Talley turned back and reached for her, and she came to cuddle in his arms. "I'm sorry," she said again. "That must have been quite a shock for you."

"Oh, no. Certainly no worse than somebody dumping a barrel of iced fish on you."

She giggled. Then, "I am sorry, Tom. It won't happen again. It's all . . . exorcised." She kissed his shoulder, and his lips, and snuggled down against him. After a while he turned out the lamp, and after a while they slept.

CHAPTER 4

During the plane trip to Indianapolis Talley was able to get out his notes on MacDonald and concentrate on them. And driving to Bloomington in his rented car kept his mind occupied much of the time because he hadn't been there before and had to watch the road. Except for those times, he drifted in the warm eddies and pools of new love and remembered passion. Jane had accepted his invitation to spend the coming weekend at his home in the country.

•

"Professor MacDonald? I'm Thomas Talley."

"Yes, Mr. Talley. How do you do?" MacDonald gave a firm handshake that belied his age. "Call me Sandy."

Of course he would be called Sandy. How could Alexander MacDonald, with his grizzled, close-cropped but still reddish hair, be called anything else?

"Would you like to take a walk out on the campus?" he said. "It's a little . . . quieter there."

Not many people were on the walks between the brick buildings. Here and there a couple, or a lone reader, sat under a tree. MacDonald and Talley found one of their own.

Talley started his recorder, put it between them, and began. "I've read over the transcript of your debriefing, but I'd like to go over it again, fresh. Sometimes something new will strike me."

"Of course. Where would you like me to begin?"

"Well, first, let me just check: you haven't done anything like this before, or had any other kind of . . . assignment . . . since you left the air force."

"The Air Corps, it was then. No. I never had any thought of making a career in it, although they asked me to stay on after the war."

"With the start you had you'd probably be a general now."

"I don't know. I wasn't really cut out for that life. As you may have heard, in World War Two a lot of pilots got rank quickly. It was kind of a joke. Fighters were a young man's game, because the older ones kept getting knocked off, and they had to give the rank to somebody."

"What did you fly?"

"P-Forty-sevens. That was a great airplane."

"Europe?"

"Yes."

"So, it came completely as a surprise to you when the agency approached you."

"It certainly did."

"But you accepted right away."

"Oh, of course. I hadn't liked the idea of a life in the air force, and I was damned glad they didn't call me up again for

Korea. I'm not any kind of a flag-waving superpatriot, but when they asked me—I guess I just thought of it naturally as my duty. And I was glad for the chance to go to that seminar.''

"You aren't a Chekhov scholar?''

"No. My field's seventeenth and eighteenth century, primarily England. But I thought it would be interesting, and, hell, everybody likes to travel. I'd never been to Prague.''

"How did you feel about the CIA using you, and using a cultural event?''

"Didn't bother me. The Russians do that kind of thing all the time.''

"You knew it would be dangerous?''

"Oh, yes, I guess so. The people who contacted me were very open about it. Well, maybe 'dangerous' isn't the right word. They made it clear there would be some risk.''

"What risk? How did they put it? What did they tell you might happen?''

"They said that Czerny would give me something, some papers, a document to bring out. They said that it would appear to be something perfectly innocuous; I wouldn't have to hide it, or try to sneak it through, or be worried if anybody saw it in my baggage or wherever. They said that he would probably give it to me in some natural way. They didn't know how he'd do it. That would be up to him—whatever he could arrange—but it wouldn't involve any midnight meeting in a back alley kind of thing. They said I shouldn't have anything to worry about—otherwise they wouldn't be sending someone like me—but that, of course, there was always some risk.''

"What did they tell you about meeting Czerny? There was a protocol?''

"They gave me a red and white striped necktie. Told me to wear it at the seminar. They said Czerny would recognize me by that, and he would approach me. When we met, I was then to confirm my function by saying something about how I'd like to see the Czech countryside, especially the Moldau. The river. It didn't matter exactly how I said it, so I could work it in naturally if there were other people around."

"Okay. You handled all the arrangements for going to the conference yourself?"

"Yes. I applied to attend. I was just going to attend—not as a participant giving a paper. I had to pay my own expenses—hotel, meals, registration fee."

"You paid those out of your own pocket? And your air fare?"

"I got some travel money from my department. And the CIA guys told me they would reimburse me for the rest, afterward."

"So you didn't get any money in advance: no government checks, no official-looking mail."

"No."

"Okay. Tell me about the trip, about what happened."

MacDonald looked off across the green lawns for a moment. "Well, I guess the place to start is when I arrived in Prague. At the airport. I had had to fly to Frankfurt and change planes there. When I got to Prague, my baggage—my suitcase, I only had that and a carry-on—wasn't on the plane. They said.

"There were a lot of us from the States, and others from England and the Netherlands, on that flight. All of the Americans, and some of the others, were missing their baggage. I guess if you were going to the seminar from anywhere in the West, that would be the flight you'd come in on, and there

was somebody from the Ministry of Culture there to meet us.
A really good-looking girl, but wearing a gray suit. I mean, it
looked like a uniform, even though it wasn't. But she was
very sympathetic, and she tried to be helpful. She talked to
the airport people. They tried to say it wasn't the fault of the
Czech airline—that the baggage hadn't been transferred prop-
erly by TWA—but since some of the Europeans were missing theirs, too, that didn't wash. But there wasn't much we
could do. They said they'd have our things for us by the next
morning at the latest. I was a little worried, since that necktie
was in my bag.

"I see now that I should have had it in the carry-on. Then
again, maybe not. We had to open our hand baggage to go
through customs, and they poked around pretty well. I don't
know what they might have done if they'd found it there, but
I'm sure—from the way it all worked out—that they'd have
had 'Plan B.'

"But beyond worrying what would happen if I didn't get
the tie back—whether I could find one in Prague—beyond
that I didn't think anything about it, because everybody was
affected.

"They had a bus for us. I think the bus was gray. I don't
know—the weather was gray, the hotel was gray, all of
Prague looked gray to me. They say it's supposed to be a
beautiful city. I don't know.

"I had dinner in the hotel, went out and walked around
with some of the other people who were going to the seminar, then went back and went to bed.

"The next morning, half an hour before the first session,
they paged me. When I got to the desk the girl from the
ministry was there, and she told me they'd found my bag, but
that I'd have to go to the airport to take it through customs.
She had arranged a car for me. It was waiting.

"Not the bus again. Nobody else seemed to be going. To tell you the truth, I didn't like that. But why should I be worried? There was absolutely nothing incriminating in the bag, or on me, or anything. Why should I be worried?

"The driver was just a little guy in a dark gray suit. He had the door open for me, just like he was a capitalist's chauffeur. I said something to him, but it seemed that he didn't speak any English.

"Now, the trip to the airport should have taken maybe forty-five minutes, given there was morning traffic. Well, we started off. Of course I didn't know the city, but I recognized generally that we were going the way we'd come the night before. All of a sudden, he cuts right, then left, then right, weaving through these narrow side streets.

"I tried to ask him what the hell he was doing, but I couldn't understand what he said, of course. He kind of jabbed with his hand, and I figured he was telling me he was taking a short cut. Only sometimes he'd make two rights, or two lefts, so he'd be going back where we'd been.

"Then all of a sudden we come down this very narrow street, and there's a barrier, some workers, a little section of road torn up front of us. No sign to warn us before we got to it. Well, I didn't see any, and that turns out to be a big point. The driver starts to back, but a big truck has come up behind.

"My driver gets out, waves the truck back. The truck starts to back up and bumps into another car behind him.

"All right. For the next hour and a half I just sit there while they all go through a thing of arguing about the situation, getting the police. . . . You see it?

"I got out once. My driver comes running back telling me to wait. I assume that's what he was telling me. Big sign language.

"What would I have done even if I hadn't wanted to wait? Where the hell was I? Who was I going to ask?

"And anyway, I've seen enough spy movies—I knew what was going on. I just got back in the car and waited, and kept telling myself it wasn't really like that, and they couldn't know about me, and they couldn't prove anything.

"I was really surprised when they finally 'got things straightened out,' and we went right on to the airport.

"Then we had another game. I had to wait in an office for another half an hour while they found my bag.

"Then they took me down to the regular customs clearance section, gave me my bag, and asked me to open it there on the table. There were lines of people at the other tables. I was just in the regular room with the tourists. I was expecting, you know, a couple of heavies in leather trenchcoats, and some sharp-looking officer with a nasty smile. I guess staging scenes in my mind is an occupational hazard of having worked in theater most of my life.

"All there was was this little, fat, bored-looking guy, and he asked me to open my bag, and he sort of poked around in it. And then he said 'Okay' and looked away.

"Of course, when I'd opened the bag—it's one of those with a strap that holds your ties right on top—the red and white tie was gone.

"But what was I going to say? What was I going to do? Stand there and yell, 'Hey, somebody stole my spy-tie'?

"I just picked up my bag and walked back to where I'd left my driver, and he took me back to the hotel.

"Of course, by then I'd missed the morning session, and the afternoon session—the one where Professor Hovey read his paper—had already started. I had to take a seat at the back.

"After a while I picked out Janos Czerny up near the front and tried to figure how I could make contact with him—I mean, by that point I knew there wasn't going to be any transfer of papers. At least, *I* sure as hell wasn't going to take delivery of any. But I thought maybe I ought to warn him. And I thought about how maybe that wasn't a good idea. And I was trying to figure what the hell I *should* do when it finally got through to me that Hovey was wearing a red and white striped tie.

"At that point it suddenly became very clear to me that I should get the hell out of the secret agent business altogether. I hope that doesn't sound chicken, Tom."

Talley had been staring down at the grass between his ankles, letting MacDonald's story make pictures in his mind. He looked up at the older man. "It all sounds to me like the kind of nerve and kind of decisions that got you through sixty-three missions and here to tell about it, Colonel.

"Then what happened? You saw them arrest Czerny?"

"Yeah. After the session was over we all went into a reception room next door. Champagne, canapés. Even though I'd missed lunch I was too scared to be hungry, but I crammed some down, and sort of drifted from group to group of people, for cover. On one side, frankly, I didn't want to seem to have any interest in Czerny at all. I mean, doesn't everybody have a red and white striped tie when he travels? But it was obvious something was going on, and if I got back, I supposed somebody would want to know about it. And I guess I wanted to know.

"But there isn't much to tell. Czerny must have contacted Hovey—I didn't see that. But I did see them go across the room and sit on a couch there. After a while, Hovey gave Czerny some papers, and Czerny gave Hovey some, and all at once there were a couple guys there. Then some uniformed police came in—big entrance—and moved everybody back. They did a big production arresting them, taking them out.

"There really wasn't much fuss, though. Most of the crowd in the room didn't know exactly what had happened at first. Nobody ever came near me."

Talley continued looking down for several moments. Finally he said, "How close were you?"

"I was across the room."

"The room was crowded?"

"Well, there were a lot of people, but it was a big room. I could see all right."

"Czerny and Hovey were sitting on a couch at the side, in plain sight, then, even to somebody across the room."

"Oh, yes. Well, I couldn't see them every second, but . . . Yeah."

"Nobody bothered you at all after that?"

"No. The seminar was pretty well a loss after that. Somehow the word got around that Czerny had been caught passing something to an American agent, and every—"

"That got around? How soon?"

"Oh, by the middle of the evening. After that, they went through the motions of the seminar as best they could. Some of Czerny's friends left in protest, and the East Europeans tried to carry on as if nothing had happened, and the rest of us went through the motions."

"You stayed, though."

"I thought it was better not to seem to be trying to get out fast. I just sat tight and listened to a lot of bullshit, and went on the bus tour with everybody else."

"No trouble when you left?"

"None. They hardly went through my luggage at all."

"What happened with the luggage of the other people? Were you the only one who had to go to the airport?"

"Yeah. I heard that late in the morning a van showed up at the hotel with all of it, and a customs man, and he went through it with the owners right there in the lobby at noon, between sessions."

"Well," said Talley.

"Yeah," said MacDonald.

"I guess that's all for now, Sandy. Thank you very much. I don't know what this means, but I'm sure what you've told me will prove to be important."

"I don't suppose you'll tell me anything about this, will you, Tom."

"No."

"No. I know I should just put it out of my mind. But I can't help wondering how they knew about me. It gives rise to some kind of disturbing speculations, doesn't it?"

"I think you should just put it out of your mind."

•

For Professor Hovey, the arrest had the quality of dream, of nightmare. Instant by instant the images were vivid. The two men in dark suits, who somehow no longer looked at all like scholars, appearing at either side of the couch, speaking in that harsh, consonant-crammed language to Czerny. The phalanx of men in uniform, booted and belted, bearing down on him. Czerny looking up, mouth open, eyes wide, rising as if to stand like an oak in defiance; then, like that oak blown by a hurricane, twisting to and fro in bewilderment, his arms swinging at his sides until they were taken by two policeman. Two others raised Hovey from his seat. More surrounded him, and Czerny, and marched them out.

But he had no sense of time, of continuity, of one event leading logically to the next. Surrounded by those gray and leather figures, he had sometimes the sense of being walked though passageways, sometimes that mechanisms conveyed him. He knew he sat for a while in an automobile while lights flashed past him.

He began to focus when they photographed and finger-printed him; the procedures were familiar. But only when the police left him alone, sitting on a straight-backed wooden chair in some small windowless office, did any sense of reality return.

It may have been that leaving him there was a stratagem to demoralize him more, giving him time to wonder what would be done to him, to let him terrify himself with more horrors than they had chained in their cellars. If that were the plan, they had made a mistake.

Gradually Professor Hovey's heartbeat slowed. Though only a little light came into the room diffusely through a frosted-glass panel in the door, he perceived the space around him clearly, three-dimensionally again, with recognizable objects—desk, wooden swivel chair, desk lamp—in conventional relationships. He recognized his situation as one he had experienced before.

When he and the others had locked themselves across the armory door, they had known they would be arrested. They had known they would be arrested the time they blocked the recruiters and when they defaced government property.

Perhaps on the first occasion Professor Hovey had had a sense of bravado. After that he knew better. Having his arm broken cured him of any enjoyment of heroics. While it was mending, though, he decided that he would never let the bastards break him, no matter what they did. Like any sensible person he would try to preserve himself, he would avoid pain, he would not be unnecessarily provocative. But he would accept anything they might do, he would suffer them to beat him, even to kill him—he didn't care if they did; he would prefer that to letting them break him.

During the course of his seven arrests and the three months he spent in a county jail, Professor Hovey had had both arms, three ribs, and his nose broken, and had lost four teeth. He might have been killed the time the police put him in a tank with several hulking men who tried to rape him; but when it became clear that he was able to fight back well enough so that they would have to beat him insensible, the jailers had turned on the fire hose.

Professor Hovey had had extensive experience with arrest. He had learned to wait, to hold worry under control. He had become a keen judge of balances of power, of what he could get away with. There were, he had learned, the good cops, who would treat you decently no matter what they thought of you as long as you didn't give them a hard time. There were the sadists, with whom you must never cross eyes. He had learned to distinguish those from the cowardly bullies who could be faced down, and the tricky ones who would try to intimidate you into incriminating yourself or your friends by using threats they couldn't carry out. While the tactics for dealing with each type differed, the essential strategy with all of them was not to be foolishly provocative, but never to appear abject.

For a while he sat leaning forward, elbows on his knees, hands clasped, looking at the floor. For a while he slipped to the front edge of the chair, stretched his legs out, leaned his head back on the wall. After half an hour he took off the necktie and his jacket, folded the jacket as a pillow, and lay on his back on the desk.

Occasionally during that time people passed along the

corridor outside the office. Twice, a hand rattled the latch. Professor Hovey kept his breathing regular, looked up at the ceiling letting his imagination try to make pictures from the fine cracks in the plasterwork. He rigidly refused to let himself wonder, speculate, or try to plan. He was able to achieve enough tranquility so that the only aspect of his situation that troubled him immediately was the need to relieve his bladder.

After more than an hour (he couldn't be sure of the time, since they had taken his watch and other personal items), the door suddenly banged open and a young police officer strode into the room. Seeing Professor Hovey relaxed on the desk rather than hunched with worry in the chair startled him and made him halt abruptly. The second policeman almost crashed into his back.

The officer covered his surprise by shouting "Attention!" at Hovey, and something in Czech to his subordinate.

Professor Hovey sat up without haste, and was swinging his legs over the side of the desk when the policeman rushed to him, grabbed his arm, yanked him to his feet, and spun him around to face the desk.

The officer stomped to the swivel chair and sat, slapping a folder down before him. He turned on the desk lamp. He opened the folder and made a show for nearly two minutes of studying whatever was inside. Professor Hovey watched him, trying to counter his fear by concentrating on observing and classifying the man's performance. Then the officer twisted the shade so the lamp shone up on Hovey's face.

"Lawrence Charles Hovey. That is your name?"

"Yes."

"Professor Doctor Lawrence Charles Hovey. You are a professor?"

"Yes."

"And a doctor?"

"Yes."

"And a spy."

Professor Hovey remained silent.

"And a spy, yes? An agent of the Central Intelligence Agency, yes?"

Professor Hovey remained silent. The desk lamp was not really that bright. It had blinded him at first because his eyes had been accustomed to the dimness of the room. They were adjusting, and he could begin to see the officer's face. The man was young, younger than himself. He wore a thin mustache that he allowed to grow downward slightly at the sides of his mouth; when he pressed his lips together it increased the effect of sternness.

The officer suddenly raised the folder and smacked it down on the desk again. "Answer! You are an agent of the CIA, yes?"

"Can I go to the bathroom?"

"What!"

"May I go to the bathroom? I haven't had a chance since noon."

"You want to go to the *bathroom*?"

"Yes."

"You want to take a bath?" The officer seemed to think that very funny. He repeated and explained it in Czech for the guard's benefit. "Now, Professor Doctor Lawrence Charles Hovey, you are a spy for the Central Intelligence Agency, yes?"

"I really need to take a piss. To urinate."

"Answer the question!" the officer shouted at him. He glared at him, then let one side of his stern mouth twist. "Answer the question, and then you may go and take a bath in your piss."

Professor Hovey stared back at him for a moment, then calmly unzipped his fly and began urinating with force against the front of the desk.

For one instant both the officer and the guard, stunned with incredulity, could only gape. Then, at once, the officer jumped up and back, crashing his chair into the wall behind him, shouting a command.

The guard lunged toward Hovey, who turned to meet the attack. A dark line appeared in a slash across the guard's leg. As though splashed with acid, he sprang backward.

The officer shouted again.

Although the guard was trained, and brave enough to disarm a man pointing a pistol or wielding a knife, this weapon was new and far more terrifying. Just out of range he lurched side to side, feinting. But Professor Hovey swung back and forth to counter him, and—despite constant direct orders from his superior—the guard could not bring himself to pounce.

Finally Hovey's ammunition ran out. The guard threw himself on him, carrying him back to the wall with a thump that knocked Hovey's wind out. Still pressing him against the wall, the guard drew back enough to swing one arm and cuffed the side of his face full strength. He would have done it again, but the officer shouted.

More shouts, more orders. Hovey made use of the moment while the guard was hesitating to slump as much as he could, get his hands up over his face and his elbows together so his arms could protect his chest and stomach.

But there were no more blows. The guard grabbed his arm, jerked him away from the wall, and propelled him out of the room. He did bang Hovey against the doorjamb, and slammed him against walls as they went, but he did not hit him or do anything that might injure him seriously.

Somewhere along their passage another guard joined, taking Hovey's other arm. Between the two of them he was jerked and shoved into an elevator, out into and along another, darker, corridor, and thrown into a cell.

•

Talley had intended to wait until he was home again to call in a report to Walter Simson, but the picture that MacDonald's story had put into his mind bothered him more and more the clearer he saw it. He began to feel a tingle, that tickle in the back of his mind. He finally pulled into a service station along the highway and called from there.

"No, not a lead, Walt, not exactly. But what MacDonald told me about Czerny's arrest—about the way he was handing over the papers to Hovey—doesn't make sense. I mean, why would he do it in plain sight like that? Off at the side of the room, where anybody who was looking could see him?"

"I don't know, Tom. Purloined letter? Make it look innocent—you know, do it in plain sight, because that would be the last thing anyone would expect him to do if it was anything he shouldn't do? Or . . . I told you how arrogant he is."

"No. I mean, maybe—sure, anything is possible. But I don't think it makes sense, not if he had reason to believe he was in real danger—I mean danger on this particular transfer. And especially not if he believed there was a possibility he was being betrayed. He may have been arrogant, Walt, but I can't believe the man was a fool."

Simson was with him. "And if he didn't believe he was in any special danger, then why have the backup channel to get the material out? Yeah, you're right. That would tend to strengthen the hypothesis that the Czechs fed us the stuff. That is what you're thinking, isn't it?''

"Yes. Look, Walt, I know we thought the best approach for me was to work on the Hovey line first; but I've got an itch on this. I think we should go both ways at once. I think I ought to go back over and talk to the guy who contacted the attaché.''

"Yeah. I think you're right. But that may be a problem.''

"Why?''

"I don't know who he is. He came to Military, so naturally they're holding his identity.''

"Oh, shit, be serious. I mean, maybe that is how those things are done, usually, sure. But under the circumstances—''

"That's the point, Tom. *Especially* under these circumstances, they're not going to want to let any of *us* know.''

Talley took a deep breath to control his anger. "Well, the backup is the line that ought to be looked into next. If you—your committee—is serious about looking into this at all. And if you're not, what the hell am I wasting my time for?''

"Okay, Tom, okay. I'll see what I can do.''

•

"Cartwright says that you should make up a list of questions, and he'll have one of his people ask them.''

Talley didn't respond for the first moment out of incredulity, and for a second moment as he tried to control his anger. He looked out of the window by his worktable. The view of field and mountain usually soothed him, but the provocation this time seemed too great.

"For chrissake—! Are you serious? Are they serious? Make up a list—and then, for follow-ups, make up *another* list? Is that how those assholes think you do a debriefing? By proxy? No wonder they came up with the numbers they did. We are not exactly flush with leads on this thing, Walt. I think this may be one, and if we're going to crack this—I am not going to fuck around playing sillyass chickenshit chain-of-command games! Now, you get that guy's name!"

"Well, I'll surely try, Tom, since you put it that way. I'm sorry to have upset you. But at least I'm glad that you seem to have developed some real feeling about this thing."

•

Professor Hovey did sleep that first night, for perhaps as much as two hours altogether.

The cell they had shoved him into measured barely four feet by eight. Along one side, bolted into the walls, looking more like an instrument of torture than a convenience, was a bench made of iron: iron framework, iron slats. It might be used as a bed, but there was no mattress or pad or any kind of covering, and even a sideshow thin man who tried to lie there on his back would have one shoulder pressed to the wall and the other over the edge. A naked light bulb shone from the center of the high ceiling—too high to be reached even if one stood on the bench. Except for the bench and bulb and the metal-skinned door, every surface was poured concrete. The cell was cold, and it stank.

He sat for a while, perched on the edge of the bench. The
wall chilled his back too much to lean against. When he tired
of sitting he lay as best he could, curled on his side. Gradually he warmed the metal slats, but as he could not soften
them or endure his body's pressure on them for too long at a
time, he had to shift from one side to the other.

Through the thin hours he held himself drawn up against
the iron, the concrete, and the cold, against doubt and de-
spondency. Though he played the mental games he had
learned in similar situations—blanking his mind or distracting
it—he could not prevent himself from knowing those situations were really not similar.

A different pair of guards came for him, finally. They
stood outside the doorway and motioned to him, then walked
him without touching him—one on either side—directing him
by further gestures. At one point they came to a men's room,
which they let him use before taking him on. They brought
him to an office, knocked, heard a reply, showed him in, and
closed the door behind him without entering themselves.

Compared to the cell, and to the first room where he
had been taken, this office was spacious. Clearly it was the
office of a person, not merely a room for some function.
There were pictures on the walls, shelves with books and
some personal bric-a-brac. A couch, two armchairs, and a
low table offered a place for informal conversation at one
side. The desk stood beyond. On the wall opposite the couch,
windows—though screened now by tipped venetian blinds—
admitted the light of a sunny morning.

"Please sit down, Professor Hovey." The man behind the
desk gestured toward a chair facing him across it.

He was an older man, white-haired, but not at all bald-
eagle-looking like Janos Czerny. The hair was soft, and full

at the sides and back, receding in the middle to reveal a high forehead. His mustache was white, too, thick, and combed outward from the center.

Professor Hovey crossed the room and took the indicated chair. Although the other man had papers spread on the desk in front of him, he did not play the bureaucrat's game of making his visitor wait while he read them. He simply watched Professor Hovey seat himself, with an expression neither severe nor benign—although the lines of his long face suggested he might take either expression, be either schoolmaster or jolly uncle, with equal habit and ease. His eyes neither twinkled nor burned, but did have the brightness of keen perception.

"I am Dr. Benda," he said. "Doctor of Laws. I am in charge of the investigation of this matter." He spoke with a distinct accent but with almost flawless grammar.

"To begin, I apologize for your treatment here last night. The young officer whom you met has done very well in cases involving—the latest, I believe, was a burglary gang. He should not have been advanced to this kind of case without having been given better instruction as to the methods appropriate for dealing with it.

"To be even-handed, I must say that your own behavior was not that of a civilized person. We do acknowledge the provocation, though, and will assume now that apologies have been extended and accepted on both sides.

"When you leave here, you will be taken to a different sort of cell, and you will be given breakfast."

Professor Hovey tried to guess, to sense, what kind of man this Dr. Benda might be—his rank, his function. *In charge of the investigation.* A policeman, secret police? He wore no uniform; he was dressed in a tweed jacket. *Doctor of Laws.*

A prosecutor? What he looked like, Professor Hovey suddenly decided, was a law school dean.

"Now," Dr. Benda said, "I have had you brought here in order that I may explain your situation to you.

"Later this morning you will be taken before a magistrate to be charged. An attorney will be provided to defend you, and he will confer with you, but as the proceedings will be in our language, naturally, I thought it would be helpful for you to know in advance what will occur.

"A prosecutor will tell the magistrate that you were seen receiving a document from Janos Czerny. At your trial, witnesses will testify to this; this morning will not be a trial, and the magistrate will accept the word of the prosecutor that such witnesses exist. The prosecutor will then present this document."

Dr. Benda spread typewritten pages, each in a separate plastic envelope. He picked up a small pair of forceps, carefully took hold of one sheet, and pulled it half an inch out of its cover.

"Please look at this paper, Professor Hovey. You will see that it is of very good quality. Note in particular the fine finish, the coating that gives it such richness. There is no paper of this quality manufactured in Czechoslovakia. Janos Czerny will probably say he bought it in France, but the truth is that it must have been made in your country. We will not try to prove that, but we will prove that the coating has a very special property: its molecules can be rearranged by electromagnetic stimulation. At the actual trial, we will show how the molecules on these pages have been arranged by equipment in Janos Czerny's possession so that information can be read from them: information about the placement of weapons intended to protect the lives of the people of this country against attack by an aggressor.

"Look here." He pushed one page closer to Professor Hovey, and pointed to smudges on the paper that were circled by rings drawn on the plastic over them. "We will show that these are Janos Czerny's fingerprints, and these are your fingerprints."

He drew all of the pages back to himself and piled them. "On the basis of this presentation, the magistrate will, we are sure, order you bound over for trial. Given that this is a case involving state security, you will be held in custody.

"As I have said, you will be provided with an attorney. You also have the right to engage one of your own, even to bring one from the United States to be associated with your defense if you wish to do that—if you can afford to pay for it, or have someone who will pay on your behalf.

"You also will be given the opportunity, after you have been before the magistrate, to speak with someone from your embassy. Your embassy has been notified of your arrest. Do you have any questions about these procedures?"

"Can I call home? My . . . family, my college?"

"No. I am sorry. Such contact must be made through the representative of your embassy. Later, you will be permitted to write letters, and to receive them. They will be subject to examination, of course. Is everything else clear?"

"I think so."

"Good. I hope you will see, now, that despite the first impression given you last night, our system of justice here follows the norm of all civilized nations. After the formalities of this morning are completed, I will be talking with you again. Please feel free to ask me about anything you do not understand." Dr. Benda nodded once, smiling briefly—not with warmth, but enough to show he felt no hostility. "The officers are waiting outside."

For Professor Hovey the interview had been like someone piling ton upon ton of lead on his heart. For a moment he thought he might be too weak to lift the weight and rise. Yet he was grateful for having been told his situation. and for Benda's manner toward him. He forced himself up. "Thank you," he said.

Dr. Benda nodded again in acknowledgment, then as Hovey was turning, seemed to remember one more detail. "Oh. I do not wish to alarm you, Professor Hovey—the penalty has not actually been invoked upon a person like yourself in many years—but you should at least be told: as in your own country, the maximum penalty here for espionage is death."

CHAPTER 5

Talley began watching for her at four o'clock. He knew that was foolish. She had an exam until two, she would probably walk home and change clothes before starting, and it would take three hours for her to drive up. She had said she would see him between five-thirty and six. But starting at four he went to the window every time he heard a car on the road below, and at a quarter to five he shut down his processor and gave up all attempts at working.

He had cleaned his house that morning, set the table. After lunch he had made all the preliminary preparations for dinner. He checked everything again. A few of the wildflowers he had picked for the table had wilted. He removed them, went out to the edge of the woods beyond his lawn, picked another half-dozen violets. The violets grew there in profusion among white barren-strawberry blossoms. He knew he was perpetrating a pathetic fallacy, but it did seem to him that the earth had burst into bloom to greet his new love.

He knew he was making a fool of himself. Tom Talley,

ex-CIA, the fastest mind in the west. Even if he hadn't ever waited out in the cold for somebody to come over the wall with the microfilm, he had been a sort of a spy. Spies are supposed to be tough. He was tough. He was a man able to keep cool under pressure. Yet here he was practically scurrying about in a frilly apron, picking at lint on doilies. God, what a fool a man can be for love!

But what the hell, he thought. If Marc Antony could throw away half the world for Cleopatra, Tom Talley could let himself be beguiled from his work for a day. With the knowledge of what he was doing as a lifeline, he allowed himself to plunge into the purple pool of pulp fiction passion.

The spring weather was glorious; she would be having a beautiful drive. He was thrilled for that.

At five-twenty she turned in from the road and started up his drive. She had packed that morning so she could leave directly from work. She had exceeded the speed limit nearly all the way.

He was outside to meet her before she reached the house, and had gotten to her door before she had turned off the engine.

"Hi," she said, looking up at him.

"Hi."

He showed her around outside, and then through the house. She delighted him by seeming truly to see and appreciate the things he had done with it.

He hadn't planned it: it was only the natural sequence of room to room that brought them to the bedroom last.

"Oh, what a wonderful bed!"

"I got it at an auction. I . . ."

Then they weren't looking at the bed anymore, and then they were clutching each other, pulling at each other's clothes, almost falling sideways onto the bed.

•

The long spring day gave them sunlight for two hours yet after they came downstairs again, and brightness glowed warmly in the sky even after the sun had set behind the hill. The intensity of their desire for one another now relieved, they lingered over the soft white wine, talking with a sense of quiet, of total intimacy.

". . . the divorce was mostly my fault, I think. If 'fault' is the right word at all. There were things on both sides, but I wasn't able . . ."

"Larry was a lot of fun. At first. He's an interesting man, brilliant, witty. He has his own slant on things—shakes up your own thinking. I like that. He has an attitude, though, that if you don't agree with him, it's because you just aren't seeing things clearly. He used to try to be very nice about trying to explain in a way that suggested you'd *missed* something, not that you were stupid. Over the past year or so he'd stopped trying."

When they found themselves both yawning, they went to bed without making a point about it. This time they were relaxed in their lovemaking, massaging one another's backs, fondling and giving pleasure to each other gently.

•

They ate breakfast on Talley's porch, looking out at the apple trees and the lawn bright with dew in the fresh morning. Then he showed her around the neighboring farm, introducing her with pride to Charley and Old Jim.

They took a picnic lunch down through the meadows and across the pasture to the little river fed by Talley's brook. A grassy bank two yards wide lay there below the pasture level, out of sight. Bluets and violets spread across the grass; windflowers clustered beneath the newly leafing trees. Birds sang and called from all around them: a robin to their left, warblers in the bushes across the stream.

He told her about his friends, about the life of the community. "When you go to see someone for some purpose—you want to borrow something, or you need help—you don't just come up and ask. You always 'visit' for a while—talk about the weather, gossip, anything. I mean, the sense has to be that you stopped by to see the person, and then, 'Oh, by the way . . .' You don't deal with people just in terms of business, of a function—like they were machines that you just come up and use.

"And with the real old-timers, you don't even ask for anything. Not unless the other person is family, or a really close friend. One time, not long after I bought the house here, Old Jim drove up. And after he'd said something about the weather, and admired my garden, he mentioned that the cows had gotten out of the pasture and he was going to try to round them up. He didn't ask for help. If I wanted to come along, I could—and I did, and he thanked me. But if I hadn't volunteered, he'd have just gone on and tried to do it himself."

"Is that a matter of not wanting to impose, or of not wanting to obligate yourself?"

"Maybe a little of each. Or . . . I think it's more of that Yankee independence: a person should make up his own mind and do what he wants to do without being forced, or required, or obligated, or having anything laid on him."

After eating their lunch, and drinking May wine with it, they lay back drowsily against the rise. They stared straight up, allowing themselves to be half hypnotized by the gently fluttering lacework of budding leaves on the branches over-head. Jane lay against Talley's side, her head on his shoulder. After a while he turned and kissed her cheek, and then put his hand on her breast.

"*Again?*" she asked.

"Why not?"

"*Here?*"

"Nobody can see us. It would be very D. H. Lawrence."

"If you want to be D. H. Lawrence, we should put flowers in each other's pubic hair."

"Well, I'm beginning to think he knew what he was talking about."

•

Talley had been correct in his assurance that no one could see them on that lower level by the river. Chip Bolander guessed what they were doing, though, because that was what he would have done—without the flowers. From the shadowed place that he had found at the edge of the woods half a mile from Talley's house, he had watched through his binoculars as they crossed the meadow with their picnic basket and went down out of sight.

So that his car might not attract notice by being parked on the road shoulder all day, he went back to his motel for a few hours. He was sure Talley and his girl friend weren't going to take off on him.

•

It was Saturday, and Talley and Jane decided to have an ethnic evening. They drove into town, cruised Main Street with the car windows open, not playing their own radio, but listening to the blasters of the kids who went by them. Then they went to the movie, bought popcorn. Jane clutched Talley's hand and buried her face half against his shoulder in the more terrifying parts.

•

Bolander saw them safely into the theater, and felt sure they weren't going to go anywhere that night. He cruised a couple of the local lounges, and saw two women he thought he probably could make, but one was too skinny and the other old. He finally went back to the motel and watched TV.

•

There were high clouds across the sky in the morning, but the weather report promised no rain before the next day. Only Walter Simson's call, coming before they set off for a walk in the woods, disturbed their idyll, and the interruption was brief and brought good news in compensation.

"Maxim Alexandrovitch."

"*Alexandrovitch?*"

"The pianist."

"Oh, I thought you meant Maxim Alexandrovitch the paperhanger. Or Old Alex, the plumber."

"Okay, Tom. So you're a man of culture. I'm sorry. Yes,

him. I'm sure he's not in the information business regularly, like Czerny was. I think it was probably a one-time thing. Whoever set it up to get the material out of Russia—Czerny himself, or . . . whoever—must have used him because when *he* called an ambassador he'd get a reply. I don't really know, because DIA isn't telling any more than they have to. Maybe they thought they could set up something with him on a regular basis; more likely they just wanted to keep his name to themselves on principle and to spite us.''

"Well, his name is all we need right now. Congratulations, Walt.''

"It sure wasn't easy. I was considering threatening to resign, but I don't want to use that if I can help it. That's one you only get to use once or twice, and I may need it for something bigger before this is finished. I had to go up to the director, and he called a powwow, and we called his friends on Oversight and told them that if DIA wasn't going to cooperate with their information, then we didn't see why the agency should be open, and maybe this would just have to be handled internally after all. We'd never have gotten away with that position on our own, but Senator Weismer took it as though it were his, and ran it through. So, you can go see Alexandrovitch.''

"Terrific! Where is he?''

"Vienna. He keeps an apartment there, and he's going to be there all next week. DIA is handling it so he'll know you're coming, and you should contact a Major Howard at the embassy as a courtesy; but you can have your go at him by yourself.''

"Great! I'll go tomorrow. Flights for Europe usually leave in the evening, so I should be there by Tuesday morning. I'll get back to you on Wednesday. Maybe we're finally going to get this thing going!''

•

So Talley rode down to Boston with Jane. She had planned to go back late, but since they would now be together anyway, they made the trip after lunch. They stopped at a supermarket to buy groceries and a Sunday *Times*. Talley made elaborate club sandwiches for supper, and they sat side by side on the Victorian couch and read.

•

Bolander had lost them for a while after they had left Talley's house. They surprised him by going on down the road, the scenic route, instead of back into town for the interstate. But it didn't matter. Bolander had recognized Jane by then. He had raised his eyebrows and made a face to himself in surprise. When he realized what had happened, he simply went back the quicker way by himself and was parked two blocks beyond Jane's house by the time they arrived.

•

"This is a wonderful bed," Talley said.

"Yes. I like yours better. It's so-o-o soft."

"I mean the bed—the head- and footboard." Propped slightly on the pillows Talley could see the footboard in ornate silhouette against the windows.

"Oh, yes. It really is magnificent. In the nineteenth century you didn't just flake out on a pad, did you."

"I should say not. When you were people of substance you retired, pater and mater familias, in a proper bed."

"Anytime you're a person of substance, Tom, you can pate and mate my familias. Even if it's not proper."

"Ow! I don't know which is worse, your jokes or your mind."

"Don't mind my jokes, it's my baloney that's wurst."

"Cut it out! Now, I am not going to lie here and be your straight man all night!"

"That's obvious."

"Then again, if there ever was someone who could set a man straight . . ."

Since their lovemaking they had lain side by side, the sheet kicked down, letting the barely moving night air cool them.

After a few moments Jane said, "I'll bet Larry's great-great-grandfather would turn over in his grave if he knew all the things that had gone on in this bed."

"He must have done a few of them himself."

"Oh, I didn't mean that. I meant what you were saying about the bed as an institution. He was a banker, I guess a pillar of the community and all that. If he'd known his bed was being used by . . . well, for purposes of *sin* . . ."

"This was Larry's great-grandfather's bed?"

"His great-*great*-grandfather. Most of the really good old pieces in the house were his. What's the matter?"

They had been lying without touching, except that Talley had let his palm lie on her belly. He suddenly had taken his hand away.

"Then this really is *Larry's* bed."

"Well, yes. What's the matter? Tom . . . I was Larry's lover. You've been screwing me blind for the past three

days, and you don't mean that that didn't bother you but now
you're all upset because we've done it in his bed?''

"I . . ."

"That's ridiculous!"

"I can't help it!"

"What is this, some kind of masculine code of honor?''

"I don't know. It just . . . doesn't feel right."

"Well, Jesus Christ! Maybe you'd better just sleep on the
floor!" She flung herself onto her side, away from him.

After a moment he touched her shoulder with his fingertips. "I'm sorry."

"How do you think that makes *me* feel?'' She was weeping.

"I'm sorry. It was a stupid, irrational thing. Don't turn
away. Please."

She did turn back to him, and cuddled against his side. In
a little while, she slept. Talley didn't sleep for a long time,
and then not well.

•

Dr. Benda's explanation about the proceedings had made
Professor Hovey feel better. As he had been told, as he
would have expected, they were conducted in Czech, but
they might have been unintelligible to him even in a language
he understood, so quiet were they.

They took place in a small courtroom that looked much
like the ones where he had been arraigned at home. He was
not brought to stand before the magistrate, though. He was
seated between his two guards. His attorney, with whom he
had spoken for less than a minute, and another man who was
obviously the prosecutor, stood before the magistrate's bench.

The prosecutor did most of the talking, and produced the papers Dr. Benda had shown. The attorney and magistrate sometimes asked a question. All of the conversation was carried on in an undertone, as mere routine. The attorney must have entered the plea of not guilty, as he had said he would, "pro forma, at this point." The magistrate said something, waved his hand. It was over in three minutes.

Professor Hovey imagined how bewildered he might have been, how that might have increased his anxiety, had he not known what was happening. Knowing gave him the illusion rational people have that when they understand a problem they can solve it.

The illusion that everything would be all right was strengthened when he met the man from the embassy.

"George Tillinghast." The man had a good handshake, and was able to look grave yet smile at the same time: the expression periodontists use to convey that though the condition may be serious it can be remedied.

He was younger than Professor Hovey, which was disconcerting. Hovey thought of himself in the way most of his academic colleagues did: as a bright young man, even an enfant terrible. The people on campus who were younger than he were students. Tillinghast wasn't a student, but his being younger made Hovey wonder instinctively whether he could be competent.

Tillinghast had his own uncertainties about his station. He wore a three-piece suit and dotted tie, and—when he thought about it—tried to take the little pause before speaking, and to use the careful construction, of his immediate superior. But he was a young man, and he had been popular among his fellows at the Fletcher School for his imitations of stuffed-shirted dignitaries who came to lecture, and he still felt most comfortable when he could deal with people as people rather than by protocol. He was sure that with practice he would be able to blend the approaches into a dynamite style of diplomacy.

As he sat down across the little table from Professor Hovey he raised a finger in front of his lips and rolled his eyes. Then he took out a small notebook and a pen. "First of all, are you being treated all right? Any rough stuff?"

"No. A little last night, but nothing serious. I even got an apology for that."

"What happened?"

"We had a disagreement about where the bathroom was, and when I could use it, and they threw me down in the dungeons for a while. But they put me in a cell this morning—I've had rooms in college dorms that were worse. I've got no complaints." Professor Hovey's tone was that of a varsity man to a scrub, a man who could handle pressure with grace. It hardly broke at all as he added, "I just want to get out of this."

"Man, I believe it!" Perhaps that was too much on the personal side. Tillinghast pushed himself up in his chair. "Well." He clicked his pen, drew a short vertical stroke at the left of one line as though to frame a paragraph. "We'll want to look over the charges and specifications against you before we can reach any firm conclusion as to how to proceed, of course. However, our tentative, preliminary assessment is that this whole thing is a frame-up to get Janos Czerny. Everyone knows what a pain in the ass he's been to them, and they must think they found a way to solve the problem without making him a martyr. But this . . . what they've done here is really unbelievable. It's got to be one enormous bungle. Heads will roll. I mean, the idea of using an international seminar, picking a distinguished scholar like you—evidently at random—planting some sort of phony document on you, or whatever they did . . . The repercussions from that are going to be far more of an embarrassment than any that Czerny might have been causing them.

"Ah . . . I . . ." Professor Hovey faltered, thinking of Tillinghast's signal that the room might be bugged.

"Yes?"

"Nothing."

"Well." Tillinghast made another vertical mark. "We'll lodge a protest, of course." Then he made a horizontal, laid down his pen, and looked at Professor Hovey. "But the Czechs have already made such a big thing of this—given who Czerny is, it's already front-page news all over the world—that . . . to put it to you straight out, there's no way but they will have to follow through and have a trial, just to save face. I have to tell you I don't think they can back down on that.

"Now." He took up the pen, put a stroke on the next line down. This was the place for the blend of styles, because he had to get the reassuring message to Hovey, and make it seem like he was talking only to Hovey, yet hope they were bugged, because the message was for *them* even more than for Hovey. But, Tillinghast liked to think, doing jobs like that well was one of the skills of his chosen profession.

"Our line probably will be to help them see what a really very bad idea it was to involve you, and to help them to find a graceful way of admitting you're innocent: you know, you merely happened to be chatting with Czerny at the moment they picked to swoop down on him. The arresting officers jumped to conclusions. A careful review will show that— whatever accusations they have to make about Janos Czerny— you were merely an innocent bystander. By investigating and establishing that, Czech justice will be vindicated, etcetera, etcetera."

Professor Hovey looked steadily at Tillinghast as he looked

at those of his students who tried to dazzle him with invention so that he might not notice that they hadn't actually read the assignment. But in this case, though he knew the fraud, he didn't want to find the exact phrase that, jerked on, would topple the pile back onto its heaper. He wanted desperately to believe the story was plausible.

•

"I'd like to make a statement," he said.

"Ah. Very good." Dr. Benda took a single sheet from a stack of paper at one corner of his desk, uncapped a fountain pen, and looked up expectantly.

Professor Hovey registered surprise.

"I am a little old-fashioned," Dr. Benda said. "I prefer to take notes and statements myself. Please."

"I met Mr. Czerny for the first time in my life following my paper at the Chekhov seminar. At the reception. I was talking with—"

"Please. A little more slowly?"

"I was talking with a group of people. Professor C. K. Taylor of Birmingham University, England, was there. I didn't know the others, but I'm sure you can find out who they were.

"As they can testify, Mr. Czerny came up to *me*." Professor Hovey went on, describing Czerny's praises, *his* request for a private conversation, *his* suggestion that autographed papers be exchanged. He concluded, "If, as you say, Mr. Czerny's paper had some kind of secret material hidden on it, I knew nothing of that. I can only assume—if what you say is true—that he thought I would be able to get the material out of your country without suspicion. That is, that he intended to use me without my knowledge.''

He allowed only the barest note of indigation to sound in the last. While eating his lunch, and in the time since, he'd rehearsed that effect in his mind—as he had the straightforwardness with which he'd presented the facts before it—so that it all might sound thought-through and sincere, but not prepared.

Dr. Benda was nodding as he finished writing the last words. ''Yes. Good,'' he said. Then he read the entire statement aloud. ''Correct?'' he asked.

''Yes.''

''Good. Please, will you sign at the bottom. And put there also the date, please. Good. This is very clear. Thank you, Professor Hovey. I appreciate your cooperation.'' He smiled again at Hovey.

The smile was reassuring. Everything since the proceedings in court had been reassuring. When the guards had returned Professor Hovey to his cell, he found his clothes had been brought from the hotel and put into the open-shelved cabinet. He had bathed as best he could in the little sink, and changed underwear, socks, and shirt. At noon a large bowl of thick, spicy soup and two slices of dark bread had been brought to him.

His sense of well-being had continued into Dr. Benda's office. The shades on the windows were up. The view was of a courtyard: Hovey had been able to catch a glimpse of other wings of the building now sunlit in the early afternoon. A once bright, now cozily faded floral-patterned fabric covered the couch; the two chairs were covered in leather polished by comfortable use; the carpet was soft and tweedy, the threads in warm browns. He caught that glimpse of the outdoors on one side, and one of landscapes in the prints on the other. Dr.

Benda had risen to greet and wave him into the chair again,
not at all like a prosecutor about to interrogate a criminal.

"So." Dr. Benda put the statement into the top drawer of
his desk. "You must appreciate that although I am very
pleased to have your statement, it will be necessary to pursue
some points and ask you questions. While it may be true that
you are not guilty of any crime in this affair, you are involved. We must ask for your continued cooperation in help-
ing us determine who *is* guilty. Are you willing to help
us?"

"Of course."

"Good. So, first: When did you apply to be a participant
in the seminar?"

"In February. February third, I think it was."

Dr. Benda made note. "I understand that the seminar had
been announced last October. Why did you wait until so late
to apply?"

Professor Hovey explained about the foundation's offer of
support.

"Ah. I see. Please, the name of the foundation, again?"
Dr. Benda took down each answer—the address of the foundation, the method by which Professor Hovey received his
airline ticket, every tiny detail—each on a separate line in his
careful, neat longhand.

"So," he said after an hour. "I think this will be enough
for this time. I may not wish to speak with you again for
another day or two; perhaps you would like to take some
books to read?" He turned to the shelves behind him. Below
the uniform leather-spined sets of references were two rows
of odd ends. "What have we in English? Charles Dickens?"
He pulled out a volume. "*Nicholas Nickleby* might help you
pass the time. *Great Expectations*?"

"Thank you. That's very kind of you."

"Not at all. And I thank you once more for your help."

"I'm glad if I am able to help. I'm sure you understand that I'd like to get this over with and get out of here as soon as I can." Again Professor Hovey felt he had gotten the right tone in his voice, communicating that he was worried enough to be honest, but a man of character who would not grovel: on both counts a man whom Benda could trust.

He was worried, of course. If they used drugs on him, or a lie detector, and asked the right questions, even just *one*— "Were you acting for the CIA?"—they'd have him. But as long as all he had to deal with was Dr. Benda . . . A sharp man, no doubt, but old school, like the kind of elderly professors he'd been getting past for years.

•

"Hi."

"Hi."

Already they had a ritual: the moment's pause, the monosyllabic greeting, the embrace.

Then Jane pushed away from Talley. She carried her briefcase on a hook of two fingers through the arch into the living room and dropped it, kicked off one shoe and the other, flopped down in an armchair. "Oh, God!" she sighed. "What a day!"

"Students wearing you down?"

"No. My colleagues. Faculty meetings. I think there's some kind of . . . Boudreau's Law: the time a faculty spends discussing something varies directly with its triviality. Would you believe we argued for two hours and twenty-five minutes about whether two shorter papers could be considered equivalent to an honors thesis; and, if so, whether they had to be designated for honors consideration before they were written, or whether— Yaaarrrgh!'' She clutched her temples and shook her head like a madwoman.

"There, there." Talley sat on the ottoman, lifted one of her feet to his lap, began massaging it. "It was just a nightmare. Just a bad dream. In a minute you'll wake up."

"Oh, I hope not. Oh, that is so nice. Thank you."

"Do you want a drink?"

"Just some wine." She made a limp attempt at rising.

"I'll get it."

"I'll let you. There's a jug in the fridge."

Talley brought a glass for each of them.

"Thanks."

He sat again, began massaging the other foot. "Supper's ready whenever you want it."

"You made it?"

"Just a casserole and salad."

"I thought you were going to work."

"I did. Read through a bunch of stuff. It didn't take long to do the casserole."

"You really are a liberated man, aren't you?"

"Yeah. I'm going to make some lucky woman a lovely wife." He said it not quite looking at her.

But she looked at him steadily for a moment while she sipped her wine, then turned away.

He had thought all day about what he might say, how to say it; he'd worked out a dozen different forms of words. Still it surprised him to hear himself saying one of them. "Which brings up an interesting subject, don't you think? Or do you?"

"Marriage?"

"Possibly. It's a great institution."

"Is it?"

"Yeah." Then he went on, "I didn't mean I think we're ready for that now. We'd have to find out a lot more about each other. I just mean I'm ready to find out."

"How?"

"Well, I can work anyplace I can plug in my processor and get mail and phone calls. And you . . . you have weekends, holidays, intersessions, the whole summer . . . I thought we could go back and forth."

"Live together."

"Yes."

"With the idea that it might work into being married."

"We could hold the good thought."

She looked at him in silence for a moment, and he could see tears coming into her eyes. "Thank you," she said.

"Oh."

"What's the matter?"

"When a woman says 'thank you' that way, it means she's touched but she's not going to say yes."

"Oh, Tom." She leaned forward quickly, put her hand on his. "I just . . . I just don't know about marriage. I have lived with men; I told you. But . . . it was never on the basis of 'til death us do part.' And they haven't lasted, any of them. And I don't know whether that's because of the particular combinations, or because . . . of me. I'm not sure I can be married, Tom."

"Well, how about the just living-together part?"

"Could you do that? Wouldn't you always be thinking . . . ?"

Talley smiled ironically. "There's a story about Alexander the Great. The priests in Egypt taught him all their magic, so he would be able to do miracles, but then they told him the one last secret: while he was saying the charms he *must not* think of the left eye of a camel.''

"Yes. That's what I meant.''

"What would it matter? God, Aunt Tilly would never believe it: I can live in sin with you just as long as I *don't* want to make an honest woman of you.'' Then he caught himself. "Or can I, anyway? I mean, was this it? Have we already had it all—wham, bam, thank you ma'am—and it's over?''

"No. I hope not. I just . . . I don't want you to get hurt, Tom. I can't commit myself . . . and I doubt . . . I don't want you to get hurt. I . . .''

Suddenly she flung herself out of the chair and into his arms. She was crying. "I . . . I think I love you. I do. And I'm frightened.''

Talley held her, rocking her, feeling that the time of the singing of birds indeed had come.

•

Chip Bolander lost Talley on the way to the airport. The surveillance might have seemed an easy one, since Talley hadn't moved much—neither from his house over the weekend nor from Jane's that day. But Bolander had had to do it alone. He couldn't park in one place all the time, and he had to eat and go to the john sometimes. It was a mark of his professionalism that he hadn't assumed Talley and Jane were in safely for the evening, and gone off himself; and a tribute to his skill that he was able to follow them without being noticed when she drove Talley to the inn to catch the limousine.

But the bad luck of being cut off by an aggressive driver in a truck too big to be argued with, and then a changing traffic light that couldn't be run, let the limousine slip out of his sight. By the time he got through the tunnel and onto the four-lane approach to the terminals, there were five identically colored limos at varying distances ahead. They turned one by one into different entrances, not making the circuit past all terminals, but going only to the ones their passengers wanted. Bolander had no way of knowing which had been Talley's destination.

He cursed quietly but didn't give up. He went on around and into the parking garage. People usually got to airline terminals at least thirty minutes early. He couldn't check all gates from which there were going to be departures during that time unless he took off his clothes and ran around in his shorts pretending to be training for the marathon. But he could make a try, and he might be lucky—why not?

First, though, there was a simpler plan. He called Jane.

"Hello. I'm trying to reach Tom Talley. I got this number from his answering machine."

"I'm sorry, Tom's not here now. He just left on a trip."

"Jesus Christ. I need an appraisal of a flash report I just got from my man in Bangkok, and I don't know if I should— Did he leave a number?"

"No."

"An address? This is really urgent!"

"No. I don't think he knew where he'd be staying. He's gone to Vienna."

"Vienna! What the hell's he doing in Vienna? Okay, never mind. Do you know when he'll be back?"

"It's just a quick trip. He expects to be back again on Wednesday."

"Wednesday! Okay, maybe I can stall— Okay, thanks a lot, ma'am."

"Who should I—"

But Bolander had already hung up.

CHAPTER 6

In a way, Professor Hovey had actually enjoyed the next two and a half days. All through the autumn he'd worked day and night on his production of *Uncle Vanya*, during the days conferring with his designers, checking the technical work, getting in extra time with his leading actors at odd hours around his and their classes, then going into the regular rehearsal every evening from seven until eleven. Six days a week, and then seven the last two weeks. He was known for driving his casts, but also for the polish of his productions. The effort had meant he'd had to work straight through the Christmas break and intersession to prepare the new course he was offering. And that course was an overload in addition to his regular schedule. He hadn't minded the work, the pressure. He liked to work, he liked to show what he could do, and he was coming up for tenure that year. To all of those stresses had been added both the excitement of preparing for the Chekhov seminar, and the tension of playing a secret agent.

111

He had been running on nerve for months, so how could he regret having all those pressures lifted from him, being prevented from working by circumstances beyond his control, being locked in a comfortable room, with nothing to do but sleep and read? It was better than when he'd fallen off a platform at a rehearsal and sprained his back: this time no one brought him papers to grade.

He worried, of course. He went over and over his situation. How had it happened? What would happen to him? He had realized by then that the CIA had deceived him, used him. They hadn't reformed; they were as bad as he'd always said they were. He'd always hated everything they stood for.

But the agent who had called on him after he'd been invited to the seminar had made clear that the agency was the true source of his grant, and that unless he accepted the assignment, it would be withdrawn. He had countered Professor Hovey's anger by appealing to respect and support for Janos Czerny. What person of Professor Hovey's sympathies and principles wouldn't want to help Czerny? And he had given those soothing assurances that there would be no danger.

Professor Hovey had worked and been successful at convincing himself that the appeal to help Czerny had been decisive in winning his reluctant agreement, that he had not been swayed by consideration of the effect going or not going to the seminar might have on his chances for tenure.

Although he knew his arrest was justified in that he *had* been acting as an agent (however much deceived), and though, therefore, he worried, he also was confident he'd be released. The position that Tillinghast had said the embassy would take, his own story to Dr. Benda, and the truth—all of them had a common element: he was an unsuspecting pawn. His treatment during these days suggested the Czechs already recognized it. Once he had testified that, yes, Janos Czerny had put into his innocent hands a paper of whose real nature he had no suspicion, they would have no reason to hold him longer.

The truth would come out, however. He'd get the bastards, tell it all. As soon as he was safely home again— He saw himself getting off the plane, reporters crowding him. Only a simple statement to them at that point to say that the CIA had deceived and used and endangered him (the tickler headline—he knew about publicity). Then a full press conference. He saw himself in Washington, testifying before the Congressional committee. And then the book. The TV appearances. The lectures. He'd get the bastards who'd screwed him and make himself a million dollars doing it!

That prospect, so appealing, more than compensated for the cycles of worry that led to it again each time.

Meals were brought to him. They were hearty, and flavorful enough. Though he recognized the cooking as institutional, and the fare as simple—wurst and sauerkraut, roast pork and dumplings—it was exotic enough to be interesting.

Each morning he was taken out to the courtyard. He would have liked to run, but of course he hadn't the right shoes, and the cobblestones would have been a danger to his feet and ankles anyway. He walked around and around at a rapid pace, and got his heartbeat and breathing up that way.

The first time out, his guards had started to walk with him, one on either side as they had brought him through the corridors and down. But they broke into laughter. Clearly they didn't feel the need for that kind of exercise; and if they understood why a prisoner might, they also thought his rushing journey to nowhere ludicrous. So they stood together in the center, smoking, stamping feet and slapping hands against the late-March cold, rotating as he revolved, or they strolled north and south between the lines of hacked-back trees while he boxed the whole compass.

The same two guards accompanied him each day, and brought his meals. They were young men, as young as his freshman students. They spoke a little more English than he had picked up of Czech—that is, just enough to say "Good morning," "You like?" (his food), "Yes," "Thank you," and "No." Each time they met he taught them and they taught him another word or two of each other's language, and they all took great amusement from their efforts.

Professor Hovey had seen young men like these cheerfully try to break one another's collarbones playing football, meaning no harm by it. He had no doubt that they might break his if he gave them reason. But there was no reason. He never thought of trying to escape. He could enjoy his enforced holiday because of the certainty he soon would be released.

On the afternoon of the third day, then, when Jan and Harry came for him and brought him to Dr. Benda's office, he had no apprehensions at all.

The old man was standing by the couch, looking somberly at one of the prints hung on the wall. "Ah!" he said, turning. His tone seemed to be one of pleasure at seeing Professor Hovey again, but he didn't smile at all. He gestured toward the chair where Professor Hovey had sat before and, without further word, watched him cross the room. He stood with his head tipped slightly forward, so that he looked up under his heavy white eyebrows. He didn't move, at first, and Professor Hovey had to twist in the chair to look at him.

"I am sorry to have detained you, alone, so long. Time was needed to verify some facts. You have been comfortable?"

"Very. This is the nicest jail I've ever been in."

"I am pleased to hear so. The food has been of good taste?"

"Yes. No complaints." Professor Hovey had by then sensed that Dr. Benda's questions, his tone, had an edge, held a purpose beyond polite inquiry before getting to business.

"And, no doubt, you have felt more comfortable in this possibly frightening situation by being allowed to wear your own clothes instead of a prison uniform."

"Yes."

"And Charles Dickens has perhaps distracted your mind from worry."

"I'm very grateful, Dr. Benda."

"Are you?"

"Yes. What's—"

"Then why have you abused me!" Dr. Benda lunged forward a step, then deflected his charge, gathered and held anger back into himself with crossed arms, and paced behind Professor Hovey toward the far corner of the room. "I have treated you in a courteous and with-hands-open manner. I have allowed you privileges unusual for any prisoner, much less one accused of spying—of making in danger the lives of my country people!"

Professor Hovey had twisted the other way. He saw Dr. Benda's back as the man stood, apparently trying to calm himself.

"Endangering," Dr. Benda corrected himself. He took a deep breath, and turned. "And you have lied to me. And you think I am an old fool, and I will not discover you have lied."

"Dr. Benda . . . I haven't lied. I have not told you one lie." Of course he hadn't. He had carefully thought through every word of his statement: every one was true. Professor Hovey's voice could ring with sincerity because his statement was true, and because he sincerely wanted Benda to believe it. And because thinking that he had lied seemed to distress

so personally the old man whose good treatment he could
appreciate by comparison with his other incarcerations.

Dr. Benda whirled and glared, then strode past Professor
Hovey, around to the front of his desk. He grabbed up a
sheaf of papers, thrust them across.

"Here! Find for me this foundation that gives you money!"

Hovey looked at the sheets, first at the heading—United
States Government Internal Revenue Service . . . Nonprofit,
Tax-Exempt . . .—then at the list of names beneath. They
were in alphabetical order. The one that had sponsored him
should have been on the third page. There was the Fitzgerald
Family Foundation, and the Fitzwilliam, but there was no
Fitzmorris.

He tried to remember the letterhead. Had there been any
other name? Any initials? He saw only (in the sharp, classic
dignity of Caslon type, in strong, raised, black print on heavy
paper) *The Fitzmorris Fund.*

With the sense of a man alone on a sinking ship searching
through every pocket for the life belt-locker key he knows he
hasn't got, he looked down for *Fund*, then ruffled the corner-
stapled pages over to the last in hope of finding an addenda.
"I . . ."

"Yes? It is that my weak old eyes fail to see what is there?
Or perhaps you think there is some explanation? Perhaps this
foundation has so much money to give away that it does not
object to giving some to your government—it does not ask
to be exempt from taxation? Perhaps you think *I* try to
deceive *you*—that I have had this document manufactured.
So. Refutation!"

Dr. Benda threw a thick volume at Professor Hovey. It
was the Washington, D.C., telephone directory. "Please,
refute me."

Professor Hovey knew the key would not be between the pages of that book, but he looked there anyway.

"So?"

"Dr. Benda, I . . . I don't understand. I . . ." Hovey knew he was drenched in sweat. He had to grip the phone book tightly to keep it from slipping from his quivering hands. He swallowed, got his mind in gear again.

"Dr. Benda, what I told you is true. I did receive a letter from—it said it was from that foundation. They paid for my plane ticket. I'm telling you the truth."

Dr. Benda had been leaning forward, propping himself on straightened arms over his desk. He waited a moment, then came upright again. "Are you?"

Professor Hovey looked directly into his eyes. "Yes."

Those dark eyes narrowed, and the white mustache twitched to one side. Dr. Benda turned and walked back to the picture where he had been at the first. "Come here, please, Professor Hovey."

Professor Hovey laid the book on the desk and, feeling as though all his weight, his substance, had gone into his feet, went to join Dr. Benda.

"Look here. A charming scene, is it not?"

The print showed a bucolic landscape: meadows, peasants with a wagonload of hay, a distant village, an onion-domed church. A river wound from left to distant right-of-center.

"Yes."

"Do you know what it is?"

"No."

"The river Moldau."

Professor Hovey tried to look blankly mystified.

"I understand you have an interest in it. Come." Dr. Benda waved abruptly toward his desk.

The two men returned to their usual positions. When Professor Hovey had seated himself again on the edge of his chair, Dr. Benda opened a drawer.

"This was not returned to you after the night of your arrest." He held up the red and white striped tie. "Nor can it be, since it is required as evidence."

Professor Hovey licked his lips but couldn't think of a thing to say. His heart surged, trying to drive the liquid ice through his body.

"Perhaps you think I have played on you a trick by not telling until now that our security apparatus knew in advance of your mission, knew in advance of the means by which you would identify yourself to the traitor Czerny. Perhaps I have deceived you. It was my hope that because of what I know of you—your association in the past with the causes of peace and antifascism—that possibly you were not fully aware of what you were doing. Perhaps you were somehow deceived yourself and did not know the identity of those who sent you. But since you have lied to me in the statement you gave, since you have persisted in this fiction that you came here only as a scholar supported by a foundation, then I see that—whatever your past—you are a conscious, willing spy."

As Professor Hovey gaped, swallowed, tried desperately to think of something to say, Dr. Benda pressed a button at one corner of his desk. The corridor door was flung open, and the two guards rushed in. Benda snapped orders to them rapidly, loudly. Then he looked back down at the young man so stunned, so slack.

"Mr. Tillinghast, from your embassy, has asked to speak with you again. I have told him we will permit this now, briefly, before we begin our serious interrogation of you."

Dr. Benda spoke again in Czech, and the guards strode up to flank Professor Hovey, half lifted him from the chair—

since he seemed unable to raise himself—and walked him from the office.

This time there was no joking. The young men were set-jawed and grim, gripping Professor Hovey's arms. They were not rough, but they steered him as they would: they moved him: he only churned his legs automatically, only to keep them under him, only so he wouldn't be dragged.

Down two flights of stairs, into another wing of the building, into a room divided by a waist-high wall and metal mesh above it, bare but for a high stool on either side. They deposited him on the one on his side. They closed the door but stood by it, in the room with him, watching him.

Tillinghast came into the other section. For an instant he registered shock at the room, the presence of the guards. But to let an opponent disconcert you is to give him advantage. He drew himself up, crossed, and sat on his stool as if he were familiar with these facilities, that they were prescribed by ancient and honored protocol. He leaned his attaché case against the wall and adjusted the sharp crease of his pin-striped trousers. He almost lost his decorum, though, as he peered through the mesh and perceived Professor Hovey's expression.

"Are you all right?"

Professor Hovey shook his head negatively, then up and down.

"Have you been beaten?"

Again he was answered by a headshake. He looked carefully into Professor Hovey's eyes. "Are you drugged?"

"No. I . . ."

Tillinghast didn't expect the answer to answer his question; he tried to diagnose it from Hovey's eyes, his manner. "How are you, then?"

"I'm— What's happening? What are you doing to get me out of here?"

Not a narcotized reaction. Probably only the effects of worry and depression. Tillinghast wanted to bring relief. "Well, Professor Hovey, we're working on it. The ambassador himself has been dealing with it personally. We had a staff meeting just this morning. It's number one . . ." But he had only those palliatives, no cure. "It seems, though, there's been a new development."

"What?"

"Well, it seems like they're determined to do the whole nine yards, have a big show-trial production. They answered our protest by informing us that they have evidence you were working for the CIA. If they try it, it'll blow up in their faces, of course. I mean, they'll put themselves right back in the cold war: freeze off the tourists, trade, etcetera. If they can pick on you, they could pick anybody. Naturally, we made a discreet inquiry, and of course the CIA denies they ever heard of you. I mean, seriously, privately—for our own guidance. So, the position now seems—"

"They can't do that!"

"What?"

"They can't leave me hanging!"

"Ah . . . Exactly what do you—"

"They've got to get me out of here!"

Tillinghast didn't know quite what to do. Again he assumed the conversation would be recorded, and those guards might not be as uncomprehending as they seemed. But though he half knew the futility, he instinctively hunched forward toward Professor Hovey and lowered his voice. "Careful, Professor. Watch what you're saying."

"They know!"

"Ah . . . I don't think I understand." Tillinghast suddenly
thought he did, but didn't want to.

"Benda knows! I *was* sent here by the CIA! Dr. Benda
knows the whole thing! They've got to get me out of here!"

"Professor Hovey, ah . . . I must assume, sir, that you've
been subjected to some kind of metal duress and suggestion.
We've been assured—"

"No! Goddamnit! God— They can't—"

"Professor!" Then Tillinghast hunched again. "Professor,
even if you were . . . I mean, purely for the sake of argument, even if we imagined you were on . . . ah . . . in some
way connected . . . you can't expect that it would be admitted. Now, if that were the case—purely as a hypothesis—
why, I think you'd be advised to hang tough. Something
would be done eventually . . . I don't know . . . it's not my
area, but—I would imagine—eventually some kind of exchange . . ."

"No! Now! They've got to— They can't— Help me!"

"Professor, I'm out of my depth here. Now, what I'm
going to have to do is get back to the embassy and report this
development. I assure you, though, sir, that your country
will stand behind you. You can count on that. Now, you just
hang tough, and we'll get back to you."

•

Back through the corridors, up the flights of stairs, guided
again between the guards, Professor Hovey went like a
sommambulist. He began to get his mind going again, finally,
only when seated once more in Dr. Benda's office. He'd
been deceived, used, and now he was being abandoned. They

were going to deny him, try to turn their own bungling into propaganda.

For the first time, the old man was not waiting for him, and Professor Hovey sat by himself at the desk, the guards inside the room, by the door, behind him. He faced the chair where that shrewd inquisitor would sit—that inquisitor from whom (he knew now) no secrets could be hidden.

Late afternoon in March: already the sun had set. Its last light colored the sky a dirty purple-brown, and there were thin streaks of silhouetted cloud as though someone had tried to sweep a sooty surface and given up for making things worse.

He wasn't left alone long. Dr. Benda returned, went to his place, but remained standing. He turned on a reading lamp, one shaded so that it threw no glare into Professor Hovey's eyes but directed all its light down onto the desk top. He took papers from a drawer and began spreading them.

He spoke without looking at Professor Hovey. "I wish, first of all, to apologize for my manner in speaking to you earlier. The fact is that you remind me of . . . a certain young person for whom I have an affection. Therefore, I felt offended personally when you tried to deceive me, and was angry. However, neither affection nor anger nor any other emotion should be permitted to intrude in matters of the law.

"Furthermore, it is to be expected that you should try to deceive me. I should not have allowed myself to be personally concerned, disappointed in you.

"Now, we shall begin without emotion to cut our way through deceptions."

Again he leaned forward on stiffened arms and looked down at Professor Hovey. Reflection struck his face, emphasizing its stern lines and making his eyes gleam, though they seemed all the darker under the highlighted eyebrows.

"So. Do you wish to declare truthfully who sent you here? We shall not try to force a confession from you. Despite what the propaganda of those who rule your country has told you, we do not use such methods. You may persist in claiming you were sponsored by this imaginary foundation if you wish, but I must tell you that, at your trial, when we prove by United States government documents that it does not exist, your attitude will be taken very much against—"

"Dr. Benda?"

"Yes?"

"What's going to happen to me?"

"You are going to be tried for espionage."

"Then what?"

"You will be found guilty. I do not prejudge from bias. You are guilty. The evidence is here." He tapped the papers under his fist.

"Then what?"

After a moment, Dr. Benda let himself down into his chair so that he could look levelly at the young man. "I do not believe you will be executed. Such things are not done anymore, and—whatever your guilt—you are not a professional spy. On the basis of sentences that have been given in your own country to persons found guilty of trying to steal your nation's military secrets, I expect you will be sentenced to thirty years at hard labor. You will probably be assigned to one of the camps from which workers are drawn for military construction projects."

"What would happen if I confess?"

"I do not wish to offer any inducements in order to secure a false confession."

"Please." Professor Hovey's hands went out in supplication. He saw them, and felt they had demeaned him. He clasped them in his lap. "You know what's true, and what's false."

"I believe I do."

"I didn't know Janos Czerny was going to give me any papers, any secrets. I didn't. I was sent by the CIA to meet him. I was only supposed to give him a message."

"What message?"

" 'I'd like to see the Moldau sometime.' "

"That was merely the recognition code."

"That was the message. That was what they told me. They never told me about any papers, that I was to bring anything back."

After a searching pause, Benda asked, "Is this true, my boy?"

"Yes."

"Then I believe you have been very badly, very unscrupulously used."

"Yes."

Dr. Benda looked steadily at Professor Hovey. Although his stare was as keen, it seemed somehow less stern. He folded his hands before him on the desk. Professor Hovey had not noticed before how large they were, how gnarled the knuckles. He let the old man look into his own eyes for as long as he wanted; there would be an end to deception.

Finally Dr. Benda spoke softly, as though to himself, but in English. "It is not right," he said. Without explanation he turned and used the telephone that he lifted from the shelves behind him. He spoke a few words, hung up again.

"We will try," he said. "Now." He took a page from his stack of paper and uncapped his pen. "Please begin."

"Where?"

"Wherever you like. Wherever this began for you."

Ten minutes later they were interrupted by the telephone

ringing. Dr. Benda seemed to report, to explain, then—in a
careful way—to argue. For an instant his face fell, and he
looked quickly at Professor Hovey and then away again.
Although he frequently inserted the words the guards used
that Professor Hovey recognized must mean "Yes, sir," his
tone became stronger. Finally, as though his hearer were
facing him, he held up a hand, then seemed to introduce a
new idea. He listened, nodding abruptly in unseen agreement. He said "Yes, sir" twice more, then hung up, turned
back to Hovey. He opened his hands and shrugged.

"The authorities insist that there must be a trial, and there
must be a sentence, and it must be served. An example must
be made. Other people like yourself must be deterred, must
understand they cannot threaten our security and escape because they are amateurs and claim they didn't know the
risk."

Professor Hovey closed his eyes. But he clenched his jaw,
too. He wouldn't weep. They wouldn't break him; he wouldn't
ever let the bastards break him.

"But, but, but . . . It is not so bad as it seems."

Professor Hovey looked at him again.

"We can make what you call a bargain over the plea. You
must plead guilty. You must confess fully. For this cooperation and spirit of . . . what word? Repentance? Not right, but
you understand . . . you will be sentenced to a minimum
security facility for five years—with the possibility of reduc-
tion in time for good behavior. Will you consent to this?"

"Thank you, Dr. Benda. Thank you." And Professor
Hovey did weep.

CHAPTER 7

The airliner hurtled down the runway and then tipped them sharply backward, and shot up into the deep blue sky. Talley dozed through most of the short night and even for a while after they'd run up to the sun.

Although a little neck-achy and gritty of eye, he wasn't really tired when they reached Vienna. He took the bus to the city and called from the terminus.

"Major Howard." The officer's voice was firm and businesslike, but not abrupt.

"Good morning, Major. This is Thomas Talley. I believe you're expecting me."

"Right. You're all set up to see the person you want to talk to this afternoon. Fifteen hundred. I thought you might want a little rest first, after the flight."

"Thanks. I appreciate it. Do you want me to come over to see you?"

"Right now? No. Not unless you need something. How about lunch?"

"That would be fine."

"Do you know Vienna?"

"Never been here before."

"There's an outdoor café in the Volksgarten. Nice on a day like this."

"Sounds great."

They determined how they would recognize each other, and agreed on a time. Talley got a hotel through the reservation service at the terminus, and took a taxi. The hotel was small, old, and—despite being just around the corner from the cathedral—quiet. He went straight to bed and napped for two hours so fatigue wouldn't sandbag him that afternoon.

If Talley had ever worked as one of that tiny minority of people in intelligence services who really are spies—field agents, those who are the heroes and villains of films—if he'd had that kind of experience instead of sitting at a desk trying to draw conclusions from masses of facts on paper, he might have spotted the men who had followed him.

•

Talley felt he would like Vienna. He walked through the center of the city to the park where the café was. All of the building facades were of stone: substantial, solid, but in no way hard or grim. In the clear spring sunlight they were warm, mellow, some creamy beige, some dark brown, trimmed with heavily carved cornices and windowcasings, niches and reliefs, statuary, all elaborate, exuberant, fantastically flamboyant. Smartly dressed people strolled in and out of chic-looking shops, traffic passed along the streets but without the haste, the rush to be finished here and on to business somewhere else that he sensed in cities that he knew, American or Asian. Jane had been to Vienna; she'd told him he'd like it. He thought of her, of coming back with her. Again, he never noticed the man behind, or the one across the street.

Major Howard was as he had described himself: tall, thin, with short hair gray at the sides, wearing a light gray business suit. He had arrived early enough to get a table before the noon rush. Talley had no trouble recognizing him. They got business out of the way quickly—all too quickly for Talley, since there was so little the major could tell him.

"All Alexandrovitch said was he had been given some papers to pass on to us. He didn't know what they were, couldn't vouch for them in any way. He refused to say who had given them to him—only that we were to know they had come out of the Soviet Union and from Janos Czerny, and that they were to be sent to the highest levels of military intelligence before they were seen by the CIA."

Talley admired Major Howard's restraint in offering the last without comment, even in tone of voice or lift of eyebrow.

"I don't imagine," Howard went on, "that I'm telling you anything you don't already know. I'm sorry, but that's all there is."

Talley stared at the bubbles rising in his glass of beer. Their lunches hadn't come yet, and he didn't want to drink much. "Are you in intelligence, Major? If you can say."

"Aren't we all? But, no, I'm not actually in intelligence. I did my combat in Vietnam, and my garrison in Germany, and now I've drawn a diplomatic tour—I guess because I must have been a good boy. Why?"

"I just wondered. Well, no, you haven't told me anything new. But hearing you tell it suggests an interesting point."

"Oh? But I don't suppose you'll tell me what it is."

"No." Talley smiled.

Major Howard smiled back. "I didn't think so."

"But maybe, after you've told your people that I said there was something interesting, and they think about it, if they figure out what I meant, maybe *they'll* tell you."

Their lunches were served, and they enjoyed them very much, sitting in the pleasant light of the sun shining through the yellow umbrella over their table. All of the umbrellas seen against green foliage and the white blossoms of chestnut trees, the white-clothed tables, the other patrons lingering over their glasses after their leisurely meals, gave Talley a sense of festive holiday. Despite the excitement beginning to simmer in him as the back of his mind prodded at the thought Howard had put there, he forced himself to loll and absorb the Viennese sense that nothing is so serious as to hurry through lunch for. Never mind his work—his own or Simson's; if he hadn't wanted so much to be with Jane again, he easily might have changed his reservation and stayed another day, or week.

"I have a stop to make," Major Howard said as they parted, "but I'll be back in my office by four-thirty if you need me."

Talley had an hour to amble through the Volksgarten and another park to Alexandrovitch's apartment. He wasn't followed there. As soon as where he was going was clear, one of the men went to a telephone box and placed a call.

Talley strolled, pausing to admire the beds of red and yellow tulips. He paid his hommage at the Strauss memorial, and was suitably impressed by the Rathaus, the huge and many-steepled city hall. He tried to tune himself to the harmony of that city: to its excess in moderation, its controlled indulgence, its life both vigorous and gracious, its sense of having learned to live not merely wealthily, but well.

His own growing excitement, though, kept sounding a jarring counterrhythm and discord. It had been set off by hearing Major Howard repeat the story that Alexandrovitch said the papers he had brought came from Janos Czerny, out of the Soviet Union.

Talley had never been a spy, had never worked at procuring intelligence, but he knew a little of the basics about it. He knew the importance of secrecy, of compartmentalizing, of what they called "cutouts."

The papers had been passed along some chain: Alexandrovitch had not had them directly from Czerny. Naming Czerny with them as they went from link to link increased the danger to him each time. To say, moreover, that they came from the Soviet Union compromised the entire chain by giving a clue to the identity of at least one link.

The only legitimate reason Talley could think of (discounting the possibility of stupidity on the part of everyone involved) for passing these unnecessary facts was that someone thought they were necessary. It had been assumed so far that the someone was Czerny, himself, sending the message he'd been betrayed. But that message would have been clear in his arrest and in the "military intelligence before CIA" delivery. Czerny may have wanted to be *sure* it was clear, but . . .

It didn't feel right. Czerny had been passing material of one kind or another for years. He wasn't an amateur. He probably could have found a way to identify himself positively without such risk. That line of thought led toward the conclusion that the reason for the identification was illegitimate—meant to mislead.

It was just a whiff, just one little fact suggesting a possibility. But picking out that one scent and tracing it was Talley's skill. He tried to tell himself that Alexandrovitch wouldn't know much, and probably wouldn't voluntarily reveal anything, and it all might be a dead end. But his blood was up; he was on the chase.

The closer he came to the pianist's address, the slower he tried to make himself walk. Even so, he was three minutes early. He went on to the cross street and back. Alexandrovitch lived in a building that was one of the units behind a block-long facade. Vertical lines of trim expressed the common walls between sections, and there were separate entrances, but window and roof levels had been maintained.

A pair of elaborately paneled wooden doors secured the entrance to Alexandrovitch's building. Or would have secured it. They were open, held by wooden wedges. Talley imagined the concierge was putting the sweet spring air to work to freshen his lobby. There was a bell, a button centered in a gleaming brass disk, for calling him, but since the doors were open, Talley decided to go in unannounced. He was expected.

At the back of the lobby were an ornate elevator, one of those filigree cages in an openwork shaft, and a wide stairway boxing the shaft on three sides. No gnome in livery waited to operate the lift—it had been converted to function by buttons—but it delighted Talley all the same to ride in it.

As he rose, the sound of a piano being played grew louder. Before he had reached the fourth, the final floor, he had recognized the music as Beethoven's *Hammerklavier* sonata. Alexandrovitch's controversial style, his attack, could be identified even at that distance. He must have been practicing to increase his strength. He was certainly banging it out.

The elevator opened directly across a little hall from the apartment's entrance. Evidently there was only one flat on each floor. Talley walked across to the door. A note was taped to it.

"Mr. Talley," it said. "I am practicing, and may not hear

the bell. Please do come in, to the music room on the left of the drawing room.''

Talley was reluctant to go in. He felt privileged to be hearing this private concert. But he had business to transact, and Alexandrovitch was still in the first movement. He was playing straight through, at performance level. If he continued that way, it would be at least half an hour before he stopped.

With an uncomfortable sense of intruding, Talley opened the door. He could see into an entrance foyer. Directly opposite, double doors stood open in an archway leading into some sort of sitting room.

Suddenly Talley was very ill at ease beyond his initial sense of awkwardness about the situation. Maybe he had seen too many suspense films, he thought. He had an urge to whirl and check behind him. He did glance over his shoulder. But then he stood for another moment, rationalizing. He had no objective reason to believe that anything was amiss.

Carefully, gingerly, standing with his knees flexed, ready to spring away, he shoved the door so that it swung fully open.

He moved half a step forward and pushed on the door again to make it pivot on around and against the wall so no one could be hiding behind it. He darted his head in and out, in and out again, checking left then right.

Feeling that he was being a fool he stepped into the foyer. At least no one would hear him over the music if there were anyone there who shouldn't be.

Talley crept to the archway. Its doors stood ajar, at right angles to the wall. He could peek through the gap where they were hinged, one side, then the other. He could see no one. He got down on one knee so that he could see under the furniture in case someone were hiding behind it.

With one part of his mind he kept telling himself how

absolutely absurd he was being. If he didn't believe there
might be some danger, then his actions were ridiculous. If he
did, then he was a fool not to go away. As he rose again and
stepped carefully into the sitting room his perversity astounded
him. Curiosity, determination to know, refusal to leave a
question unanswered: it was his too familiar vice that moved
him on, appalling his rationality. He was the alcoholic, home
from the cure, cold sober and knowing the consequence, who
uncorks the bottle and pours himself the fateful slug.

Sunlight streaming through the large windows cast cres-
cents of light and scalloped shadows, interlaced, from the
sheer—what else could they be?—Austrian draperies. Curves
upon curves, they fell over the figured carpet, the floral
upholstery of furniture carved with rococo swirls. Through
the open doors to his right, Talley could see partway into a
dining room equally ornate. Maxim Alexandrovitch, a throw-
back to the great piano-pounders of the gilded age, had
clearly adopted their tastes as much in decor as in rubato and
trill.

Partly from a sixth-sense intuition that something was
wrong, partly from the feeling that even if it weren't he
shouldn't barge in, Talley opened the door to the music room
cautiously.

The first shock came from what he could see of the room's
appearance as he swung the door inward. It was totally
contemporary in style, paneled with vertical wooden strips
stained a dark brown. After the brightness of the sitting
room, Talley had a moment's difficulty seeing in the compar-
ative gloom. The shades had been drawn. They were slatted
blinds, not curtains, so what light came through came in
narrow bars. Where it struck the floor it striped it regularly,
but dashing against the walls, it shattered into broken streaks.

The pattern, here so rigidly straight, there determinedly irregular, confused the shapes of objects.

The first he could identify was the black grand piano, huge, squatting, gleaming darkly like the carapace of a giant scarab, the sweep of its lid a half-raised wing.

He wanted to flee. Not from the fantasy of a monstrous insect, but from the suddenly sensible knowledge that he shouldn't be there, which came as a second shock when he realized the music wasn't coming from the piano at all. He saw the sound's source on the wall to his left: the rack, the lighted dials. He almost moved toward it, then hesitated. Someone might be in another room, using the music to cover—who knew what? To stop the sound would reveal his own presence, locate him. He did take one step in that direction, looked across the room, and froze.

Maxim Alexandrovitch sat tied to a chair. His eyes stared at Talley's, wide with pain and horror. He slumped, twisted to the side. His face was twisted in agony. His arms, under the rope, were twisted across his knees; and his hands, his fingers, were twisted, splayed, broken. Winding rivulets of blood ran across his face from the gunshot wound in his temple.

Forcing down his urge to whirl and flee, Talley held himself there, still, while his mind raced. He might not have been heard coming in, assuming the killer were still in the apartment.

He began to edge carefully toward the door.

But if the killer were still there, he would surely have heard or known somehow, since the note on the front door gave warning that Talley was expected.

Talley paused again.

The note must have been forged, to lure him in.

His heart pounding, he waited for whoever had trapped him to come in and shoot him, too.

No one came in. Maybe they were waiting to get him as he came out.

Why should they wait? They could have killed him at any moment from the time he entered the foyer.

With a resolution more from intuition than from his incomplete analysis, Talley took a breath and stepped back into the sitting room again. No one was there.

He went back out to the hall. The elevator was down. Despite his growing feeling of safety, he wouldn't have wanted to close himself in anyway. He started down the stairs.

Halfway down to the second floor, he heard the two-toned howling of police cars rapidly nearing. For a moment the sound filled him with relief; his impulse was to call the police himself. But their imminent arrival made him pause.

Who had called them? Talley understood at once that he had been lured into the pianist's apartment, and the police had been called in order to associate him with the murder.

So what? He couldn't really be framed for it. He could establish who he was, his business. Major Howard would explain. Talley didn't understand why some enemy wanted him found there, but realization that they did kept him standing. He could hear the police cars drawing up outside.

He turned and started back up the stairs. If they wanted him caught, then he should want to get away.

He knew the stairs ended at the fourth floor. He had seen no way to go farther up, nor any other back down. But he sensed that there had to be some alternate passage—a service stair, a fire escape.

Two at a time he took the steps, dashed back through the open door—snatching away the note—into the din of Alexandrovitch playing his own death music. He turned right, to the dining room, past the polished table that was long enough for twelve to dine there, through the serving pantry, and into the kitchen.

The apartment was a rectangular ring around the central hall and stairway. With similar buildings to either side, the windows were all at front and back. A white plastic table and four chairs sat between the two in the kitchen. Beyond them, in the right-hand wall, was a door.

Talley went through it, and found the service stairs, and thought he'd escaped. He went down three steps and knew he was trapped. The sound of footsteps of at least two men carried up the narrow shaft from far below.

He dashed back into the kitchen, shoved aside a chair, opened the window, and leaned out to look to the sides and over the wide cornice. There was no fire escape anywhere. Below—probably fifty feet below—he saw the brutal surface of a stone-paved alley. Across it, another building twinned this one.

He paused for an instant, choosing between evils. What was really so bad about being found? He didn't know, but he felt a sudden rage at whomever had killed Alexandrovitch, and was trying somehow to use him.

He went out the window, onto the ledge. He pulled the window leaves closed behind him. He couldn't latch them, of course, but that might not be noticed at first.

He stood, carefully, facing the wall. He had never suffered from acrophobia, but felt more comfortable facing that way just the same. The ledge was at least fifteen inches wide. "No problem," he told himself. He'd painted his house standing on a narrower plank. He might have turned and walked along the cornice, but he chose to sidestep, keeping his hands against the wall.

Getting past the next window was a little tricky. Its thick casing and trim projected onto the ledge, narrowing it. By compensation, the cornice over it gave him handholds. He kept his eyes on it, didn't look to the side to see the sky, the clouds, so close above, or the tops of buildings that would remind him that the ground was so far below.

The more hazardous obstacle was the vertical trim that separated building from building. It jutted nearly a foot from the wall.

He was playing a game, he told himself: he was standing on the ground playing some kind of game as kids do. He came right up against the projection and pressed one palm against either side. He focused on the joints of the stonework, tried not to let them make him think of the ones in the floor of the chasm behind him. He took a breath and slid himself around. For two or three seconds he was aware that his back was out beyond the ledge.

He wondered if the police had reached the top floor yet; when they would notice the unlatched window; when they'd look out; whether they'd be able to see past that obstacle. He thought they wouldn't see—not easily, not without leaning far out—but he wasn't sure. He could only be sure of not being seen by not being there. He tried to hurry.

He approached the first window of the neighboring apartment. Again he sidled right up to the casing, then carefully, carefully, leaned his head back to try to see in. He saw only white, and realized the window had been opened inward and the curtains drawn closed.

Cautiously, he moved across. Between the drapery panels a gap let him peek in as his head went past. In the shaded room an old woman sat propped up in bed, her head back, her mouth open, eyelids closed.

He went on. With a comfortable breadth of cornice under

his feet again he could move quickly between the windows. He reached the second one of that room. Its draperies were closed, too, but not as carefully; nearly six inches of space divided them.

Talley set himself carefully, then went past in two quick steps. He knew he'd thrown a shadow into the room. He heard the woman snort. He froze. She muttered or moaned to herself, and was silent again.

He let out his breath, and started on. With any luck the next window should give onto the landing of another service stair. He was going to make it. Even if the police had reached the fourth floor by then, even if they looked out the window, he doubted that they'd see him now unless they leaned very far out. They'd have no reason to do that.

"Hallo," a little voice called.

Talley froze again. No, it couldn't be anyone calling to him.

"Hallo."

Carefully he turned to look over his left shoulder, saw no one.

"Hallo, Mann."

He looked over his right shoulder. Slowly he turned to put his back against the wall. Still he saw no one.

"Hallo, Mann."

Directly across from him a tiny head seemed to rest on a windowsill. It grinned at him, wide mouth pushing up fat, rosy cheeks.

Talley raised one hand and rocked it, waving. The child giggled with glee. Her own pudgy hand came up into sight above her head, and she flapped her fingers up and down against her palm. *"Hallo, Mann,"* she piped again shrilly.

Talley waved again and began sidestepping toward the window. The little girl turned away. He could hear her babbling, but the voice no longer carried and echoed down along the buildings. Perhaps she was bored with him already. Only a few more moments—

"*Hallo. Was tun Sie dort?*" Head and shoulders showing above the baby was a sister old enough not merely to wave to a passerby at any altitude, but with a beginning sense of the proper and the strange.

Talley waved. The little one grinned and flapped her fingers again. The older peered out from her long light brown hair half shyly, half suspiciously. The younger would be the vivacious girl, the older the serious. She would not be put off. "*Was tun Sie?*"

He raised a finger to his lips. Didn't children love secrets? Didn't they want to be part of conspiracies? He winked.

"*Was tun Sie dort? Muti! Muti!*" The girl turned and disappeared.

Talley moved quickly up to the window, peered around the casing. It did look out from a service landing. He pressed his hand against the glass. It was secured.

His sense of time was distorted, he knew, but he was sure that by now the police had climbed all the stairs, the front, the back: squads of policemen, pouring into that apartment, one (at least) at every window, checking, finding that kitchen window unlatched, opening it, looking out.

"*Hallo, Mann, hallo, hallo.*"

Half kneeling, leaning against the wall, holding the casing with one hand, trying to hurry, trying not to lose his balance, trying not to think about losing his balance, Talley fumbled at his shoelace. He could hear the older child, back somewhere inside her house, demanding attention. He slipped off the shoe, brought it up to the hand holding the casing—afraid to bring that one down—and turned it heel upward. He struck once, hard and sharply, smashing in a pane next to the latch handle. He grabbed it, got the window open, swung around and through it.

"*Sehe. Muti! Da! Ein' Mann!*"

"*Wo!*"

Talley had dropped to his knees below the window. There was a pause, and then he heard the mother begin, "*Lotti, Ich habe dir fünfzen hunnert mal gesacht—!*"

He crawled over to the stair and went down backward on hands and knees like a child until sure his head would be below the window when he stood. But he didn't remember to put his shoe back on until he had passed the next floor.

•

Reaching ground level at the back of the building, creeping out into the alley, keeping close to the wall, Talley imagined scores of policemen craning from windows above him. No one shouted, though.

At the alley's exit he turned right, away from the street the apartment faced. He went to the corner, right again, down toward the Ring and the one part of the city of which he had any knowledge at all. It seemed important to be able to locate himself precisely when he called Major Howard for help. He crossed the Ring and headed back toward the Volksgarten, whose green foliage he could see ahead.

The greenery, and his sense of direction, were the only guides he had. He saw the Rathaus, not recognizing it at first from the other side. While he was far short of panic, he was truly frightened. Trying not to be obvious about it, he kept scanning around and behind him to see if the police—or anyone else—were following him. Because of that focus, the

monumental buildings seemed insubstantial. The passing traffic, the pedestrians, seemed two-dimensional. All were like
slide-photo scenes flashed too quickly onto screens around
him.

He reached the Volksgarten and the café again, and located
a telephone box. Then he remembered that Major Howard
had not been returning directly to his office. Talley checked
his watch. He wouldn't be able to reach Howard for at least
another half hour. Should he talk to someone—anyone—else
at the embassy? He decided he should not.

Although the fight-or-flight reaction was wearing off, Talley was still too tense to sit and wait. He walked on through
the park, back the way he had come from his hotel, deliberately slowing his pace to calm himself further. He was
successful enough so that his attention turned from escape to
trying to understand the meaning of what had happened. He
had to wait for traffic at the thoroughfare that ran through the
Heldenplatz. When he crossed he walked a few steps further,
then sat on a bench at the edge of the lawn by the wide path.

A crowd of questions competed for his attention, but he
recognized only the most immediate, the one he had ignored
before: why had someone wanted to associate him with the
murder?

He couldn't imagine that anyone would be out to get *him*,
Tom Talley, so he rephrased the question: why did they
want to implicate an investigator for the CIA? Put that way,
the question answered itself: discrediting the CIA was a
major aspect of this whole Czerny-Hovey affair.

From that point of view, the setup was neat. It would be
believed either that the CIA had tortured and murdered
Alexandrovitch for its own purposes, or—since the frame
probably wouldn't work—that someone else had done it to
prevent the CIA from reaching the man. Which showed they

knew Talley was coming. Which would suggest to all of the foreign intelligence services, who would inevitably hear about the incident, that the CIA was penetrated.

That final possibility was the one Talley was supposed to be investigating. Given his feelings about the agency, he might actually have been pleased if he proved it true. But the fact that the enemy seemed to be trying to prove it made him doubt; and their trying to use him as a pawn for the purpose made him angrier by the moment.

As his thoughts turned first from his immediate predicament and then from the theoretical problem toward the crime itself, its horror finally began to come fully upon him.

For some minutes he stared ahead, not seeing the leaves fluttering in the breath of breeze, not aware of the warmth of sunlight that the older strollers so enjoyed. Lovers walked by hand in hand. A woman with hair like a golden helmet stalked past, a German shepherd prowling at heel on either side. She looked like Brünnhilde among the Nibelungen as she crossed the path of a busload of Japanese who were just being deposited on the plaza. They all snapped her picture.

Gradually Talley became aware. He heard birds singing, the chasing children shrieking, giggling.

He could not believe what he heard and saw. He could not believe that these joyous sounds, this broad and bright and fecund afternoon could be, not slatted, not broken, twisted in shadow. And then he couldn't believe that room could be enwebbed somewhere within the lily of such a day.

None of his speculations had suggested that he was still in immediate danger now that he was far away from the apartment. So it came as a complete shock when the two men sat, one on each side and very close, on the bench beside him.

He had known he was out of his place, known from the moment he perversely went into Alexandrovitch's apartment despite his misgivings. His place was at a desk, not in the field. He didn't know what the risks in the field were, much less how to take or avoid or escape them. He had realized all that long before the men sat down, before one of them jabbed him with what had to be a pistol muzzle.

The man on his left smiled; the one on his right—holding the gun under a raincoat folded over his arm—didn't.

Talley was out of his place, but his mind was now concentrated wonderfully. His first thought was, "What can they do?" It was afternoon in a public place. People passed by. All he had to do was to get up and walk away. What could they do?

They could shoot him. If the movies were true, the sound of a silenced gun was no more than a can of beer being opened. No one would hear it. The passersby were scattered across the stone-paved plaza. If one came close—like the young woman approaching now—they could shoot her, too.

He and the man to his left watched her go by. The one with the gun looked only at Talley with all the expressiveness of a mackerel.

Talley calculated. If he jumped up and tried to run toward other walkers farther away, the man would shoot him, and then he and his partner could jump up too, shouting "heart attack" or "get an ambulance," and run off before anyone really comprehended what had happened.

The man on his left smiled again, probably with contempt at the shock and fear on Talley's face. Talley was afraid, but although he was no field agent accustomed to functioning calmly in the face of peril, he had disciplined himself for years to focus his thinking against the distractions of any emotion.

Why was this happening? They must still want to connect him with the Alexandrovitch murder. He'd taken the note from the door; how could anyone know he had been there? By his fingerprints, of course. He'd left those on the doors, the windows.

Talley understood fully. If the police had caught him in the apartment, these men's purpose would have been accomplished. Now, the police were left with the task of finding the man who matched the prints.

The man on his left looked right. Talley did too. No one was anywhere near on that side. The man looked left, and Talley checked as he did. The Japanese were approaching, obediently two by two behind their guide. No one followed close beyond them. After they'd passed, the pair would either invite him to walk or simply shoot him there.

The group began to go by. Those on his side took in all of the scenery they were passing through, but politely avoided eye contact with him.

"*Ohayo gozaimos,*" Talley said in a very tight but quite loud voice. Startled, several of the people stopped, and one or two of those behind bumped into them. Talley went on quickly, asking if they were enjoying their visit. As he had the attention of eight or ten already, he rose and stepped toward them asking whether they had come from Tokyo.

While Talley's French was execrable, and he knew no other European language at all, his Japanese—learned for the sake of his business—was reasonably good.

The whole procession halted. Everyone was curious to see who was speaking, and it would have been rude of those who did to go on. Talley introduced himself to the two men closest. He and they smiled and bowed and smiled back and forth. Talley said he didn't want to interrupt their tour, but might he walk along with them? They said they were honored that he should wish to do so.

He kept his hands jammed down in his pockets so that

their shaking might not be noticed. His shirt was soaked with perspiration. His voice was high, and he was aware that he was making mistakes in grammar. Still, he knew that he was safe; he had escaped. And even beyond the relief of escaping death he felt the exhilaration of having gotten himself out by his own wits. He might not be a cloak-and-dagger spy, but he'd been able to get himself out of his predicament as skillfully as any of them might have done.

He didn't look back until they had reached Joseph II and were spreading around him to appreciate from all sides his rearing horse and his banner held high, and to find the best angle to photograph him. To Talley's shocked surprise, one of the men was still there, hanging back at the edge of the paving. The other man had gone around the group and was ahead, over closer to the palace.

Why hadn't they gone? He was safe now, wasn't he? They couldn't get him and then escape easily while he was with a group that large; and if they didn't leave him, all he had to do was to tell one of the Japanese . . . tell him . . . say . . . what? Not that he was being stalked by killers and to call a policeman for him. Involving him with the police was what the killers wanted. They must be assuming that he'd try to avoid doing it for them. Well, Talley decided angrily, they were right.

The guide blew a little whistle, and everyone quickly fell in behind her. She began leading them off to the right. Talley was told the group's next stop was Schönbrunn Palace. Their bus was to meet them out on the Ring. The man he was speaking with asked if Talley had seen that palace, and, learning he hadn't, said how unhappy he was that Talley couldn't go with them. To his immense sorrow, all of the places on their bus were taken.

If Talley couldn't avoid contact with the police, he certainly preferred to make it himself rather than let his pursuers attract attention to him their way. But he would try to escape clean. The men must have expected that decision. The one ahead of the group had crossed the narrow drive and was walking along its edge, between Talley and the lot full of cars that disfigured the courtyard in front of the palace. The other man closed in a little behind. They weren't going to let him simply flee. The only way he could win in this situation would be to keep their own risk in shooting him too great, or to trick them by making some kind of fuss about himself without actually arousing any serious police interest. Attempting the latter precluded his darting between any of the buses parked along his side of the drive and dashing to lose himself among the parked cars. The men hunting him would either see him and shoot him, or create enough commotion for a few moments to draw the attention of one of the policemen who stood up the stairway by the palace entrance.

The guide stopped across from the Neu Hofburg to tell the group about the museums in that wing. The tour did not take them inside, but they might return in their free time next morning. Then the guide turned and led them all toward the Ring. Talley could see the bus already there.

He felt himself starting to panic, and fought it back. They were coming to the main thoroughfare of the city. There were people everywhere. Traffic. There would be a thousand ways he could cover himself—or at least one obvious one: he could just step into a crowded shop, or a café.

The group reached the bus, which had found a place by the corner at the head of the line. Talley looked back and forth in horror. There were no shops, no building entrances of any kind. Along the Ring to his right, fenced from the sidewalk, was the park. To his left—also fenced—was the Hofburg.

There were no shoppers, few people strolling on that side of the avenue at all.

The guide stood aside and smiled and bowed slightly to each of her charges as he or she stepped up through the door. Talley stood, still trying to chat with those tourists who, out of politeness, stayed at the back to be the last to leave. But the movement of the others seemed to draw all of them, as though they were being pulled into the bus by some steady force. They were like grains of sand being sucked in, and when they'd all gone . . . The two men stood just away, flanking.

Surely they couldn't expect to shoot him right there on the main street and get away with it! But Talley could see that they did. The stocky man with the raincoat draped over his forearm and hand stood sideways to Talley, the pistol that must be under it pointing directly at him. He could shoot and then disappear back into the park before anyone realized what had happened. They could expect to get away with it if Talley let them.

But he guessed that they didn't expect they would have to shoot him. The other man, the more expressive one, was smiling again in a way that seemed to say, "Nice try, but no cigar." The look of contempt was gone—maybe he thought Talley had feigned fear back at the bench just to put them off guard—and he shrugged slightly, as if to a fellow professional who had lost this round and now would end the match in a way that would be safest for all of them. He seemed confident, but not overly so—a fellow professional might still try to make a break for it. He was standing with his arms crossed, and only someone with a reason for looking might notice that his right hand was inside his unbuttoned jacket.

More than a dozen of the tourists had boarded the bus.

Two or three times that number stood along its side waiting their turns. When all of them had stepped up . . .

"But I have been very impolite," Talley said. "I haven't introduced you to my friends," he went on more loudly. "I'm sure you'd like to meet them. They're international film stars. We're here planning a new picture." The heads of the nearest Japanese turned suddenly to look at him. Talley nodded toward the dark, dull-eyed man with the raincoat. "That's Sylvester Stallone—you know, *Rocky*."

"Ah so?" The name swept along the line of tourists. Cameras began coming up.

"Take his picture! Ask him for his autograph! He'll be glad to give you his autograph!"

Two of the Japanese at the end of the line smiled at the gunman, bobbed bows, began shyly to move toward him. Seeing the ice broken, three more, and then half the crowd joined them, circling the man.

"And this"—Talley gestured toward the other man—"is Steven Spielberg, the director of *ET*!" The man was no longer smiling. He took an uncertain step back. Talley grabbed the arm of the Japanese to whom he had been talking and began to lead him. "Steve, this is Mr. Watanabe. Mr. Watanabe, this is Steven Spielberg." Talley stepped behind Mr. Watanabe, shoving him onward with one hand while he turned and waved to the rest of the tourists with the other. "Come on, everybody! Get Steven Spielberg's autograph!"

As the other half of the line surged forward, Talley ducked behind them and then around the front of the bus.

CHAPTER 8

"**O**ur problem is not so much a lack of facts, as that none of them suggests a single conclusion."

Walter Simson had placed himself, as the President does with his cabinet, at the center of one side of the long table. The position suggested he was merely one among the committee members, yet would allow him to control the discussion as he might not have been able to do if isolated at an end. Simson spoke in the confident voice of a man who took his authority as understood, but low enough that the others had to attend to hear him. He met the eyes of every man in turn as he spoke.

Talley, sitting at Simson's left, kept his own eyes down toward his notes. He had not wanted to be there at all. He did badly with committees. He had learned to deal with two people at once, or even three sometimes, but he always tried to meet with a single executive of the companies that hired him. The sensitivity to another person that served him so well when he did, his ability to adjust his approach intuitively to that other's character and style, failed him with groups. Perhaps confused by conflicting reactions, he had no sense of being in touch. He overcompensated, came on too strong. He lectured. He preached. He seemed either defensive or domineering—in either case, angry.

But Simson had been firm, had said, "Just give the facts, answer questions. I'll do the summary."

"I think the best way to proceed," Simson said to the group, "is in terms of our two hypotheses: that is, by examining the evidence for each. As you'll see, some facts work as evidence for both of them. You know—this proves A, except that it could have been planted deliberately, so therefore it proves B. I think we can deal with that problem best by looking at each alternative as a whole before we get at them point by point.

"Now, Hypothesis One is that this whole thing is a put-up job, not only to get Czerny, but to get the agency by planting the *false* idea there's a penetration. Hypothesis Two is that the penetration is real. Mark, why don't you start on One?"

"Yes, sir." Mark Wallinsky got up. He was one of Simson's new smart young men, tweedy, of course, but very trim, hair as short as his predecessors' two agency generations before. He turned the cover sheet of the chart on the easel set up behind him. "I've set this out in chart form because I think a graphic presentation is clearest.

"Now, here are the names of everyone we know who had any knowledge of any part of this whole affair." The names were listed in a column down the left. "Here"—he pointed across the top of his chart to headings for other columns— "are the individual bits of knowledge. *Czerny* means the knowledge that Janos Czerny was passing military material. This one is for knowledge of the secret device by which he . . . encoded . . . the material. *Seminar* means the knowledge that he was going to pass something at the Chekhov seminar. This one is the recognition protocol. This is the identity of our contact.'' He pointed to the items one by one. ''That Tom Talley was working for us. Maxim Alexandrovitch's identity. That Tom was going to see Alexandrovitch.

''So, we have a grid: people and knowledge. Now, where a block is darkened in, that means that person had, or reasonably might have had access to, that bit of knowledge. I should say we determined this by checking reports, signals, minutes of meetings, memos—all the documentation—and by interviewing everyone concerned—or who had any contact with any part of this—to reconfirm what was talked about, who heard it, and so forth.

''I think you can see the point of this procedure right off in the chart. There is nobody who has all his blocks darkened. Nobody, no single person knew, or had access to, everything. For my money, gentlemen, this proves Hypothesis One by simply negating its opposite. Are there any questions?''

Simson looked back and forth. ''Henry?''

''Yes. That's a very useful chart, Mark. Makes your point very clearly. Nice presentation. However, while it seems to show that no single person goes through on every line, there are a couple of places where at least two people—if my visual sense is working here—there are a couple of pairs— who overlap enough to . . . Well, it is only an assumption that a penetration would be an individual.''

The man on Talley's left exploded. ''Now, wait a goddamned minute, Henry! I'm not going to sit here and let you take evidence that proves there is no penetration in the agency, and try to turn it around to say we're riddled—''

''Sam, I didn't say the agency was—''

''That's fucking bullshit!''

''Gentlemen!'' Simson, lacking a gavel, smacked his palm

on the table, then smiled with pained benevolence. "Gentlemen, we are here to examine the evidence and make what we
can of it. Henry's point is valid. As we go on, we can
evaluate how plausible it seems."

Talley smiled only to himself. Walter is so good, he
thought. Each man could believe the chairman had pretended
to smooth the argument impartially, while really vindicating
him and cutting his opponent.

"Other questions? Colonel?"

"Thank you. Mark, I just wondered if there is any *positive*
evidence—anything *nobody* on our side knew, something the
Czechs had to know and which they couldn't have gotten
from us."

"Ah . . ."

"I think we'd better let Tom handle that, since he's been
doing the external work."

Talley looked up at the air force officer sitting down the
table from him. "No," he said. "There's nothing, so far,
that either proves or disproves the hypothesis that the Czechs
masterminded the whole thing. There's nothing they had to
know that we didn't know. But also, every step of the way,
there's a way they could have known without any information from inside the agency.

"First, they undoubtedly had had Czerny under some surveillance before he ever started passing military product. And
there are any number of ways they could have known when
he did. Obviously they organized his schedule to get him to
pass this particular material at the seminar.

"They could have learned the recognition protocol in the
same way we did: the Frenchman could be a double.

"They could have identified the contact we sent in at least
two ways. One, he's a former military officer who is not a
Chekhov scholar and who registered for the seminar late.

There's nothing outrageous about that, but if they knew somebody was coming, he would be easy to spot. Or, two, they saw the striped tie when they checked everybody's baggage. Either way. Or both.

"As for Alexandrovitch and me . . . that's not as clear."

Another uniformed man broke in. "If we hadn't had to give up his name—"

The man named Sam, whom Talley didn't know, cut over him. "If we hadn't had to go outside this committee to get it—"

"Gentlemen! Go on, Tom."

"Well, if they had set it up to pass the duplicate material through Alexandrovitch, then obviously they already had his identity. They—"

"Not necessarily. Excuse me, Tom. They could have put it into a line without knowing where it would come out."

"That's true, Colonel. But it still remains that they *could* have known. If so, they could just have watched him, maybe tapped his line, bugged him somehow, and known I was coming to see him."

"What about the decoy?" someone else asked. "What about this asshole Hovey?"

"There's no question in my mind that he's genuine, that he was set up," Talley responded. "That's based on everything we know about him, the report of the embassy people who dealt with him, what he says himself—he writes a lot of letters home, and naturally we read them. Yes, of course he could expect that and be writing for our benefit, but . . . that's not the way it feels to me. I'm confident about him.

"And I'm sure that the legwork in setting him up was done by an American. Well, possibly Canadian, but the point is, I think he was a native speaker of English. I think he served in the military, and worked—or works—in one of the intelli-gence or security services.

"Again, though, this doesn't prove anything either way. Someone inside the agency could have known him, could be running him, or he could have been turned from outside. Unfortunately, people of ours have been turned before."

The man called Henry asked, "I assume we're trying to find this man?"

Simson nodded. "We've run the personnel lists with all the variables we have on his description. We're matching the people we've pulled out against a composite of identikits. If we think we're getting anywhere we'll go back to the people who met him, and then run checks on all possibles. It's going to take a while."

"So," the colonel said, "there's really nothing conclusive either way."

Talley nodded. "That's right."

Henry broke in. "That creates another problem with Mark's line of reasoning. Even if we accept—for the sake of argument—that no one in the agency could have given them *everything*, it's still possible that they got key information from an agent and the rest for themselves."

"Walter, if you don't mind my saying so"—the elderly man who had chosen to sit as if by habit at what might have been the chairman's seat at the table end spoke, and everyone turned to him and was silent—"it has been useful to look at these two possibilities whole, but now I think perhaps we should go over the details more carefully."

"Absolutely, Senator."

There was a moment in which everyone seemed to wait to see if the senator would begin, himself. Then someone asked, "What about that Frenchman? If he is a double, can't we . . . Are we watching him?"

Sam replied. "Harry, when he shits, we smell the paper."

"And?"

"Nothing, so far. Personally, I think he's our ringer. But nothing, so far."

Someone else asked, "Doesn't what they did to the piano player prove . . . I mean, why do that unless they were trying to trace back the net that got out Czerny's material? Which would prove they hadn't planted it."

Talley had given much thought to the point. "First of all, as Walt said before, the Czechs might have done it to make us think what you just said. And in either case—even if they had set it up themselves—killing Alexandrovitch would make an example to frighten others who pass things they don't want gotten out. And of course, waiting to do it until I got there would further seem to suggest a leak in the agency."

"Tom and I have been discussing that last point," Simson put in. "They went to some trouble and risk to themselves to make that suggestion—trying to involve Tom and the agency with the murder. Now, elementary reverse thinking would lead us to say that since they tried to suggest there is a leak, then there isn't one. However, they were so ham-handed about it that one is tempted to reverse the reversal, and reverse it again, until we reach the point of having so many conjectures that we just don't know—and that's obviously exactly what the Czechs want."

For another hour and a half they went over the puzzle, piece by piece, and still could not agree what the picture might be.

Walter Simson finally attempted to summarize and lead toward a conclusion. "The situation seems to be that at present we cannot prove or disprove either hypothesis absolutely. Nothing new in that, is there? As usual, we have to make the best evaluation we can on the basis of incomplete material. What do we want to suggest as our current, tentative assumption? Subject to revision should we get something from the surveillance on D'Avignon or an identification of the legman here. What do we think is the more plausible, the more likely of these alternatives?

"Let me put that first to the two men who've been working most closely with the data on this.

"Mark?"

"Well, Walt, I've already said what I have to say. I think it's a put-up job by the Czechs, and it's right there." He waved at the chart behind him. "To go against those facts you have to invent all kinds of conspiracies, and I just don't think that's plausible."

"Okay. Tom?"

Talley kept his eyes on the paper in front of him. "In the absence of anything conclusive, I agree that the most likely, the most plausible probability is that the Czechs set this up . . . but—"

"Thanks, Tom. Now, I guess if someone would like to formalize that by making a motion . . ."

Sam was quick. "I do so move. I mean, that we accept as our conclusion—"

"Excuse me."

Simson held up a hand to stop Sam in mid-motion. "I'm sorry. Colonel?"

"I don't think Tom was quite finished."

"Oh, weren't you, Tom? I'm sorry. Please."

Talley began, still looking down. "I . . . ah . . . I agree that Hypothesis One is the most probable, but we don't know for sure. And . . . I mean, maybe we'll never be sure, but we haven't done everything we can do to find out."

"What would you suggest?" the colonel asked.

Talley looked up at him. "Get Professor Hovey back."

"What?"

"Jesus!"

"How?"

"Why?"

The last question was the one Talley had prepared to answer. It had come from somewhere down the table to his right, so he looked in that direction.

"Hovey was there," he said. "When it happened, when Czerny and he were arrested. He was the one they got to confess. How did they do that? What did they tell him? What would that tell us about what they knew?"

"We can't do it," someone said. "We've tried through every channel."

"Fuck the channels! We could break him—"

"For chrissake, Sam! We're not playing cowboys and—"

Simson banged on the table steadily. He no longer looked benign. "Colonel?" he said to the officer who was sitting quietly, one hand raised politely for attention.

"I'd just like to ask Tom further . . . I'm sure we all realize the possible implications of what he's suggested, so I'd like to ask you, do you really think having Professor Hovey back, debriefing him, would give us a definitive answer?"

"I don't know, Colonel. It might. More probably, it won't. I just advise you that if you don't get Hovey out, you haven't done everything that could be done to get your answers. Whether you care is up to you. For myself, I'd like to know. Frankly—some of you, maybe all of you know my background—I don't give a damn if the whole agency gets canned because of this. But . . . one of the finest musicians in the world was tortured and murdered. And I was nearly aced myself. I'd like to know about that. If there isn't anything more to know, then I want to know *that*! I'm not going to be

satisfied until I do know everything I can know. If you're
satisfied, okay. You draw whatever conclusions you want to.
I am not satisfied!''

●

"You changed the bed." Talley spoke from the archway
into the dining room. Jane was putting his supper onto the
table there.

"Yes," she said. "I . . . I thought . . . since it bothered
you."

"What did you do with it?"

"I just exchanged with the one in the guest room."

"It must have been hard to do by yourself."

"Not really. I kept the same mattress and springs. *They're*
new." She was trying to keep her tone matter-of-fact, but a
thin edge cut through the last.

He went to her and put his arms around her from behind.
"Thank you."

She straightened, and leaned back against him, her eyes
closed. "I thought of putting all his furniture there. But there
isn't room. And I couldn't have moved some of it—the
couch. And then . . . the things we bought together—they're
half his."

"I know."

She turned, still within his arms, but drawn back so she
could look at him. "I can't move Larry out of my life and
not leave any trace of him, Tom."

"I know. I know. It was a pretty stupid kind of scruple.
I'm sorry."

"No. I don't know . . . half the time I think it was stupid, and silly. And half the time I think you were right." She smiled and touched the side of his face with a finger. "But I like it that you have even silly scruples, because so many people seem to have none at all." She broke away from him. "Come on, eat your supper before it gets cold."

Talley sat. He hadn't eaten for eight hours; he should have been ravenous. But tension had tightened his stomach so that he hadn't thought of food. He wasn't sure that he could touch what she had prepared for him.

She had met him and driven him back from the inn. "Oh, God, I'm glad to see you," she'd said at first, before they'd embraced. And then, as they were driving away, "I was so worried about you."

"Why?"

"It was on the evening news yesterday about Maxim Alexandrovitch being murdered. I just knew, somehow I just knew you were involved. I got scared."

"Why did you think I was involved with him?"

"Weren't you?"

"Why would you think so?"

"I don't know. Your going to Vienna. The fact that he was a Russian. I kept telling myself I was imagining things. But I wasn't, was I?"

"No."

"Can you tell me about it?"

"A little. Later."

She had kept her eyes on the road most of the time, glancing at him quickly. "You look exhausted," she'd said.

"A little tired. Jet lag."

She had begun chattering about school, obviously only to distract him.

He had been grateful both for the distraction and for the postponement. So shocked and horrified had he been over

Alexandrovitch's death and his own narrow escape, in angry
reaction he'd been so fixed upon finding the truth, that
he—the meticulous analyst—had not, until getting on the
plane for Boston, thought about what bringing Hovey back
might mean in relation to Jane. Not that thinking about it
could have made any difference. But he was tense about
having to tell her. Would she still love him, live with him,
when Hovey was back?

He took a spoonful of chili. She had said, "I wanted
something you could sit right down to. I knew you'd be
famished." He chewed, and made himself swallow against
the lump in his throat. "Thanks," he said. "For supper. And
the bed."

She put down her spoon, stared at him for several moments, then smiled. "I'm glad you had to go away," she
said. "Distance doesn't always make the heart grow fonder.
Sometimes just the opposite. I mean . . . I think it can be
good to be apart from someone you're involved with. The
separation allows some perspective, some objectivity."

Talley nodded.

"It was being apart from Larry that made me see I really
had to break with him. That I could. I'd wanted to for at least
a year. But somehow I couldn't do it. There were good
times, good things—things about him I'll always like and
admire. Maybe when I'd get almost up to it, they'd sway me
back. Or maybe I didn't have the courage to face him with it.
I'm not usually the submissive type, but . . . Larry always
knows he's in the right. He just *looks* at you and you believe
it—that it's *your* fault. After he was gone I began to realize
how much he was undermining me.

"And after you'd gone—while you were away, when I got
so worried about you—that's when I decided to change the
beds. Not to be too symbolic about it. I'm writing to Larry."

"What?"

"I'm telling him what I just told you. And that I'm sorry to do this to him now, but that I just can't wait for—"

"Have you mailed it?"

"No. I'm not quite finished. Why?"

Talley had been working steadily at the chili, which tasted like sawdust to him. He put down his spoon.

"Jane . . . I have to tell you . . ."—he swerved—"I have to tell you something about what I've been working on." As briefly as he could—wanting to give full detail just to make the story longer, but disciplining himself—he told her. He was violating the oath of secrecy he'd signed, but he had to.

"And so the only thing left to do is to see if Larry himself can make things clearer for us."

"But how can you get him released?"

"We, ah, we're going to try."

"But the State Department already—"

"We may be able to find another way."

"How?"

"I can't say."

"But if there's a way, why wasn't it used before? Do you really mean that the government can—could have gotten him out before, and didn't do it, and now—*now*, just because they think they can use him, *now* they're willing—"

"It's not like that. I really can't talk about this, Jane."

"But what— You don't mean you're going to arrange for him to escape!"

"I really can't—"

"But he could be killed! Or if they catch him, he could be sentenced— Tom!"

"Well, do you want him left there?"

"No! I . . . But not put in danger! That's . . . that's worse! You're not doing it for *him*. You're doing it because *you* need—"

"*I'm* not doing it at all!" It was a lie: Talley knew it even as he said it. "*I* didn't decide. I—"

"What if Larry is killed? Who will be responsible?"

"He won't . . . They won't do anything that will put him in danger."

She snorted.

"They won't!"

"How can you say that? How can you be sure? There's bound to be danger. Do you care? Or do you really just care about getting an answer for your mystery!"

He slashed back. "And do *you* really care about what happens to him? Or do you just want to keep him away so you won't have to face him!"

She stared at Talley, her face flushed. "That was a rotten thing to say."

He could not continue to meet her eyes. "I'm sorry."

"I do care what happens to him," she said after a while, "but I was relieved when he was arrested and kept there, and I didn't want him to come back. I guess I still don't. The more he asks me to wait—tells me he's counting on my waiting for him—the more I dread seeing him again."

He risked a glance. She wasn't looking at him, either. She was hunched forward, her forearms on the table. He slid his hand near hers.

"I guess I don't want him back either," he said, "and then I guess I do. I guess I want you to tell him."

"You mean, to see if I will tell him?"

He nodded.

Jane moved her hand next to his, brushed her little finger against his. "I will, Tom. I am. I'll finish my letter tonight."

"I . . . ah . . ." Again he could not look at her.

"What's the matter?"

"Were you going to tell him about me?"

"Yes. I think I have to be honest with him."

"Are you . . . were you telling him my name?"

"Yes. Why? Do you want me not to?"

"I'm kind of caught . . . I seem to have a conflict."

"What?"

"I don't want you to write to him about me, who I am. I guess I don't want you to write to him now at all. I want to talk to him. I need for him to be willing to talk to me, to be open with me. He has to be in good spirits about getting home. It has to be that way if I'm going to find things out. You must know what that's like. Your own work . . ."

"I know what it's like to be on to something, yes. But in my work no one is hurt or put in danger. And I don't have to lie to anyone in order to do it."

"No, because you're dealing with the past. You hope that what you write may have an effect now, maybe change some thinking, but you're right: nobody is going to be really hurt by it. Well, that's the difference: people are going to be hurt—they *are being hurt*—by what I'm working on."

He paused, looking into her eyes steadily now. "Maybe I am hooked on solving the mystery. I do get hooked, get involved, get to care—they tell me I get to caring too much about knowing it all, getting it absolutely right. But this problem is not just academic. And I'm not asking you to lie. Just to . . . wait. Until after he's back."

"And you've talked to him."

"Yes."

"While you're talking with him, though, you'll know."

"Yes."

"And he won't. Doesn't that bother your scruples?"

Talley tried to meet her stare. He managed for several moments. Then he pushed away his bowl. He took off his glasses and laid them aside, put his elbows on the table, his face down in his hands. He rubbed his face, trying to press away fatigue. Finally he turned toward her again, supporting his head on clasped hands.

"Yes, it does," he said. "So, what do you think I should do about it? Should I resign? Drop this whole thing?"

"Would you?"

He looked at her for a long time. "Yes," he said. "For you, I would. But *should* I?"

"That's not fair. It's not fair to put it on me."

"You're right. I'm not. I just wanted to know what you thought I should do."

"Do *you* have to do it?"

"No. They asked me to because they—the man in charge of it, anyway—thought I was the best person they could get. I don't know if I'm conceited enough to think that's true, but that's the way it was put to me, and I took it on, and I think I've been doing some good work. I've told you what's involved. Should I drop it?"

She looked back at him for a long moment. "No. You shouldn't drop it. Should I—should *we* deceive Larry?"

"No, we shouldn't."

"Choices."

"Yes."

"Where will you question him?"

"I don't know. The agency has places: houses in Maryland, Virginia. It won't take very long."

"And then you'll let him come home?"

"Yes."

"And I can tell him. Welcome home, Larry!"

CHAPTER 9

Professor Hovey hummed to himself as he swept. When he reached the end of the corridor opposite the one where he'd started, he turned and looked back with pleasure and pride. The hallway ran east and west. Early in the mornings light shone directly through the window there and, for a few minutes, seemed to become a solid substance, filled as it was with motes from his work. Moving in it was a pleasure almost sensuous, watching his highlighted arms swinging rhythmically, seeing his black shadow carving changing shapes in the three-dimensional luminescence. He began at that end partly because the light from behind showed clearly any soil or sand or debris that might have escaped him otherwise, and partly for the satisfaction of looking back and seeing the sunlight gleam along his spotless and polished cement floor.

The polish, the wax, had been his own idea. Using it on cement, he knew, was a common practice at home; evidently it was unknown by those in charge at his camp. Suggesting it had made the prisoners who did the other floors angry with him at first. Previously, they had had only to sweep, and to mop now and then. After his first week doing just that, Hovey had managed to communicate his thought to the guard who supervised him, overcome the man's incredulity, and finally get the request sent up through channels. Eventually a can of liquid wax and a second mop were delivered to him. Then Professor Hovey's corridor glowed.

His supervisor had been impressed. He brought his own superior to see, and then an officer came. On the week following, the other three corridor custodians were issued wax and mops. Naturally they were displeased at the additional work, until they discovered that waxing the surface made the daily sweeping far easier. However, none of them was as careful as Professor Hovey about putting down the wax, nor about the sweeping, so his floor remained the shining exemplar.

He knew it, as they did not, because his floor was the uppermost—the fourth. He could see the others as he went down the stairway at the end of the hallway to the room where they all ate. He enjoyed the knowledge of his accomplishment in secret, not needing the admiration of his fellows to confirm it, and shrewd enough not to arouse their envy.

Professor Hovey was the only prisoner from his floor who did go down. He was sure that at least some of the other cells had occupants at various times, but he never saw them. He had been absolutely forbidden to open any of the spy-holes that the guards could use to look in; and although, as a matter of principle, he ordinarily did at once anything authority forbade him to do, this time he recognized and obeyed his limits.

Professor Hovey recognized that he was being given special treatment in a special kind of prison. Dr. Benda had indicated that would be the case, without specifying exactly what his circumstances would be. Before the end of his first week there he had deduced that he was not being kept in a true prison at all. Most of the inmates, like the ones on his floor whose cells he cleaned after they had been taken away, were transients.

Like himself, he believed, the others were in some sense political prisoners. Those of them who did eat, work, and socialize together were forbidden to talk about "political matters." Although they sometimes alluded to their past lives, their homes, they never discussed why they had been sent there, nor did they ask him.

His final clue was the nature of the place outside and around the "jailhouse." He had been brought there in a closed van, and knew about his surroundings only by what he could see from his cell and corridor windows or from the prisoners' yard. What he saw was more buildings, of relatively recent poured-concrete construction similar to the one he was in, to and from which went men in uniform. He was sure, therefore, that he was being kept in a detention facility at a military base.

In addition to the prisoners he never saw—they always were brought and taken away at night, after he was locked into his own room—there were only a dozen like himself, longer-term residents who functioned as part of the institution's staff. He and three others worked as janitors for their floors, the rest in the kitchen or the offices on the ground floor. They were all, he recognized, "trustys": incarcerated, but not—beyond that—being punished. He appreciated that status. He had read about gulags, about being quite literally sent to the salt mines. He believed he had escaped that fate but narrowly, by the good fortune that assigned the kindly Dr. Benda to the Czerny case.

Hovey was aware that Dr. Benda had become almost a

surrogate father to him, and he accorded the man more affection and respect than he did his true parent. He believed his feeling was justified. His father was distant and cool: Dr. Benda, though dignified, seemed always truly concerned about him. His father held rigidly to opinions based on snobbery, bigotry, and received ideas; Dr. Benda was thoughtful, flexible, sensitive, and fair.

Dr. Benda had understood the conflict that having to testify against Janos Czerny was causing a man of Hovey's ideals. He had acknowledged that Czerny's previous dissent might be seen in a favorable light. But he had been convincing in his argument that passing information to fuel the arms race violated those ideals. Furthermore, he had emphasized, Professor Hovey was in no way betraying Czerny (who had been caught and would be convicted on the basis of information obtained from another source); rather, Czerny and the CIA had tricked and betrayed him. His testimony would be no more than a statement of that fact, one that, surely, he intended to make when he returned to America anyway.

Hovey assured the old man that he did indeed plan to make that statement publicly.

And then—in his total frankness and fairness—Dr. Benda had warned that testifying and confessing in the Czech court would carry its own risks: the CIA would try to discredit him; they might seek to twist or distort what he said, to use him again somehow. They might even—Dr. Benda had paused, and then apologized, suggesting he might be quite wrong, unnecessarily alarmist, perhaps unfair to the CIA, but Professor Hovey ought at least to be given some warning—they might even try physically to prevent him from telling his story. It would not be right to urge him to make this confession without apprising him of all risks.

Professor Hovey had been willing to take them. He had

been eager, and grew more so each day. Almost as much as he yearned to be home and free, he burned to revenge himself on his true jailers.

He fought against waves of rage that made him want to smash something—even his hand against his cell wall—and against soul-chilling depression, with his routine, by concentrating on detail, by the satisfactions he could find in simple activities.

After his morning's chores he studied Czech. Dr. Benda had found a set of texts for him, and he had begun working with them before his trial. He was now on the second book, the intermediate level. As he already had French and German, and had been working at Russian, he knew how to go about learning a new language. He was progressing well. Dr. Benda had also given him a tiny Czech-English dictionary, which he carried always in the breast pocket of the jacket of his pajamalike uniform. Several of the other prisoners spoke English, but increasingly he directed conversation into their own language.

At eleven o'clock each day he went down to the fenced yard at the back of the building, did some sit-ups, and ran—rain or shine. If the weather was good, he came down again in the afternoon and worked at his writing, sitting on one of the slat benches, enjoying the brightness of the early summer. He could go up and down at will during daylight hours. Steel gates could be swung to close each floor from the stairway, and were closed at night, but he had never seen them closed during the day.

Prisoners were forbidden to be on any floor or in any cell but their own. He had been so instructed by the officer who received him into the place, and had heard the warning restated by the older prisoners as they put the new boy wise at his first supper. Guards made unscheduled inspections each day, and might appear at any moment on other business, but as long as the few rules were observed, the prisoners were permitted to go as they would to and from the yard or the dining room where they played cards or chess before curfew in the evening.

It was a tolerable existence, in some ways even pleasant, so Hovey often hummed to himself and was bearing up well. Though sentenced to five years, he sometimes let himself hope he might be freed after only one; more realistically, he expected to have to serve two or three, and steeled himself for that. To help himself do so, he contemplated the small fortune he foresaw himself making from his story.

He communicated his good spirits when he wrote home. He wrote to his dean and chairman expressing sorrow at the problems his absence was causing them (a very noble gesture, he thought). He thanked them both after receiving word of the award of tenure. He assured them that his being away would not be a complete loss to the college: he'd work on the Chekhov versions he'd been going to seek a grant for. In a way, he said, the government had made the project possible without all the bother of going through the grant process. He thought that sort of remark would be acceptable if (as he supposed to be the case) his letters were read by the CIA when they arrived in the States, as well as by the Czech censors. But, believing Dr. Benda's warnings, which merely fed his previous opinion, he did not reveal the depth of his anger or the exposé he planned to make.

Writing to Jane was more difficult.

"As my letters are read by a censor here—and probably by the CIA, too—I'm inhibited about saying plainly what I feel. What I want you to know, though, is that I miss you terribly. I've had a lot of time to think about us, and sort things out. I see things I didn't see before, about us—about me. When I come back, things will be different. I'll be different.

"It's asking a lot to ask you to wait, to be there when I do come home. Especially the way things were before I left. I can only say I hope you will be there. Thinking of you being there is what keeps me going through this bitter and lonely time. Understanding that is why I know our relationship will be different. I hope you will let me prove what I'm saying is true, that you will let me prove my gratitude to you for standing behind me through this ordeal."

Professor Hovey was totally truthful and sincere in what he said. He did not consider his sincerity compromised by his calculation that the way he'd said it would make it impossible for Jane to desert him.

•

All but one of Professor Hovey's fellow prisoners were older than himself by ten years or more. Despite their baggy uniforms, and the short haircuts they were required to give one another, most of them looked like men who had exercised at least moderate authority in whatever professions or careers they had followed. There were two exceptions: the artist and the Jew.

The artist identified himself as such by spending his free time sketching. He was a man of about Hovey's age, with a similar tension about his mouth and intensity in his eyes. He and Hovey might have become close friends, but he committed a form of suicide ten days after Hovey's arrival.

The prisoners were permitted to listen to the radio in the dining room in the evenings. The station they tuned to played classical music, but there was a news report at eight. In those days Hovey's Czech was not good enough for him to under-

stand much of anything said, so he never knew what incited
the artist. All he knew was that the man made some comment, and all the other prisoners froze for an instant, and
then one of them spoke up loudly about the move his opponent had made.

But one of the guards sitting on the other side of the mesh
wall that separated the prisoners' section from their own had
heard. He raised his head and asked, sharply. The artist
retorted sharply. The guard put down his cards, stood, and
rebuked. The artist was insolent. All of the other prisoners
stared in motionless horror. A second guard rose. Both of
them picked up their submachine guns and came into the
prisoners' section. The artist defied them. He began a tirade.
The guards rushed upon him, yanked him up, jerked and
shoved him from the room.

A Haydn quartet began playing from the radio.

After a moment, Hovey asked the man across from him,
"What's going to happen to him?"

The man flipped his hand dismissively. "Labor camp."
Then he advised Hovey again. "This is a good place—for a
prison. But do not . . . what? . . . shake the ship. Do not
make the guards angry."

Getting along with the guards was not difficult. They knew
the trustys were not hardcases. If some of them sometimes
indulged in the petty displays of subordination that the roles
of guard and prisoner seem to mandate, they were never
vicious. Except one of them. Except with the Jew.

That guard came to the prison six weeks after Hovey.
Within a day the prisoners had learned that his first name was
Karel and that he liked to make people laugh. He did so by
laying about with a wit like a pig's bladder. He made jokes at
the prisoners' expense, but at the guards' and at his own as
well. Like boys jollying and proving each other with shoves

and shoulder-punches, they all could laugh at the blows whether they fell on another or on themselves, believing no real offense was meant.

Except for Travnicek, whose name was not Jewish but whose face was. While Professor Hovey could take Karel's insistence on joking about being an American and an intellectual, and Krafka grimaced ruefully every time they all were reminded of his age and presumed impotence, and the young guard Jiri would merely flush and grin at the jibes about his virgin horniness, Travnicek would not laugh at the slurs on being Jewish.

It was not clear, really, whether Karel became increasingly vicious because of a true hatred of Jews, or simply because Travnicek wouldn't laugh with him. The guards and some of the prisoners continued to. Hovey and the others stopped, and looked away in silence when he started on Travnicek—which seemed to incite him more. His attacks became physical: bumping into Travnicek, trying to trip him. Travnicek stopped going to the yard or the dining room, except for meals, when Karel was on duty.

The crisis came on a day when they were given their mail. It did not come every day. Evidently the censors, or whatever authority, waited until a quantity had collected and then sent it to the prison all at once. Even so, there wasn't much of it. With the exception of Hovey, whose friends and colleagues wrote without fear, to help keep up his morale, the prisoners received letters only from their immediate families.

They all, therefore, could recognize at once the envelopes addressed to them. They could have accomplished the distribution themselves much more quickly had the letters simply been dropped onto a table. But regulations, or practice, seemed to require that a guard read off the names and put each envelope into the addressee's hand. And so they had to endure that eternity of waiting for the word, the touch of love, the assurance that another world existed and might be returned to.

Karel brought the mail out to the prisoners' yard that day, just before the noon meal. The other guard with him was Miros. Karel held the eight or so letters in his left hand, read the name on the top one, handed it over with his right. He called out Novotný's name, Hovey's. Then he paused and slowly crumpled the third envelope into his fist. Then he called out the next.

Everyone knew at once. They didn't have to look at Travnicek. Hovey did, and saw him standing upright, his arms straight down by his sides, his fists clenched.

Karel read on, and handed over all the other letters. "That's all for today," he said. "Except for this advertising for salve for infected foreskins." He tossed the wadded letter up and caught it as it fell again. "Anybody here got an infected foreskin? Travnicek? No. This wouldn't interest you." None of the prisoners was reading. They all watched Karel. He was grinning slyly, and though he looked mostly at Travnicek, he glanced at the others from the corners of his eyes as he always did to enjoy their amusement at his joke. None smiled back.

He tossed the letter again, and then fumbled the catch. It bounced out away from his fingers.

"Oops. Can't litter the area. Travnicek, pick up the trash."

For a moment the prisoner didn't move.

"Pick it up, I said."

Travnieck stepped forward as if wading through sand, bent, and picked up the letter.

"Give it to me. I'll throw it in the garbage for you when I go."

Travnicek rose. He held the letter like an object of blown glass.

"Give it to me!" For an instant the smirk was gone. Then it sidled back across Karel's face. "This is a pretty exclusive sporting club here, you know. I'm surprised they let Jewboys in at all. You better do what us stewards say, or you'll get your membership canceled. Give it to me."

Travnicek walked slowly up to him.

Karel suddenly put on a face of concern. "Unless it's something you really need. I mean, if it's something you really need, then of course . . . You just tell me if you really need it. Just ask me."

Travnicek extended his arm and dropped the letter into Karel's open hand.

"Well, then, I guess it isn't anything important, is it. I'll just take it along." He turned and moved two steps away, still looking at Travnicek over his shoulder. He turned back again. "Nice paper, though. Maybe I'll use it to wipe my ass."

He tossed the crumpled ball high into the air. A breeze across the yard pushed it sideways. He lunged to catch it again. Whether he intended to prolong Travnicek's ordeal by playing the same trick over, or whether he did miss, the wad bounced once more, up, away from his hand. This time it landed closer to Hovey.

Everyone stood still, Travnicek staring at his letter, Karel at Travnicek, the others at Karel, in dread that he would put them all through it again. Nearly noon. They stood on short shadows.

Professor Hovey had been holding his own letter clenched in his left hand, quivering with a cold fury that was making him almost sick. In that moment of stillness, though, suddenly he was calm.

He took the long step forward, leaned, and picked up the letter.

"Good boy, Yankee. Don't want trash around the area. Give it to me."

Professor Hovey opened the wad and smoothed the envelope. He felt the pleasant warmth of the sun on his forehead tempered by that gentle breeze. He walked over to Travnicek.

"Hey, shit-brain! You bring that here!"

Professor Hovey extended the letter. As Travnicek reached to take it, Karel charged. Full arm swinging, he smacked his hand down on Hovey's shoulder to grab and spin him backward.

Hovey let the jerk pull him. To Karel's force he added his own: right hand against left fist, full strength in both arms driving his left elbow back into Karel's stomach. As Karel began to fold and fall away, Hovey controlled his own fall, spun with its momentum, and smashed the heel of his right hand into the point of the guard's chin. In continuous motion he followed through, thrusting out his arm, heaving the man up and back to come crashing down in the dirt.

For one instant Karel seemed stunned, more by surprise than impact. Then he scrabbled behind him, grabbing at the submachine gun slung over his shoulder.

•

When the door was opened for the third time—which Professor Hovey thought must mean it was the fourth day—he rose from the bench, eager to have even the half loaf he assumed they were bringing him.

Solitary confinement had been a more difficult ordeal than he would have expected. In jails at home he had always been fed meals that were full, however plain. He had had a cot that was intended to be a bed, however Spartan, rather than another of those iron-slatted benches. This one, in an improvement over the one in the cell where he'd been held on the night of his arrest, at least offered the luxury of a ticking stuffed thinly with some kind of fiber, and a large rag that could be referred to generically as a blanket.

Otherwise, the cell, in the basement of the building, was almost identical to that first one. From time to time Hovey had tried to divert himself by fantasizing a dungeon-industry as an important component of the Czech economy: the engineers with their charts of statistics on human anatomy, testing discomfort levels of various bench designs; the production line turning them out, every hundredth tested and rejected if the quality-control inspector could sleep without waking for sixty consecutive minutes; the slop-bucket division; the design studio where they worked at achieving the most depressing shade of gray for the walls; the desperation, the layoffs, the bread-and-water lines in a catastrophic year of domestic tranquility; rippling recession as demands for bench-slat steel and spy-hole-cover hinges fell off.

The fantasy occupied his mind from time to time, and—he thought—would provide some humor for the lectures he would give when he got home. He still made himself believe he would get home. He never allowed himself to dwell on the probability that now he would not. He never allowed himself to think about the labor camp that he assumed he would be sent to.

At least he was alive. He might not have been if the other guard, Miros, had not been quick. As Karel had caught hold of his machine gun and begun swinging it around, Miros had rushed up, his own weapon leveled. Keeping it pointed at Hovey, he grabbed his partner's arm and kept him from firing for long enough for him to regain his sense. Karel had

had to release what he could of his rage merely by kidney-punching Hovey as they hurried him down to the cell.

When Hovey saw that the guards who opened the door on that fourth day had no food for him, despite his self-discipline he nearly sank down again on the bench. But he had known; he had chosen.

Back into the van, off to the mines; he was resolved to meet his certain fate with fortitude. Tiny frosted-glass windows set into the van's rear doors admitted light, but it was impossible to see through them. He had to hold to the bench, unable to see the road to anticipate its turns and twists. After a while traffic seemed to become thicker, and then he could tell they were coming into some city. It was not until they had let him out of the van in a basement garage and started upstairs with him that he realized where he had been brought.

•

Dr. Benda sat gazing toward the window when Professor Hovey entered his office. "Good morning, Lawrence. Come and sit down," he said.

Hovey tried to judge his situation by that greeting as he crossed the room to take the chair by the desk. They were back to the formality of the desk between them, not resuming the friendlier couch and armchair that they'd moved to while preparing and rehearsing his testimony for the trials. On the other hand, Dr. Benda did call him "Lawrence," the familiarity he'd adopted at that time. Hovey still called the older man "Dr. Benda," by which deference he surprised himself. He never said "sir" to any man, and always used the first name of anyone of any age or rank who used his.

"Good morning, Dr. Benda."

"I understand that you have been uncivilized again."

Professor Hovey looked at him levelly for several seconds. When he answered he tried to temper his tone of righteous anger, which he had no thought of hiding, with respect. "No. I think I was being civilized. I think I did what any *civilized* person would have done."

"You were insubordinate. You struck a guard."

"Yes. Unfortunately, I don't think I really hurt him. Dr. Benda . . . sir . . . you must know the whole story. You must know what Karel was doing. How can you say I was wrong . . . you can't say that it would have been right to stand there and let him do it."

"He was a guard. You are a prisoner."

"I am a human being."

"You might have been killed. You might have been beaten. You could have been sent off to a labor camp for the rest of your probably short life."

"There are worse things!"

"Don't be a fool! Don't play the hero!"

"I'm not. I'm not playing— And I'm not a fool. That's the point. It's a fool who thinks it's worth living when you let them fuck you over and make you—I'm sorry. I know that kind of language offends you, and I don't mean to offend you. But the fault here isn't that I hit a guard, that I was insubordinate, 'uncivilized.' The fault is— How could a man like Karel ever get to be a guard in a 'civilized' country? You— I'm sorry, but you must have lived through the Nazis, through the occupation. I can't believe you didn't resist. I can't believe you believed that the Czechs should just obey because the Germans were the guards and you were prisoners."

At the beginning of Hovey's tirade, Dr. Benda had stared at him with an expression of growing incredulity, but at the end—for just an instant—he looked down at his desk, almost as though he could not meet the young man's eyes. Then he sighed and shook his head and looked back again.

"You make your case with much power, Lawrence. And it is fortunate for you that a case can be made. However, prison discipline must be maintained. You—neither you nor anyone else—must be allowed to form the notion that you can be insubordinate over anything you take to be a slight to your status as 'a human being.' You will be for four days more in solitary confinement."

"And then?"

Dr. Benda swiveled to gaze toward the windows again. "And then—this time—things will be as they were. But take care.

"Now, I had been planning to be in touch with you on another matter. It has seemed to me a great loss that your abilities are not put to some good use.

"There is, not far from where you are . . . staying . . . a school, an institute for young people who will enter careers serving the state abroad—in the diplomatic service, Ministry of Trade, and so forth. I thought you might like to speak with them regularly, help them with their English—idiomatic conversation. Perhaps even . . . with the director . . . work up a series of lectures on aspects of American culture that could be followed by discussion.

"If this can be arranged, you will even be paid for your work. Of course, you would have to be transported and accompanied to the institute and back, and that cost would have to be deducted. But I believe there would remain a little stipend you could use for books—when you have exhausted the ones I have loaned you."

"Dr. Benda, that would be fantastic!"

"You are willing. Good. I should tell you, Lawrence, that

I have an ulterior motive in suggesting this work. Of course it will serve the students, and may help you pass your time in a more interesting way, but also, I wish that you should be able to tell when you return to America that you were well treated here. In telling you this, again I must warn you: your government may not want you to tell such a story—it would better suit their propaganda that you should be badly treated. Even best, perhaps that you should be so badly treated that you do not return at all. Now, are you sure you wish to do this work?''

"Absolutely. I don't give a— I can take care of myself when I get back. But thank you.''

"So. Perhaps thinking about these classes may occupy your mind for the next four days.''

"Thank you, Dr. Benda. For everything. Is that all?''

"Yes. Except . . .'' Dr. Benda rested his forearms on the desk, his big hands spread, and leaned over them toward Professor Hovey. "I did resist the Germans. And I believe I still am fighting for the cause of civilization and principle to this day. But, Lawrence, my boy, consider: I am able to go on fighting because I did not die for my principles at an early age.''

CHAPTER 10

It was decided that freeing Professor Hovey was impossible. At first, Talley was angry and frustrated, but as the days stretched into weeks his frustration subsided. He accepted the judgment that while at a common prison a guard might be bribed, or a truck carrying convict-laborers might be intercepted, or a raid might even be dared on an ordinary camp, there was no acceptable way to break Hovey out of a Czech intelligence service facility set in the center of an army base.

His desire to *know* subsided too. He still hoped that the surveillance of D'Avignon, or the search for the agent-impersonator would be fruitful. The latter had been narrowed to fewer than twenty men, who were being checked. What consternation, what paralysis at the agency this lack of resolution might be causing, he neither knew nor seriously cared about.

He came finally to admit that, as time passed, he hardly cared about solving the mystery at all. The college year had closed. Jane had moved up to live with him for the summer.

He reorganized his office to make room for her. They read and wrote, gardened and kept house, walked in the meadows and woods, and made love.

He had thought—accepted as inevitable—that their passion would diminish with familiarity. Instead, it seemed to grow as they learned about each other, as each became more skillful at pleasing the other. It was a period of bliss beyond any either had known. Talley refused to recognize his doubts that it could continue, and Jane held hers to herself, countering them with her joy.

A cloud would pass across their heaven each week or so, when a letter would come from Hovey. Jane would read it, and write an answer that was chatty and said nothing true, writing at once in order to have it done with. She and Talley never spoke of the correspondence, until the letter came in which Hovey told of his opportunity to work outside the prison.

"Would that make a difference? About getting him out?"

"It might."

"Well," she said, looking down at the paper in her hand, "I guess it's not a secret, is it?"

Talley shrugged, not looking at her.

•

They got to Chip Bolander in the third week of July. The FBI agent came to the storefront school at about two forty-five on Tuesday, while Bolander was working with a class of women. Bolander spotted him for what he was at once, but kept his cool. He let Manny intercept him and take him into the office, and kept right on with his instruction and coaching until the hour was finished, as if the agent watching through the big window meant nothing.

He knew it wasn't nothing. When the agent asked him if he could establish his whereabouts on those dates last winter, Bolander knew it was a lot of bad. It wasn't the worst, though, not yet. He played it straight at first: a little bewildered, cooperative, good-natured.

"I guess . . . I don't know. I mean, who remembers where he was this past January . . ." He flipped back the pages of the calendar book. "Yeah. Here. January twenty-fifth?"

"That's right."

"Right here. Class from four to five—high school club— and then the regular evening session, seven-thirty to nine. March what?"

"Second."

"Here. Same thing."

"You taught them?"

"Sure. See? My initials. Manny—my partner—worked in the evening with me. See? I don't know—he probably was around in the afternoon, too."

"Okay, Mr. Bolander. That should do it. Sorry to have taken your time. Ah . . . if we should need further verification, beyond talking with your partner, you do have lists of people who were in those classes?"

"Sure. You want them?"

"I don't think that will be necessary now. Thank you."

"Don't thank me yet." Bolander kept his expression of good humor so the agent would see the tough talk came from confidence, not fear. "Sure, we keep lists. But before I give them to you, you're going to have to get a court order. The people who sent you are going to have to prove in court they've got a reason. Now I know you're just a foot soldier like I was. So I'm not going to give you, personally, any hard time. But when you report back on me, you carry back this message for me, too. You tell them I am not going to be harassed. Okay?''

"Okay, Mr. Bolander. I'll do that.''

"Thanks. I'd appreciate it.'' He kept his voice light, kept his smile. It was the kung fu style: you're not scared, you're not angry, you don't really want to fight; only if you're forced to will you toss your opponent over your head and shove his leg up his ass.

"Now, I know what this is about,'' he went on. "The agency, the CIA, just wants to breathe on my neck. That's the only thing it could be. I'm straight-arrow. I'm an honest citizen and an honest businessman. So the only reason to send somebody around asking where I was on the third Thursday of last week, and threatening to go around and say to my students that the FBI is checking on me, is to keep me in line.

"Well, I am in line. The noodle-whips are running things by their rules, and I am retired from the wars. So you just ask them for me, very politely, to get the fuck off my back.''

•

"This is Clarence Brown.''

"Oh?''

"I'm going to have to relocate.''

"Why?''

"The FBI's checking on me. Came by an hour ago. Wanted to know where I was on those dates in January and March, when I was out East.''

"How quickly do you believe you must move?''

"It feels like I've got a while. They wouldn't have sent a

man right in to see me if they had me under heavy suspicion. But I'd like to be on my way tomorrow.''

"How did they find you?''

"How the fuck should I know? That's what I want to ask *you*. Maybe they're just running me, just fishing, because the agency canned me and they know there's no love lost. It doesn't matter, though. I'm going to have to move.''

"Yes. What is your situation?''

"It seemed like just a preliminary check, and I could show my book that says I was here. But if they come back again, get to my students, they'll blow me.''

"Are you under surveillance?''

"I haven't spotted any. I'm secure right this minute. Of course, I'll assume they're on me, and take evasive action when I split.''

"Yes. Can you get to New York City? By afternoon the day after tomorrow?''

"Sure.''

"Call at fifteen hundred. I will give you instructions then.''

•

Although Chip Bolander used "Boy Scout" as a term of contempt when he applied it to anyone over the age of sixteen, he valued his own youthful experience as a scout. He had found the motto "Be Prepared" to be a sound maxim for life, particularly in conjunction with his own, "Travel Light.''

He detected no surveillance as he drove to his apartment, nor any around it. Nevertheless, he followed his usual routine, going in just long enough to make himself a snack and watch the news before heading back again for the evening session. After it was over he went out with Manny for late supper and a few beers, and then home to turn on the late movie. While it played, though, he packed his carry-on.

He had no regret about the clothes, the furnishings, the possessions that he would be leaving. They were all good things, expensive, but they all could be replaced. Traveling light meant never owning anything you couldn't leave—never being *owned* by anything. The furniture was actually Manny's, anyway. So was the car. Technically, so was the school. The paper work was pretty involved, but what it meant was that he could clean all the cash from the safe-deposit box and walk away, and Manny was sole possessor of a business and a lot of property.

Manny would cover for him. Manny would buy him a little time, if he needed it, no matter how much pressure they put on. Manny believed Bolander still worked for the agency, that when he went off on those mysterious trips from time to time he was coming from deep cover to handle special, top-secret missions. Manny was a sweet guy but a little simple.

Still following routine, Bolander got up late the next morning, did a little shopping, went to the bank. Again, he saw no one following, but he pulled a couple of neat maneuvers in traffic to be sure. Then he vanished.

He did regret not being able to say good-bye to one in particular of his women, but only a little. Travel light.

•

Professor Hovey sat with his arms spread wide along the top of the back seat, his head up, smiling into the warm

breeze as the open car carried him across the countryside. An
outing on a fine midsummer afternoon. "Sweet are the uses
of adversity," he quoted to himself, aware how his pleasure
in the drive came from being confined all the rest of the
week. At home he'd have been in a hurry. It wouldn't have
mattered where he was coming from or going to, he'd have
been in a hurry and would hardly have noticed the day. A
vehicle like this Czech equivalent of a jeep would have
seemed too loud, the springs too stiff, the seats too hard; now
it was his limousine.

The weekly trips were a half-holiday for all of them, his
guards as well as himself. They obviously enjoyed the trip,
the break in routine, too. They could smoke as much as they
liked, and flirt with the girls who worked in the institute's
kitchen while they waited for him to give his talk and have
tea and conversation with the students. This week Miros was
driving, and Antonin, the new guard who had replaced Karel,
sat beside him in the front.

While a group of squat gray buildings—factories or hous-
ing or both—sluglike, befouled the outskirts of the pictur-
esque village near the prison, and a herd of them munched
the country from the larger town on the horizon toward the
fine old house that housed the institute, most of the drive was
through rural, rolling landscape. Along one section they drove
for several minutes in a forest.

So expansive were his feelings during the drive that Hovey
allowed himself an uncharacteristic fantasy. Sitting in the
rear of the car, with the uniformed men in front, in his own
civilian clothes that had been returned to him to wear on
these occasions, he could (despite his genuinely antiaristocratic
principles) imagine himself a squire, a great landowner out
surveying his estates.

The narrow road brought them down and around a small

hill in a wide curve just sharp enough to exhilarate them with
the sense of motion, then tunneled into the wood. Not a
wildwood like those Hovey drove past sometimes in America, a tract not yet developed, but overgrown, allowed to
grow up naturally. This land must have been seen by some
planner as a roofless factory for producing trees. The planting
might have been done by a military drill team, the saplings
inspected daily by martinets. Every youthful pine now stood
to attention, every rank, every file seen from either end as
one tree. Evenly spaced, at the corners of perfect imaginary
squares, the trees made aisles diagonally, too. Only at angles
other than forty-five or ninety degrees was a viewer's line of
sight blocked by trunks in the spaces between trunks,
succeedingly. Professor Hovey found the neatness appealing
to his sense of order, the regimentation antithetical to his
beliefs. Without attempting to resolve the contradiction, he
merely let the movement of the car through that pattern—the
opening and closing of vistas—delight his eye.

When it entered the wood, the road must have come under
the jurisdiction of the forest engineer. If it could not be made
to conform exactly to his grid, it was at least required to
renounce meandering and pass through his domain by straight
lines. The first was about half a mile long; the second, at a
right oblique, another quarter; then a final right opened the
long straight to the end.

Just before the first bend an orange reflective safety trian-
gle had been set out to indicate that a vehicle was stopped
ahead. Miros slowed to make the turn.

As they came around, the small truck they saw was not
really pulled over, perhaps because its back was piled high
with cages of chickens, and the driver feared tipping if he put
two wheels onto the soft and crowned shoulder. Standing out
on the road, the truck blocked visibility ahead in its lane. As

if recognizing the potential hazard created, one man stood beside the truck in the left-hand lane in order to signal approaching traffic. The other man knelt at a rear wheel. Evidently he had just begun his repairs: he had not yet had time to get the jack in place.

Because the truck had been halted so close to the bend, it was not possible to see whether another vehicle were coming from the opposite direction. There must have been, though, since the signalman held up his hand for Miros to wait, made a waving-forward motion toward the other way, then stepped toward the back of the truck to clear the lane himself. Because of where the truck had stopped, Miros had to coast right up behind it before he could come to a halt, even though he had slowed.

Smiling, the farmer who had signaled came up next to Miros to say a word while they waited, and the other got up and moved to retrieve the jack handle he'd laid at the side of the road behind the truck.

As they approached, Professor Hovey glanced back and forth at the men with mild interest to see what Czech chicken farmers looked like. They looked like he would have expected: one wearing a gray work shirt, the other a hand-knit brown sweater, both with dark trousers tucked into scuffed high boots, both with soft, billed caps. Both were youngish, both had lean, high-cheekboned faces. They fitted the stereotype that Professor Hovey—and, evidently, the guards—held. Until they both produced automatic pistols.

It happened so quickly, and the men were so close, that Antonin had no chance to unsling his submachine gun, nor Miros to take his from between the seats.

The former signalman said, "Get out." He and his partner waggled their pistol barrels at the guards to emphasize the command. As the guards, moving very carefully, complied, the first man let his eyes leave Miros just for an instant while he said in English, "You too, Professor Hovey. We here for free you."

Professor Hovey slipped forward to the edge of his seat but sat still for the moment that Antonin took to get onto the road and step away from the car. His mind seemed both frozen and racing. Stunned, bewildered, he seemed to himself unable to reason, to direct his thoughts, yet he understood that these men were the agents of the CIA, and therefore could not be trusted. The man on the right was making Antonin slowly unsling his gun and lay it on the ground. Then he gestured to him to step away from it, and backed off, himself, to be clear as the other man directed Miros around the front of the car and next to Antonin.

"Come," the man said over his shoulder. He and his accomplice kept their aim on the guards who were ordered to walk ahead, while the ambushers put Hovey between them.

For the first moments after they started into the forest, conflicting emotions made him almost dizzy. Wild elation at the thought of freedom whirled in alternation with doubt and fear. Why would the CIA want to rescue him, since he would denounce them as soon as he returned? Dr. Benda had warned him that they might prefer him never to come home at all. He had understood that warning: he had believed for years that the CIA would kill anyone they considered an enemy. Was this their means to kill him? But if it were, they could have gunned him and his guards at once, when they stopped the jeep.

Miros and Antonin paced side by side ahead, with the two ambushers and Hovey abreast six steps behind them, all their footfalls soft on the thick carpet of yellow and red-brown needles, moving silently like some formal procession up the columned aisle.

"Where are we going?" he asked.

"Away from the road."

"What for?"

"We tie them."

"Then what?"

"We take you away."

"How?"

"Never mind."

No, escape was not possible. They could never get him out of there, riding with them in a farm truck through the countryside. If the CIA hadn't been willing to admit he was their agent, to get him released through diplomacy or some kind of exchange, they certainly wouldn't take this risk for him now. But if they wanted to get rid of him, why wait? Why take this walk?

Of course! They wouldn't kill him and the guards and leave their bodies on the road as evidence of what they'd done. He would just disappear. That way they could get two birds at once: keep him from coming home and claim the Czechs had done away with him. It would exactly parallel what they'd done at the beginning, when they'd tricked him into their plot and then abandoned him.

How far into the forest would they go? he wondered. So straight was the row that they would be seen walking, standing, even at a long distance from the road. But not, he realized, lying. Soon they would be sufficiently far, their figures small enough to seem only humps in the ground, like scuffed-up needles, if they were noticed at all.

Hovey had always wondered why men allow themselves to be marched away to their deaths, marched to a place chosen for their executioners' convenience, rather than insisting on being inconvenient in a last, self-respectful defiance. Now he understood. One may still hope to find the chance to run; the gun may jam; the ground may open, lightning strike, the swift-winged angel fling up a shield to ward away the speeding bullet.

They were not really going far. They were not really moving slowly. There was no time merely to hope.

On his next step, instead of swinging his right foot forward, Professor Hovey lunged backward. Simultaneously, he smashed his left hand down on the one assassin's forearm, gripping so that the man couldn't bring up his pistol again, and flung his right fist full-arm-around into the solar plexus of the other man. As though his hand had bounced from his target, he swung it in a powerhouse blow back to knock the wind out of the first man, too. Stepping fully back from between them, he brought his hands back to his shoulders and shot them out to slam against each man's already bent-over back. He hoped he sent them lurching, toppling, sprawling—he didn't wait to see. Shouting, "Miros, run!" he flung himself to the left, sprinting down an aisle, darting diagonally right, left, right.

He was aware that behind him the pistols were fired, that men shouted. He ran on, weaving between the rows.

He swerved to the side, caught himself up behind a trunk. In that young forest the trees were thinner than he was, face on. Only by standing sideways could he hide most of his slim figure.

He had partially lost his sense of direction. He believed he knew, generally, where the road lay, where the aisle perpendicular to it was that they'd walked up. He wasn't sure, though, whether he now looked back toward that aisle on a diagonal or at a right angle to it. He tried to remember the turns he'd taken in running, to orient himself, so that he would know which direction to take when he ran again. He did not think he'd run far enough.

The wood had only seemed silent, he realized. Now he

heard birds twittering. From somewhere high up to his left came a tapping he knew must be a woodpecker. Those noises were small ones, though, and the woods were quiet. In that quiet he could hear distinctly, if distantly, when an automobile engine was started. The sound helped him locate the road more exactly.

He tipped his head forward to venture an eye beyond the trunk. There was no one in that aisle, nor in what he could see of the ones paralleling or diagonal to it. Perhaps the sound of the automobile, now moving, signaled the killers were abandoning the chase.

But the volume of the sound held steady instead of diminishing. Then it grew louder, seeming to move very slowly from behind toward his left. Could he have run that far, come near to the second bend in the road?

He looked again, stepped out, crossed the aisle to the next tree. Again he peered to his right, just past it.

Only the lower branches of the trees met overhead. Nearly straight-down sunlight through the boughs seemed solid shafts in the dust-filled air, but, striking the ground, it splattered, dappling the forest floor and the lower trunks. All limbs had been cut from the trees to a height of twelve feet or more.

The lines of trunks, the pillars of light, the softness and silence should have given a sense of cathedrallike calm. Instead the tranquility seemed sinister, frightening him more. He looked over his left shoulder, the other way along that line. He felt the heavy stillness was a deception meant to lull him—he turned to look behind—to dull the fear-sharpened keenness of sight and hearing, to soothe him so terror could take him off guard and strike suddenly. He continued to pivot, to look next up the diagonals behind him, his anxiety rising like the whine of the automobile engine.

Coming at him! The brown-sweatered man! Fifty yards away, crouched, loping!

Hovey spun, sprinted. The man shouted something unintelligible to him. Over two rows, Hovey cut diagonally left. To his left, a little behind him, some dark shape, roaring, sped along beyond the bars of trees. The jeep! He realized that one man was driving the jeep along the road—and he was running at an angle toward it.

He shifted direction to run—flat out—parallel to the road. But the jeep was faster. He was aware of it passing on his left. Then its sound changed, and he understood that it had turned to drive up an aisle ahead to intercept him.

He recognized that he and his pursuers were like pieces on some game board. He could escape only if he moved at angles, keeping enough trunks between to screen him and let him get beyond them.

He angled right again. He was still heading toward the aisle up which the jeep moved. He would have to cut away again. Where was the other man?

There! Almost upon him, sprinting, flashing through streaks of sunlight and shadow, keeping Hovey between himself and the jeep.

Hovey threw a frantic look toward the sound of the car. The driver had seen him, turned, and was racing up the diagonal head-on at him. Hovey swerved. But the other man—both men— They were too close now. He couldn't get enough trees between to mask him, to let him take a new direction unseen.

Hopelessly, but unwilling to be run down, he dashed into another row. Spraying dirt and needles, the jeep swung around a tree, shot forward two rows, and wheeled around another to face him out of a roiling dust cloud, blocking him.

Hovey threw his back to a tree. The brown-sweatered man lurched and almost stumbled in bringing himself to a stop. He swayed for a moment, gasping, the pistol swinging back and forth in his hand. He was too far away to be lunged at. Professor Hovey, his own chest heaving, brought himself up as straight as he could to face him.

•

He was afraid continually that he would be sick. The jouncing and swaying in darkness, disoriented; the stink of the truck—gasoline, oil, exhaust fumes—and of the chickens; the adrenaline that had been pumped into his body and not yet dissipated. There were reasons enough for nausea, he told himself. The way to deal with it was by relaxation, by fixing his mind on a point, by calming himself, by draining himself of tension.

But with every jolt and lurch, conflicting thoughts, waves of emotion swept through him. Rescue! Or were they, truly, merely going to kill him in some other place, to serve some plot beyond his comprehension? Freedom! Or had they captured him for punishment by the CIA at home? Escape! But would it succeed? What would be done to him if he were caught again? Those were the alternating crests and troughs, but under them all, dragging him, icy, twisting his stomach, was a tide of guilt.

The abductors had been angry, and frightened, and had run and shoved to make him run to the truck. They had grabbed and pushed him to cram him into the tiny compartment under the chicken cages. Yet he had remembered, and had made them pause for one instant to tell him about the guards.

"We kill them! What you think? You crazy? You run—we only going to tie them up! You run, we got to kill them!"

Miros had saved his life. Antonin had been just a boy.

They'd been killed because he'd misunderstood. Because he'd— But how could he have known? Because he'd been— They hadn't gotten word to him. Naturally he might think . . . Because he'd been *wrong*.

More than the motion, it was the guilt that sickened him, the realization that he had been, that he could be, so wrong so disastrously. The truck rocked; it swayed in ways he could not anticipate as the road curved. A little light came through cracks in his compartment, but it flickered. He pressed his feet against the end, his back against the side. That made the jarring firmer, which felt better, better than queasy floating. Gradually he fought the nausea down. It wasn't his fault. His mistake was reasonable, his actions logical on the basis of justifiable perceptions. Mistakes are made when the data are in error. He should have been told. It wasn't his fault.

As he was able—little by little, going over it, thinking it out—to free himself from the ocean-bottom quicksand of guilt, the focus of his anxiety shifted to the more practical question of escape. His abductors hadn't killed him; they probably weren't going to. Whatever the CIA might do was in the future, not to be worried over now. The immediate danger was recapture.

He tried to analyze his situation. A key element would be time. He and his guards would have been due at the institute at about three o'clock. What time was it now? His fists were up under his head, to pillow it. He struggled to move his arm far enough to get the wristwatch away from his nose so that he could read it. The space was too small even to be called coffinlike. He couldn't get his forearm crosswise in it.

He began estimating. It must have been about two-thirty when they had entered the forest. How much time had been wasted— He blocked the thought. How much time might have remained when he did leave, in the truck? Twenty-five minutes? Twenty?

How long had he been in there? His emotions had been in such turmoil that he had lost track. Five minutes? Ten minutes? More than five, less than ten. That would mean between—

Ridiculous! It was ridiculous to be guessing. He writhed, digging his elbow into his ribs, scraping his knuckles against the compartment wall. For an instant he had to fight a claustrophobic urge to thrash to try to free himself from his confinement, to scream because he knew he couldn't. He made himself stop, lie still, relax completely. Then he slowly worked his arm down. By peering down his nose he could just see his watch. It was about five minutes before three.

How long after they were due before someone called back to the base? Five minutes' grace? Ten to allow for a flat tire? Then, would the full cry begin at once, or would someone be sent along the road to check? At best, another fifteen minutes might be gained there. In either case, would the search work outward, or would the borders at once be sealed? He had to assume they were taking him toward a border. Where was the border? He had no idea where the base was in relation to any border, so far from his mind had been the thought of escape.

Too many unknowns. All that he could be sure of was that in a very few minutes they would begin to hunt him.

•

The truck slowed. It went on, but slowing gradually, not the momentary lift of accelerator and tap of brake before a curve. Professor Hovey heard the steady squeal as the driver pressed the brake pedal gently but steadily. They were coming to a stop.

Why? Had they reached their destination, or were they being intercepted? He strained to hear any sound that might inform him.

Silence. He had been able to hear the two men in the cab speaking—not their words, but the murmur of their voices. They did not speak now.

Then there were the chickens. They surrounded him. They had been still, hunkered, huddled against the movement of the truck, the buffeting of the wind. As the truck halted they began to stir and cluck. Some even pecked at his compartment.

He had seen a film, possibly more than one, of people escaping hidden within a wagonload of straw. The soldiers had thrust their swords or spears into the straw, or had threatened to. Chickens were a better idea, but if they were unloaded . . .

Expecting the worst, he was sure they had been stopped by soldiers. He lay rigidly still, soaked in sweat, certain they had been stopped by soldiers at a roadblock even before he heard the voice just beyond his head ask the driver for papers.

"Your papers," they always said. And then, "We must ask you to come with us."

The voice made some remark (Hovey understood it was about the chickens), and the driver answered, and they both laughed. The truck started up again.

By pressing himself tight against the compartment Professor Hovey was able to control his shaking enough to take another look at his watch. Three-ten. There hadn't been enough time for a roadblock to have been set up in response to an alarm. It must have been routine. He let himself go limp and dissolve into mindless relief.

•

When the truck stopped again he was not afraid. From all of the traffic sounds, the slowings and stoppings and turnings, it had been clear that they were coming into some town. At last there had been a pause and a sharp turn; the noise of the truck suddenly swelled as it was held close around them, and darkness was total. He realized they had entered a building.

The engine was shut off, and he heard a voice ask, "How'd it go?" in Czech.

"Not good, Jake."

"What happened?"

The speaking was too fast for Hovey to follow every word, but he knew what was being told.

The cages above him were removed and his box opened. The two men who had brought him grabbed his arms to help pull him up, and he stood there like Lazarus, peering around, feeling as rumpled and discomfited as the chickens on either side looked.

He saw that the truck had pulled into some kind of small warehouse, but he had no time to take in its details as the man on the ground—who must have been the one they'd called Jake—called up to him. "Okay, Professor. Let's go. We're running a little late." Now he spoke English, and clearly was an American.

"You should have told me! Who are you? What is this? CIA? You should have let me know you were going to— Of course I thought—"

"Get down here! I don't know what the fuck the problem is, but I've just got ten minutes to get you out of here. Move!"

Hovey climbed over the side of the truck.

"Take off your clothes. You're going to have to change. Your face is dirty. You can wash up over there."

Hovey saw the sink in a corner. He began taking off his shirt.

"Now," Jake said. "Listen up. There's just a few things you've got to get. Your name is Scott Johnson. What's your name?"

"Scott Johnson."

"You're from Rockford, Illinois."

"I'm from Rockford, Illinois. My name is Scott Johnson."

"Good. That's good. You've got the idea. Scott Johnson, Rockford, Illinois, you work in a bank, you're a loan officer."

Professor Hovey repeated it all as he removed his shoes and trousers and went to the sink to clean himself.

"Here's your wallet with all your U.S. ID. There are some photos in it; you make up who they are. Think of people in your own family. You're married. You're on your summer vacation with your wife. You got to Vienna on Tuesday."

"I'm married?"

"Your wife's name is Mary. You'll meet her in a minute. The two of you have stayed pretty much to yourselves, but she'll tell you if there's anybody on the bus you should know anything about."

"Who . . . what . . . ? Who is she?"

"Your wife, Mary. You met her at the bank. She was a teller. Other than that, if anybody asks you anything about her, her family, background, whatever, you just think of your lady friend Jane Boudreau. Mary knows about her.

"I'll give you a guidebook to Vienna. I've checked the things you've seen on the tours. You can read it on the bus and see what you should know about them. You're staying at the Hotel Burgenlander. There's a brochure from the hotel and a reservation receipt. Put them in different pockets. Here's some change. Here's your passport and visa. You came yesterday on the two-day tour of Prague from Vienna.

You stayed at the Excelsior Hotel. You toured the city by bus—the same tour you really took when you were there in March. You saw the show at the Lantera Magica last night. Here's a program. Now you're going back on the bus to Vienna. You going to remember all that?''

"Yes. I'll read over the stuff there.''

"Good. There isn't really much, and don't worry about every detail. This is all completely surface. It won't stand up to any real questioning at all, but it's the best we can do in the time. And anyway, if they stop you and they're suspicious enough to really dig, they're going to get you—they've already got you. But this should be enough cover for the routine once-over-lightly.''

"I'm going to Vienna on a tourist bus?''

"That's right. It makes a rest stop here—we're about halfway between Prague and Vienna, but we're right up close to the border. The bus should be pulling in in about two minutes. You're on it.''

"What do you mean?''

"We got a double for you. Close enough, with the clothes and glasses. He's been on from Prague to here.''

"He looks like me?''

"Close enough. At least, we've got to hope so, don't we.''

"Couldn't you have done something to disguise me, to make us look more alike? A beard?''

"No time, Professor. Those things have to be made for the person—get the color right and all. Otherwise they just look stuck on. Probably most of the people on the bus won't notice anything, and if they think they do, your wife should make it work. If she thinks it's you, why should anybody else doubt?''

"Won't they have closed the border?''

"You don't close a border for something like this. You just check people going through it. We don't know how close they'll be checking by the time you get there. The theory is that they won't."

"They must know I'm missing by now. They'll know I'm heading toward a border."

"You've been heading away from the nearest border to where you were. The theory is that once they do get fired up, they're more likely to look for you in someplace like under the chickens than by us sending you through this way. But I don't know, Professor—maybe you will get caught."

CHAPTER 11

"**P**ut your collar outside your sweater," Jake said.

Professor Hovey didn't react. He hadn't really heard. He was staring at the man who had come into the storeroom through the small door in the wall opposite the truck entrance.

The man was of medium height, slim, in his early thirties. He was lean-faced, his hair looked to be cut rather short, but he was wearing a hat made of printed cloth, with a narrow brim turned down all around. He wore glasses. He was dressed in chino trousers and a plaid cotton shirt with a lightweight pullover. The collar of the shirt was pulled out over the sweater.

Hovey had been startled when the man came in, and then struck by the fact that he was dressed identically to himself. It actually took him another instant, though, for full realization.

"It won't work!" he said. "He doesn't look at all like me!"

"Which one of us should be pleased about that, Jake?" the man asked.

"Put your collar outside your sweater. You're close enough." As Hovey still hesitated, Jake reached and pulled out the collar himself.

"But—!"

"You're close enough, Professor! And you haven't really got a choice. So let's do it."

The man who had come in removed his glasses, gave Hovey a nod that was both greeting and farewell, and walked past him, pulling off his sweater as he did.

With a firm hand on his back, Jake guided Hovey to the door, opened it for him, and pushed him through. "Good luck," Jake said, and went back.

Hovey found himself in a corridor leading from the storeroom to another door at the other end. On his right, as he walked down it, a door with a window in it led into a meat-cutting room. A man in a blood-smeared white apron was working there, but he didn't look up. Opposite that door were two others with the silhouette of a man and a woman on them, respectively.

There was a small window in the end door, too. Hovey looked through it and saw into a market.

No, he didn't have any choice. He pushed on the door and went through.

Immediately his arm was taken by a woman. "Let's go on back to the bus," she said. Although her arm appeared merely to be draped casually through his, she pressed it firmly against his ribs to direct him.

"What's the matter, Scott? Do I have dirt on my nose? You're looking at me like you've never seen me before."

He jerked his stare away from her. That sense of dream, of delirium, that he'd had with Janos Czerny was coming over him again. He fought it. He had acted in plays, he could do so now. He looked at her again, smiling. "Every time I see you is like the first time all over again, Mary."

The woman was, he estimated, about his own age. Her face was fuller, fleshier than Jane Boudreau's, her hair a more feminine mass of curls, but her eyes had the same appraising, calculating look, and her arm was firm and strong.

"You'll go far with a line like that," she said.

"I sure hope so."

When they went out of the market they were at one side of a stone-paved square. A dark-windowed tour bus with *Cosmos—Wien* lettered along its side stood parked at an end. The woman nodded to turn him toward it.

"You have a bad summer cold," she said. "You blow your nose a lot. You probably should be doing that when we walk down the aisle of the bus."

Professor Hovey felt in his back pocket and found a handkerchief. "Right."

"Because of your cold you just had some soup sent up to our room for supper last night, and you had breakfast sent up this morning. I went down to the dining room and ate with the group both times and assured the people at our table that you were just taking it easy, and it wasn't serious. You did eat lunch with those people today. And we did have the regular lunch in Jihlava yesterday, but that was at a long table, and we were sitting closest to different people than today. We've made a point of sitting in a different place each time the bus went out, but always toward the back."

"That other guy really didn't look like me."

"A little more than you may think. Pull your hat down a little more in front."

The bus door stood open. Mary climbed in first. Hovey had his handkerchief out as he followed her, and he seemed to be blowing and wiping all the way to their seats.

About half the seats were taken. In fearful fantasy he had imagined all of them full, pairs of heads on either side of an interminable aisle, eight eyes to each row, row after row, all fixed on his face.

In actuality, while most of the people glanced at him, they showed no interest in his passage whatsoever. One couple did smile and nod at Mary as she proceeded him, and the woman asked him, "Are you still feelin' better?"

Without lowering the handkerchief he nodded back.

"Why don't you sit next to the window?" Mary said, halting and waiting for him to sit first. "That way you can lean against the corner and take a nap if you want."

Hovey slid in to the window seat. By tipping his seat and sliding down he screened himself behind the high backs of the row in front.

The bus's engine rumbled, idling to keep the air conditioning going. No passengers had returned to the seats immediately ahead or behind. Speaking softly, her head near his, Mary asked, "How did it go—picking you up?"

He answered as his abductors—his rescuers—he wasn't yet sure how he thought of them—had answered Jake: "Not good."

"What happened?"

"They . . . nobody had told me—I didn't know . . . I thought they were going to kill me. I ran. They killed the guards."

"Oh God! Why . . . why did you think they were going to kill you?"

"For revenge, because I told the truth about the CIA at my trial. To keep me from telling any more. To get rid of me. They've got plenty of reason to want to get me."

"We're getting you out!"

"For your own reasons, I'm sure."

She seemed about to respond to that, then suddenly leaned
and pointed toward the window. Hovey turned to look. He
saw nothing of particular interest, but held his stare as he
realized people were passing and sitting in the row behind.

When they were down he turned back. "What's going to
happen?"

"Nothing. We hope. We're just going back to Vienna.
We're just about ten minutes from the border. I guess they
make the buses stop here because it's the last chance to get
some of the tourists' money. The tour makes a circuit; we
came in at a different place yesterday. You've got your
passport and your visa?"

"He just gave me a passport."

"The visa should be inside. Let me have them."

Hovey handed over the blue book. She checked inside,
then put it into her purse. Abruptly she pointed to the window again, and he turned and looked as people came and sat
in the seats across the aisle, then in those in front of them.

He was about to turn back to her, when he sensed someone
else approaching.

"Excuse me, Mary, honey, but I just wanted to see if
Scott was really feelin' better. I thought he was lookin' kinda
peaky again when he got on just now." She spoke with a
superficial hush to her voice, and used the third person in
referring to him, as though in the hospital room of someone
near death.

The hush was only superficial. Her voice, he thought, had
the timbre and carrying quality of a donkey in heat; and
respectful of his illness as she might be, she still meant
herself to be heard over the engine noise.

"I thought he was lookin' just fine at lunch, and I thought
maybe the air conditionin' was . . ."

Because he obviously wasn't comatose and could so clearly

hear her, he really couldn't continue to stare away toward the window. He fished out his handkerchief and brought it up to his nose as he turned, nodding and smiling at her.

"George and I thought that if Scott was feelin' up to snuff again, maybe you all would like to . . ."

He didn't think he could just sit there holding the handkerchief over half his face all the time she was talking. He crumpled it into his fist, but—elbow on seat arm—kept the fist against his mouth.

The woman faltered. Her eyes opened wide, then narrowed, then opened again. Still staring at him she stumbled on. ". . . have some supper with us . . ."

"Meine Damen und meine Herren, bitte, sitzen Sie sich. Ladies and gentlemen, please take your seats. *Mesdames et messieurs, prenez* . . ." A woman's voice came over the public address system.

"Thanks so much, Sally. We'll talk about it later. You'd better sit down now." Mary smiled and nodded up at the woman, who backed away still staring at Hovey. She turned to move to her seat, but stared at him once again before sitting.

The tour guide came down the aisle counting passengers. She returned to her place at the front, the bus engine roared, and they pulled away.

"That woman recognized me. I mean, she didn't. She knows."

"Maybe. How could she be sure? Anyway, it doesn't matter. Ten minutes from now she can jump up and tell the whole bus."

Hovey wanted to dash, to sprint for safety, to be in a helicopter that would fling itself skyward and dragonfly away, darting unpredictably. He had to grip his hands together tightly to contain his tension as the bus, with hippopotamal ponderosity, swayed and lumbered around the square and along the street that led down to the highway.

There it paused and waited while a military truck filled with soldiers sped past. With a great grumbling and a sense of monstrous inertia to be overcome, the bus then turned onto the road in the direction the truck had gone.

Hovey started to say something about the truck full of soldiers, then decided not to. The bus began to pick up speed. Yet it still was slow enough that another vehicle came up quickly from behind and passed. It was an open, jeeplike car, like the one that had conveyed him to the institute. A soldier drove. An officer sat beside him. The officer stared up at the bus as he passed. For an awful moment Hovey sensed that the man was staring straight at him. But the man held his head fixed, looking at all of the windows; and the windows (Hovey tried to reassure himself) were smoked and could not be seen through from the outside.

"What's going on?" he asked.

Mary paused for an instant, regarding him, before she answered. "I don't know. It's probably just the national guard going home from summer camp."

He put his head close to hers and hissed in her ear. "You and Jake and all of you—you seem to think this is some kind of TV sitcom! Do you know what they'll do to me if I get caught? They'll put me in a labor camp for thirty years!"

Mary looked at him steadily. She pursed her lips as though calculating, then nodded, accepting his estimate.

"Goddamn you! You don't care! None of you!" He threw himself over to the window again. Goddamned CIA! They'd gotten him into this, now they were jeopardizing him again. He hadn't asked them to get him out—not now, not this way. He had been getting along all right. He would have been out

soon anyway. But if he were caught now . . . What could
he say? Could he explain? Would Dr. Benda believe him?
Would it matter if he did?

The bus had been accelerating steadily. Now it hurtled
down the highway, its rumble become a roar. The sense of
mass in motion comforted him, as though that momentum
could not be halted. Maybe that's why his companion seemed
so calm: the driver was part of the plot, and would simply
keep his foot down and crash through the flimsy barrier of a
black-and-white-striped border-bar. Hovey didn't believe that,
but his mind desperately sought any way of seeing himself
safely on the other side.

The bus began to slow.

He could not see ahead. The highway had had three lanes,
the center one marked for passing first from one side, then
the other. Although not a major throughway, it clearly was a
principal route. In one part of his mind he had recognized
that fact, yet he had visualized the sort of border crossing he
had seen before on his trip to Austria and Bavaria with Jane:
a country road coming upon a spindly barrier-bar, two customs policemen, their little hut.

Slowed now to a crawl, the bus swung right. Hovey could
see directly down the road. His jaw dropped, his eyes wid-
ened, and he felt as though his innards had withered from
frigid horror.

Like a turnpike reaching a toll-collection point, the road
broadened toward the right. Concrete wedges and booths
divided it into lanes, each with its own barrier. As the bus
turned further he saw them appear one after another: one,
two, three, four. Automobiles were stopped in two of them,
four soldiers surrounding each while a fifth looked into its
open trunk. The other lanes were empty at that moment, but
Hovey's fantasy of the bus ramming through could not have

been realized there, either. Beyond the barriers, centered one in each lane, stood a rank of huge military trucks. After passing the booth-barriers, a vehicle would have to creep forward and snake to pass between them. And by each truck stood another half-dozen soldiers, their submachine guns unslung from their shoulders, held upright on hips, fingers beside the triggers.

The bus swung further, aiming beyond the farthest booth. It turned left to straighten again. Looking through the windows across the aisle, Hovey could see that they were pulling up in a wider area at the front of a long two-story building. They stopped.

He looked in terrified bewilderment at Mary.

"The tour guide collects all our passports and visas and takes them in so we don't all have to get off the bus." She nodded toward the front of the bus, where the guide already was beginning to move from row to row.

Across the aisle he could see the passengers digging into their jacket pockets and handbags. It was okay. It was normal.

Suddenly a pounding sounded on the bus's door. The driver opened it. An instant later a voice snapped out an order from the front. Mary leaned out into the aisle to look, and one of the people in the row ahead half stood to see above the seat backs. Hovey tried to slump lower into his seat.

The tour guide spoke over the address system, first in German, then in English. "Ladies and gentlemen, please have your passports and visas ready for examination here on the bus by a Czech border official." She said it again in French.

Hovey sucked at his cheeks and tried to swallow. He could feel his pulse racing through his whole body. He looked to his left, out the large window. Rays of the early evening sun struck it directly. Its heavy tinting screened out glare, but the brightness lit him—he felt—like a limelight.

Beyond the other side of the highway a flat grassy strip led to a low wire fence. A field began there, rising slightly but not enough to block his view of meadows, wildflower speckled, rolling off and toward a little wood and some buildings in the distance—a view of wide, unbounded openness.

At the bottom of the bright aluminum frame around the window was lettered *Ausgang/Exit/Sortie*, with a broad black arrow pointing up at either side. He took that in, understanding that if he lifted the casing there, the whole panoramic-vista window would pivot. The hermetical compartment would be opened to untempered air, to unbuffered noise, to any scents that wafted on a breeze. And he might fly through as easily.

It was only a flicker of desperate fantasy, he knew. And even as he gazed at the pale, gold-tinted puffs of cloud and the sky of transparent blue, two soldiers came around the bus and stood just off to one side of his window.

The first man coming down the aisle must have been an officer. His uniform was slightly different from the second man's, and he wore a holstered pistol. The second clearly was a common soldier. He carried his submachine gun, like the men outside, at the ready.

The officer moved down the aisle with deliberation, but quickly. He looked first at the occupants of each pair of seats, and took their visas and passports, barely glancing at the documents before handing the passports back, his eyes already moving on to the people across or in the next row.

Hovey sat upright in his seat. He took a very deep breath and made himself focus. They were looking for him, of course. But they didn't know where he was, or they wouldn't be searching everything that moved on the highway. That they would be looking for him had been planned for. He had a cover. He had a role. He only had to play it.

As Mary was playing. She was leaning out into the aisle, watching the officer's progress toward them with an expression of concerned curiosity but no apprehensions.

He mimicked her, leaning like a man trying to see instead of one hoping to hide.

From two rows away the officer spotted him. He skipped those rows, and came directly to Hovey's.

"Your passport, please." He extended his hand.

Hovey was aware instantly that the man's having spoken in English might be significant. On the other hand, perhaps he merely had the experience with foreigners that enabled him to guess their nationality at a glance.

Mary offered him the documents for both of them. That seemed to give him a moment's surprise. He looked at both, looked down at Mary in an appraising way, and then spoke to Hovey again.

"You are on a tour from Vienna?"

"Yes."

"When did you arrive in Vienna?"

"Tuesday."

"Where are you staying in Vienna?"

"The Hotel Burgenlander."

The officer nodded slightly as though in acceptance. But he continued to hold the documents. He shifted his eyes to look to the back of the bus, took a step so that he could survey all of the remaining passengers, and then returned.

"I must ask you, please, to come with me."

"What's the matter, officer?" Mary asked.

"I must ask you, please, to come with me," he said again and stepped down the aisle so that they could get out. When they had done so, he preceded them. The soldier, awkward as he tried to keep his weapon pointing safely upward and yet still ready, leaned backward over the laps of the people in the row ahead so that his superior, Mary, and Hovey could pass him.

The officer strode briskly. As he passed the driver and tour guide he said something, and then he went quickly down the three steps and out of the bus.

Hovey's progress down the aisle, following Mary, was like the entrance he had imagined: every face was turned to him, every head swiveled to watch him as he passed.

The tour guide stood at the front of the bus, a look of fear on her face. She altered it and tried to smile, to reassure as they approached. Mary smiled back and shrugged, and turned down the steps. Hovey didn't have a character prepared, so he imitated her, and went down too.

The soldier kept his face grim, as he must have thought duty required. Just as he turned and started down the steps himself, there came carrying over the murmur that was beginning to arise from the passengers one clear and piercing voice.

"George, I told you that wasn't Scott Johnson!"

•

The officer was standing in a large windowed office that looked out on the waiting room when they got there. He was talking on the telephone. He must have hurried there immediately from the bus. When Mary and Hovey had gotten down, Hovey almost falling from the final step, they had halted, stunned. The soldier had stepped down, nodded, and said, "Into the building, please," in Czech. Professor Hovey, his wits honed by terror, had had sense enough to pretend not to understand, nor did Mary seem to.

The soldier nodded again and pointed. He thereafter kept both hands on his submachine gun, holding it at port arms in front of himself, instead of at the infinitesimally less threatening hip rest, as he marched behind them. He stayed by the door in that posture. He did not seem to have anything to report to his superior.

"I guess he doesn't understand English," Hovey said under his breath, weak with the sense that the gallows trap had stuck—at the first springing, at least.

Mary only smiled. "I'll kill that woman," she said.

The officer stopped talking and waited. He stood with the receiver to his ear looking steadily at Hovey.

"I wonder what the hell is going on," Hovey said.

"Well, I guess they must be looking for someone, Scott."

"Well, I don't like the way *he's* looking at *me*."

"Maybe he thinks you're a spy. Where did you hide the microfilm?"

Hovey goggled with shock and horror. For an instant he felt he might collapse. His voice almost squeaked as he tried both to shout and whisper. "For chrissake, Mary, that's not funny!"

She grabbed his arm in hers and pulled herself to him, chuckling. "Oh, Scott. You get so worked up about things. We don't have anything to worry about. They checked us into the country yesterday. They probably had someone following us around—hiding under everybody's beds—all the time we were here. He'll find that out, and that'll be all there is to it."

He understood her game. "Okay, but don't say stupid things. I mean, even in the States, if you make some wisecrack in an airport about having a bomb—you may think

that's very funny and everybody knows it's a joke—they
have you in handcuffs and your luggage soaking in oil before
you have time to stop laughing. Just cut it out."

"Well, you'd better, too. If you don't stop looking so
guilty, they'll keep you here until they find out why."

There were two soldiers with their submachine guns at the
other end of the long room, and another officer type. Only
the soldier who had brought them from the bus fixed his
attention upon them constantly, but the others looked at them
often and apparently were speculating about them.

In another minute the tour guide from the bus came in. The
other officer went to her, and they spoke briefly, and she
gave him papers. Hovey guessed that they were the visas that
the first officer had not finished collecting. She left. He
waited in dread to hear the sound of the bus's engine firing,
to hear it pulling away, abandoning him.

The officer responded to something said on his line. Carrying the phone he moved to the office door.

"Come closer, please," he said.

Hovey and Mary started to comply, but he stopped them.
"You alone, sir. Please."

Hovey came up and stood just outside the office.

"Take off your hat, please."

Hovey took off the foolish hat.

The officer spoke into the phone, then listened again,
looking steadily at Hovey all the while, his eyes moving over
Hovey's face, feature by feature. "Yes," he said in Czech.
"Yes. Exactly."

He listened again, said, "One moment, sir," and held up
an opened passport so that he could look at it on the same
level as Hovey's face. "It is him," he said. He put the
passport down, took up the visa from the desk, held it up in
the same way. "Yes, sir, the visa also."

Hovey felt his legs quivering. He wondered if it was making his trousers shake. That wouldn't be a giveaway, he thought. It would be natural—for Scott Johnson—it would be natural to be nervous in this situation. Mary had given him that—he could be a character who got uptight about situations.

"Do you want fingerprints?" the officer asked.

Hovey thanked the god in whom he didn't believe for all those seminars, oral exams, tutorials, and committee meetings in which he had trained himself to show no shock no matter what might be said.

"I'm holding the tour bus," the officer said. "But if you want me to hold him for a fingerprint check, I'll let it go and keep only him."

Hovey tried to look like a man who understood nothing in that foreign language, but who was trying to learn by dint of close concentration. It gave him an excuse, he thought, for listening and watching intently.

"No, sir, he's with a woman, identified as his wife," the officer answered. "She could be," he said. "No, sir, I called you at once." He nodded. "Yes, sir. Good. Can you have me patched so that you can listen? Good."

There was a pause for a moment.

Hovey had been trying frantically to think his way into his character and situation. Should he get angry? Should he bluster and demand some explanation? Threaten to call his consulate?

Two unhurried but decisive steps forward to the office door, bringing his hand up and slapping it against the frame, gripping it. "Officer, I think this has gone on long enough. Now I want to know exactly why you're keeping me here, or I'm going to—"

He quickly plotted out the whole scene.

Maybe he should go the full bluff: present as his deduction

that they must be looking for someone who resembled himself, suggest being fingerprinted as the quickest way to settle the matter.

No. He didn't think he had the guts to go that far. And they might take him up.

But he should do something. His feel for the scene was urging on him more and more strongly that he should not stand meekly like a man who knows the ax is going to fall.

"Could you . . . please . . . tell me what's going on?" he asked. He could draw on his own real emotions to combine in his voice the tones of worry, anger, and the sense of having made a conscious decision to handle the problem calmly.

For a moment the officer seemed to be deliberating whether to regard the question as coming from an escaped spy and murderer, or from a guest who had just helped to alleviate his nation's foreign exchange problem, and whether he owed any answer to either.

"There is a technical problem concerning your visa, sir," he said. "We should be able to clear it up very shortly. Thank you for your cooperation."

"Yes," he said suddenly into the telephone, and followed that with a rapid string of words most of which Hovey could not follow, except for "tour," and "Vienna," and "identify," and his name. Scott Johnson's name. "Yes," he said, and shifted the receiver a little away from his ear, and leaned back against the edge of the desk.

Hovey's mind worked frantically to imagine what was happening. First he had been matched to a description—probably his own—then to his photographs as Scott Johnson on the travel documents. This Johnson and the missing Hovey were found to look alike. But Johnson had entered the country yesterday, before Hovey's escape, at some other place. Had he and Hovey looked alike then?

"Yes," said the officer; "yes," taking in Professor Hovey's height and bulk; "yes," looking at his hair; "yes," to his eyes and glasses; "yes," to the shape or the character of his face.

Would all those yesses build a certainty of coincidence? Or would the coincidence seem too convenient to be true?

"Yes. Thank you. Sir? This would seem to be the same man."

The officer said something else that Hovey didn't understand. He hoped against hope that one of the words was "coincidence." The next thing he did understand included ". . . hold him anyway?" He shoved his hands down into his pockets and sighed with the air of a man becoming exasperated despite a patient nature. Doing so, he hoped, would conceal his fingers trembling.

"Good," the officer said, "I'll try that."

Hovey's mind almost always worked quickly. At that moment, though, if the neural firings in his cortex could have been displayed on some screen, they might have made its entire area appear as a constant brilliant fluorescence.

He grasped that the Czechs had established to their satisfaction that there were two men who looked alike when described over the telephone. The one they were holding most likely was Johnson. If he was, and they kept him for fingerprinting or other definitive identification, the story might chill the tourist trade they seemed to be trying to cultivate. Surely they would take that risk rather than let their prisoner slip by, but if they could assure themselves more simply by . . .

". . . his wife, yes, sir," the officer went on. "Yes, sir. Good." He put down the telephone without hanging up.

His wife. Yes! How clever, Hovey thought. For the first

time ever, he was filled with an almost worshipful awe and admiration for the CIA's foresight and competence. Let the Czechs ask him anything about his "wife." He would think of Jane, and answer with a fact that Mary had, in leisure, learned by heart. Birthday? May twenty-eighth. Her mother's maiden name? Pierce. For one second his heart soared as he knew he had the exam aced and would pass with honors.

"Mr. Johnson," the officer said, "what was the date of your wedding?"

•

As they approached, the soldiers fell into two lines, one on either side, making a gauntlet for them to pass through. The angle of the sun had flattened more, casting the soldiers' shadows across the road like bars, until they were swallowed into the solid darkness from the huge, ugly, squat trucks.

Hovey's heart had stuck at the base of his throat and turned to stone. He had licked his lips and almost replied to the officer, "That's a very interesting question."

While still in high school he had calculated that it was always better to guess than to leave a blank, so at various times he had prayed, O God, let the Emancipation Proclamation have been in 1865; let the atomic number of nitrogen be nine; let the date of the First Folio have been 1625.

But what could have been the date of his wedding? Oh, yes: If anyone asks a question about your wife, just think of Jane, and answer. Oh, yes.

He could name any date he thought of for a wedding that had never happened, of course. And then the officer would go into the waiting area where Mary was and ask her, too. And his chances of getting past the border would be 364 to 1.

For a microsecond he had looked at the officer with an expression of bewilderment. Then his gaze had drifted off across the office as if he wondered why the question were asked—and he saw the answer on the wall beyond the desk.

"July twenty-second," he had said. "Today is our anniversary. We were planning to have a nice dinner in Vienna to celebrate, which is why I really would appreciate it if you'd—"

"Thank you, sir. One moment." The officer took a step forward. "Please," he said, and Hovey, as though not understanding why the man wanted to leave his office, stepped back to allow him to do so.

The officer had gone to Mary and asked his question. Agitated as he was, Hovey had appreciated her professionalism. She never let her eyes dart toward him for a signal. She had asked the officer why he wanted to know, in order to gain a moment's time. He had refused to say, merely asking his question again. She had given an answer, and then the officer had turned to stare at Hovey narrowly for several seconds.

•

"It was the only thing I could think of," she said. "Today *is* the day when you and I became husband and wife."

Hovey threw his arms around her and hugged and squeezed as best he could in the narrow space between their seats and the row ahead.

"Oh, wow!" was all he could say, and he said it over and over. He wanted to jump up and shout, but even hurtling along the highway toward Vienna, he was still unwilling to call attention to himself.

Even after the overflow of emotion at his reprieve had
subsided, and he merely grinned, now and then shaking his
head from side to side and sighing, he still repeated, "Oh,
wow!" and still held Mary's hand tightly. She seemed willing to let him do so; more than willing, she seemed to feel
the same lingering fear and joyous relief, and gripped his
hand in return.

"God," he said, "I thought for a minute there that we
were dead. I mean, I *knew* it was thirty years in the salt
mines for me." Then he thought, "What would have happened to you if they'd caught us?"

Mary looked at him steadily for a moment before answering. "It would have depended," she said. "Just for trying to
get you out, probably prison until we had someone they
wanted to exchange me for. On the other hand, if they
wanted to consider me an accomplice in the murder of your
guards—I mean, according to the rules of our game, we're
supposed to avoid actually killing each other—they'd probably just have quietly shot me."

CHAPTER 12

"**I**t is good that you are being removed from this business."

"Why?"

"Because the professor seems to have been rescued yesterday."

"No shit!" Chip Bolander revealed his astonishment in his voice, and his eyebrows rose. Only those little signs showed it, though. Otherwise he appeared calm and relaxed, leaning into the corner of the booth in the murkily lit bar at Kennedy Airport. "How did they do it?"

"I do not know the details."

"How bad will this screw up your game?"

"I do not know that, either. I assume that we would have preferred to keep him in our prison."

"Does he know enough to blow it?"

"Again, it is difficult to say. It would depend on what he might tell them in relation to whatever they might have discovered for themselves. As I say, we would have pre-

227

ferred that there were no opportunity for him to tell them anything.''

The man with whom Bolander spoke was one whom he had met in person only twice before. He was attached to the Czech embassy, or some Eastern-bloc mission, in Washington. He looked like a diplomat: exquisitely barbered and manicured, handsomely suited and shod. He was too good-looking to melt into a crowd inconspicuously, and Bolander wondered how he managed to evade the FBI surveillance that naturally accompanied him when he traveled. He had evaded it. Bolander had assured himself of that by spending twenty minutes following and checking the man, and another ten while the man checked him.

Bolander took hold of his glass of beer but did not raise it to take a second sip. He twisted it a quarter turn between his thumb and forefinger.

''If there was a way to keep him from telling them anything, would that be worth something to you?''

''I suppose it might. Do you know of a way?''

''I suppose I might. How much?''

''I suppose it would depend. Just to silence him would be worth something, I'm sure. I'm not sure how much, though, because I am not sure how much he can tell them. I would think . . .'' The man lifted his own glass and took a tiny sip. ''I would think that more important than merely preventing him from talking would be to have it appear that he was prevented from confirming a penetration of the CIA. Do you follow me?''

''Yeah. And even better if he was gotten in such a way that they wouldn't know how you knew where to get him.''

''Yes. You have something in mind?''

''I think I might.''

''That is very interesting. I would have to check with

higher authority, of course, but I think I can say that we would be grateful for something along that line. But, ah . . . isn't it rather dangerous for you to continue with this? You are welcome to use your parachute. I take it, though, that you would like to have a spare one."

"Makes for a softer landing. You want to check?"

The airport was an ideal place from which to call. The man was back within five minutes. He slid into his seat again, smiled.

"Twenty-five thousand if he is silenced quickly and prevented from possibly spoiling the game, or the same amount if an attempt is made which is unsuccessful but which counteracts anything he might tell them and so contributes to the continuation of the game. Fifty if both are accomplished: if he is removed in an appropriately suggestive and, for the CIA, embarrassing manner."

"Fifty and one-hundred."

The man smiled. "No."

Bolander smiled. "Thirty-five, seventy-five."

"No."

"No."

The man tipped his head to the side. "Yes."

They raised their glasses and saluted each other.

•

"Now, Tom, we thought that today, for the first session, at least, we'd put him there on that end of the couch. We thought you could sit in the armchair at the end of the couch, with just the little end table between the two of you. You can put your recorder on it." Walter Simson seemed less like a general disposing his forces than a faculty marshal assigning places on a commencement platform.

"Aren't you going to use the room recorders?"

"Oh, of course. I imagine they're picking us up now." He turned toward the mirror on the wall opposite the couch. "Are you getting us, in there?"

"Loud and clear, Walt," a voice answered from the ceiling.

"The thing is, Tom, he'll expect us to be recording. But if you use your machine—perfectly naturally, just as you would—then he'll think that's it. Sometimes that little trick can be useful, because if the subject sees the visible recorder is off, then he thinks he's off the record."

"When did you get into all of this, Walt?"

"Oh, I've been coming to debriefings from time to time for quite a while. I don't conduct them, though. I sit at the card table there and take notes. We've got Steve for our expert on this."

The third man was of medium height, medium weight, middle age. Talley had the sense that from that balance he could shift quickly in almost any direction. He was wearing corduroy jeans and a bulky maroon sweater with the sleeves pushed up, and he looked like a middle-level executive at home on a Saturday afternoon, getting ready to watch the football game. Talley felt sure that a quick-change of costume could transform him into father-confessor or mafia hood.

"You'll sit on the couch too?" Simson asked him.

"Yeah. Away at the other end from him. Keep a sense of openness—we're all in this together—but he'll be turned away from me most of the time talking to you, Tom. That way he can get used to all of us being here without being overwhelmed."

"You figure everything."

"Say, that's the business."

"This guy is not a spy for the opposition, you know."

"I know. He sure has helped them, and he sure seems to hate our guts, though."

"I know you guys still find this difficult to believe, but it is possible both to be a patriotic American and to hate the CIA's guts."

"That's good, Tom. That's very well put. Use it on him, just that way. Start with it, or work it in, but use it. That's the point of view that we need if we're going to get into him at all.

"That's why I think we'll probably let you handle the whole session this morning. If having you make the intro works, then let him just keep focusing on you. Let him think you're in charge. I can come in later when we start over, and we all ask questions.

"Well, are we ready?"

Simson answered, "I think so, Steve," and Talley merely nodded.

"Okay," Steve said, not raising his voice as Simson had. "Bring him in."

They all remained standing, waiting to meet Professor Hovey as though it were a social occasion, as though he were a guest.

Talley did put his tape recorder onto the little table. Using it in the way Simson had suggested was a small trick, probably a harmless one, but it seemed to him the symbol and manifestation of his larger, private deception. Hovey would sit at the couch end, he would sit in the nearby chair and pretend to be Hovey's friend, and the redundant recorder, the sham recorder, would lie between them, its tiny wheels turning.

The door opened, Professor Hovey was shown in, and the man who'd brought him left again.

"Ah, good morning, Professor. I hope you had a comfortable night." Simson crossed the room to shake Hovey's hand before the younger man might have had time to set a hostile tone to the meeting. Simson wore a suit and tie, of course, but the suit was light-colored and without a vest, so he looked distinguished but not daunting. "You are looking much more relaxed. They gave you a good breakfast, didn't they?" He radiated a sincerity of interest and concern, and even though he didn't wait for a reply to any of his comments, one would have to have been especially churlish not to be a little disarmed.

Hovey was feeling only moderately churlish. That the CIA might kill him now seemed unlikely. In fact (though he would always assert that what had happened in the forest was essentially their fault) the suspicion was severely embarrassing to him. If he still hated them, both on principle and for personal grievance, he had to acknowledge that they had gotten him out of prison and had treated him courteously since then.

"Professor, this is Tom Talley . . . and Steve McCluskie."

Hands were gripped firmly, whether to show good-fellowship or resolution, and Simson gestured Hovey to his seat. The others took the ones they had agreed upon.

Hovey sat, determined to make some show at preventing them from thinking they controlled him. "How long do you think you're going to keep me here?" he asked.

Simson still played the role of chairman. "Until we've had a chance to hear about what you've been through, and ask you some questions."

"I don't know as I particularly . . ." Hovey reconsidered. "I'm grateful for your having gotten me out of Czechoslovakia, *finally,* so I suppose I might be willing to talk with you." He was angry, but he often was angry, and knew how to control himself. So he prudently didn't add anything about how much he intended to talk *about* them. "But I would prefer to do it in my own time and at a place of my own choosing."

"I can understand that, Professor," Steve McCluskie answered in a tone that suggested he did, and sympathized. "But if you'll bear with us for just a few minutes, we'll try to give you some good reasons why you should talk with us here and now. Tom?"

Talley began to say his piece. "Walter and Steve are employees of the CIA. I am not. I was, fifteen years ago, but I quit because . . ." He went through the same story he had told Jane Boudreau. Telling it again didn't bother him. He often had to make presentations to clients; he had lectured to his classes. There was no duplicity in planning what to say in order to achieve an effect on someone. The only parts that touched his tender conscience were those where he stressed the attitudes toward the agency that he and Hovey shared. It was done to give credence to the rest of the story, of course; but doing it was a reminder to Talley of what else they had in common.

"Despite my feelings about the agency, I was persuaded to work for Walt, on a one-time contract, because he gave me reason to believe that this case involving you was not what it seemed. As a result of my own extensive personal investigation, I know that to be true. I'd like to tell you what I've found out."

Talley didn't begin with the revelation that Hovey had been duped by the Czechs themselves. He guessed that it would be too stunning if it came right off, and might therefore be rejected. He began with Janos Czerny, told the story chronologically, and brought Hovey into it from the point of view of the agency's true contact, Sandy MacDonald.

Hovey tried for a while to maintain an expression of academic neutrality. At the beginning, though, he was unable fully to mask his hostility and skepticism. As Talley's story proceeded, the skepticism deepened to incredulity.

Talley sensed that. He broke his narrative to say, "We would prefer to keep the identity of the man who the agency sent secret. But if you have any doubt about what I'm telling you, we will let you talk with him and satisfy yourself that he's genuine and that he's telling the truth."

Hovey didn't really doubt. The story rang true, partly because of its coherence and detail, but more because—without wanting to—he trusted the man telling it. Talley's deep anger against the CIA had projected clearly, even though he told about his former employment and reason for leaving matter-of-factly, even lightly. And there had been no sense that he was selling his story, trying to make it convincing by an intensity of delivery. Hovey's astonishment was that of a sane and sober man confronting a palpable whale in his living room.

And his hostility was transformed into a mixture of outrage, disillusionment, and shame. He realized how he had been deceived by Dr. Benda, how easily he had been deceived. He felt not merely light-headed, but light-bodied, as though his cells were rarefying from each other, his substance dissolving, evaporating, leaving him transparent.

He did, of course, want to protest, to deny, to refute. But he was not a fool. When Talley finished, and summarized: ". . . so you see, it wasn't—for once—it wasn't the agency pulling dirty tricks. The whole thing was set up—*you* were set up—by the Czechs . . ." Hovey merely nodded slightly.

Talley paused to let it all sink in, to allow Hovey to begin to deal with it. Steve McCluskie, though, took the opportunity to get in a point.

"That's why we've brought you here, and want to talk to you here before letting you go home again. Frankly, if we let you go now, you might be in some danger. The Czechs will know we got you to debrief you; they might like to prevent that. After we have talked with you, then they have nothing to lose—or gain—so you'll be safe."

Hovey, still staring at nothing halfway across the room, merely nodded again. Then he managed enough strength to ask, "How long will this take?"

"Three, four days—maybe a week," Talley answered him, taking back direction of the interview as they'd agreed he should.

"Can I call—I'd like to call someone . . . some people . . . to let them know I'm back."

Talley knew the answer was "no," that Hovey couldn't call what he must think of as his home and speak to the woman he would expect to be there, for more than one reason. He dropped his eyes and let McCluskie give the agency's reason.

"I'm afraid not. For the sake of security it's better that nobody knows where you are."

"Where am I?"

McCluskie decided instantly to tell him. Hovey was—unexpectedly—putting up no resistance at all; it was best to keep the sense of trust and openness between them. "In Maryland. You probably couldn't see much when you were brought in last night, but we're out in the country."

Hovey turned back to Talley, who was looking at him again with an expression of sorrow that he could read as compassion and friendship. "What's going to happen?" he asked.

Talley knew himself to be misinterpreting the question
that, he sensed, Hovey truly was asking—perhaps without
knowing it himself. Talley answered narrowly. "First, we'll
ask you just to tell the story from your point of view.
Everything, from the first contact you had from the phony
foundation."

He made his tone more businesslike because they were
getting down to business, and because he thought doing so
might make Hovey feel better. And because it made *him* feel
better.

"We'll want you to go into every detail you can think of.
When you mention a person, tell us everything you remember about him: what he looked like, what he was wearing.
Any place, any room—describe everything about it. Most of
that will probably prove to be irrelevant, but at this point we
can't tell what tiny detail might open up something.

"We'll try not to interrupt or ask any questions. After we
get your whole story—which I'm going to record—we'll go
through it all again with you, and ask questions. We'll break
it down into separate sections, and go over and over it again.
It probably won't take long for that to annoy you, since you
may think you're just saying the same things. You may think
we're asking again because we don't believe you. That won't
be the case, but people who do this kind of thing—I don't
myself, but I know about it—their theory is that if you keep
going over, to the point the person is tired, even exhausted,
maybe even getting angry, little details can pop up out of his
subconscious.

"And as you tell us things, you may give us leads to
check. When we've checked them, we may want to get at
new questions they suggest. That's why, although you may
think your story is straightforward and maybe won't take

long to tell, that's why we will be at this for so long. Do you understand?''

"Yes."

"Well, do you want to get started?"

"Yes."

•

Professor Hovey had a good memory. He was able to recall events and scenes vividly once he got started, once he fully understood how detailed they wanted him to be. By ten o'clock he had only gotten as far as the period when Dr. Benda was preparing him to give his testimony at Janos Czerny's and his own trials.

His recital began to falter then, and McCluskie suggested taking a break for coffee. McCluskie guessed that the slowing of pace of speech, the hesitations, the increasing vagueness of description were at least partly caused by emotion. Hovey was obviously an intelligent man with a high degree of self-awareness. He had managed to keep his tone fairly even throughout, allowing only the barest tinge of self-justification, of pleading for understanding and exoneration, to color his voice when he had described how and why he had been persuaded to confess.

On the other hand, since he didn't become physically agitated or use emotional language, he might only have been getting tired of talking. In either case, for this first time through, it seemed better to give him a rest.

Talley was more certain. Although he had never before been involved in this sort of debriefing, in which the questioners sought a psychological reading of the subject, he

found himself especially sensitive to what he recognized as
grief as Hovey relived his betrayal.

It was indeed pain at betrayal that Hovey felt, far worse
than the outrage when he had believed the CIA had betrayed
him. He hadn't truly been surprised then; certainly he hadn't
been deeply grieved by an unscrupulousness that was to have
been expected of them.

But Dr. Benda . . . He had trusted the old man's dignity,
his fair-mindedness, his balance of strictness and compassion, his honesty and openness, his kindness, his . . . His
poses, his sly and knowing tricks. Dr. Benda had not misled
him merely by simple fraud, by misinformation or prestidigi-
tation. Hovey felt the agony of one who has given love in
return for what he thought was love, and found he's simply
been seduced.

●

"And that's why, he said, he'd arranged for me to teach at
the institute. Do you want me to go on about what that was
like?"

Talley glanced at the other men. "Steve? Walter?"

McCluskie asked, "You have any further contact with this
Benda?"

"No."

"And was there any change in your routine at the prison?"

"No."

"Well, I think we can leave it there, for now at least."
McCluskie surveyed all of them. "You know, I think it's
lunchtime. Why don't we all have something to eat, and then
we'll give the Professor a break for a couple hours while we

go over this—you really did a terrific job, Professor. Normally, we wouldn't expect to have so much detail the first time through—and we can see if anything seems to jump out. And then we can start over it all again."

As they rose and started to leave, Hovey asked, "Is there any way . . . I usually run every day. I don't suppose I could do that, but could I go outside and walk for a little while?"

McCluskie considered. "I guess so. You'd have to have somebody with you, but just kind of around the house . . . sure."

•

"Any first thoughts, Tom?"

"Well, the two things I'd want us to do some work on—and for you to get somebody on right away—would be the additions to the description of the guy who contacted him at his home, and this Dr. Benda. I don't recall that name in any of the material I read about Hovey's trial. Hovey said Benda said he was in charge of the prosecution, but he wasn't the prosecutor. Who is he?"

"Yeah. My list, too. Anything else? If not, I suggest we sit down and listen to the recording through again."

"I'd rather not right now, Steve. If it's okay, I'd like to just let it simmer for a little while without stirring at it. Is that okay?"

"Whatever works for you. I think we have to go over it and talk about it together. I mean, that's the point of having this be a group activity. But if you want to let it settle . . . say a couple of hours?"

"Sure. And if nobody minds, I think I'll drive back down

to the village. I need to call home and check my answering
box. I am supposed to be running a business while I'm doing
this, you know.''

"Call from here.''

"I'd rather have a line that doesn't go back through Langley, if you don't mind.''

"Why would we listen to your business?''

"Habit.''

•

Talley had not, of course, mentioned to any of them that
Hovey's former lover was now living with him. To speak
with her, more than to check on his business, was the reason
he wanted to use an unmonitored telephone.

"How long will you be away?'' she had asked when
Talley got the news and told her he would be going to debrief
Hovey. She had been peeling potatoes. She had asked the
question without looking at him.

"I don't know. Several days. I'll call you whenever I
can.''

She had nodded.

"I'll call you as soon as I can, to let you know how he
is.''

"Yes,'' she had said, her hands still for a moment. Then
she had peeled faster, as though to make up the lost time.

They had not truly been able to make themselves not care
about Hovey. They were simply going on together anyway.
Talley wasn't sure whether that was ethically better or worse.
The continuing sense of guilt drove him to seek reassurance

by contact with his accomplice, perhaps, as much as did his longing for her.

He took one of the agency's cars and drove the six miles into the little village. There was a pay phone outside the gas station there. His fingers trembled as he put the coins into the slot, and his heart hammered while he listened to the ringing at the other end.

"Hello?"

"Hi."

"Tom . . ." Her voice sounded strange. He could hear tension making it tight and high just in saying the one syllable of his name.

"What's the matter?"

"Where are you calling from?"

"Jane, what's the matter!"

"Tom . . . Please . . . Where are you calling from?"

"I'm in a booth at a gas station. What's wrong?"

He heard her say, away from the telephone. "He's in a booth at a gas station."

A man's voice spoke to him. "Talley? Now, listen up, old buddy, because I'm not going to talk very long. I admire your taste, Talley. This chick you're shacked up with is a real piece. I wouldn't mind tearing off some of it myself. Now, whether I do, and whether you ever see her again depends on you. I want the professor."

CHAPTER 13

"**I**'ll give you twenty-four hours," Bolander had said. Talley had tried to protest, but Bolander had cut over him: "Twenty-four, that's it!"

Bolander had gone on. "This is a great place you've got here, Tom. I mean, a great defensive position: on a rise, in the open, clear view up and down the road, clear field of fire all around. Nobody sneaks up on you, do they? Not even at night, if you can see in the dark like I'm set up for." The last was a lie; Bolander had no night-vision equipment, but how would Talley know that? "And don't even think about anybody dropping in fast on a chopper. I'd hear it, and even if you were quick enough to catch me, I'd get her first. And don't think about a cordon back off out of sight. I've got that figured, too.

"Now, you want to see your little nooky-cookie here in the same condition you left her—or see her again, period—you get Hovey up here to me within twenty-four hours."

"I can't get him away from—"
"Then kill him."

•

Talley gripped the steering wheel hard, and in doing so kept as rigid a grip on himself. He knew what he would have to do even as his mind raced systematically through his non-options.

He could not tell the CIA men back at the house about the demand. They would not comply with it. They would not jeopardize Professor Hovey, and therefore they would jeopardize Jane. They would try to take the man holding her, not for her sake, but for theirs. They might make some effort to save her, but she would be expendable. He knew about them.

Even in reporting what had happened—as they would surely do—they would condemn her. Bolander had said to Talley, "I know you've got Hovey. I know you're with him, Tom. If you try to fake killing him, I'll know about it. You should know you can't keep a secret inside the agency." Talley couldn't question that. He couldn't even allow himself to wonder why it had been said. The man had warned that he would know if any trick were tried. It might be true, and that was enough.

He would have to comply. Some part of his mind tried to tell him it could be avoided. He would get Hovey away. At the last moment he would trick the man who was holding Jane, somehow. Fight and overpower him. Negotiate. A way would be found once he had time to analyze the situation. But even as that small part of his mind sought to reassure him, he knew he had already made his ultimate choice.

With a callousness, a ruthlessness he had never suspected in himself, he pushed aside all compunction and focused on practicality. He would find some way and kill Hovey if he had to, but first he would try to get him out of that house and take him all the way up to northern New Hampshire.

Assuming he could get the two of them away from the house at all, would he be able to persuade Hovey to go with him? He had no way to take him by force. How could he persuade him? By saying, "Your lover is now my lover; you've got to come and let yourself be killed for her, to save her for me"?

When he got to the place behind the house where they parked the cars, he saw Hovey and one of the support team walking across the field between the house and the line of trees beyond.

•

"Hi! You're getting in that walk."

"Yes. It feels good. This is really nice countryside. But I'll surely be glad when I can take a walk without somebody following me with a machine gun."

Talley smiled at the CIA man. "You guys think that's really necessary?"

"Probably not, but it's the way we do it." He shrugged and quoted. " 'Subject will be accompanied and protected by an armed escort at all times.' "

"I've had some thoughts, and I'd like to ask the professor a few questions. In private. Would it be all right if I took over for you?"

The man considered for a moment. He knew that Talley

was not in the agency, but that he was one of the leaders of
this operation. And he truly thought the regulation was ridiculous in a case like this. He shrugged again. "I guess so.
Don't get farther away from the house than this, okay?"

"Right."

"Here." The man extended the gun.

"You're serious?"

"It's how we do it. Do you know how to use this thing?"

"No."

"Push over the safety, here. Pull this back. Squeeze the
trigger. Even a ten-year-old Lebanese kid can do it."

"Then I should be able to handle it. I mean, in case a
wave of Czech tanks comes out of the woods to get him."
Talley was sweating, but somehow he managed to keep his
fingers still and his voice steady.

"You got it." The man nodded and left them.

"What have you thought of?"

Talley started them strolling, and waited a moment before
answering.

"Nothing. I had to get rid of him. Don't stop. I just got a
phone call—a message. I went out to call my answering
machine, at my home, to see if I had any business messages.
I got a message about you."

Hovey did not hesitate again in his walking, but he looked
down at Talley intently. Talley realized for the first time that
Hovey was two or three inches taller than he. And slimmer,
probably in better shape than he was, despite his wood-
splitting. And more than five years younger. He held the gun
tightly, his thumb near the safety.

"The message—I'm sure it was from the agent, the opposition's man—the one who did their legwork, who pretended
to be from the agency. He's got your friend Jane Boudreau."

"What! How . . . where!"

"He's holding her hostage. For you. They—the other side—they don't want us to debrief you."

"What's he going to do with Jane!"

"He says he's going to kill her if we don't bring you to him."

"God! My god! What are you going to do?"

"Keep walking. The agency won't do anything. Not to get her back. They'll try to get him. They'll send up a team—the FBI, police—but he'll kill her first. That's why I haven't told them. I . . . I'm not in the agency. I don't believe in . . . I can't agree to let that happen."

"But . . . but what else . . ."

Without thought, Talley pressed over the safety lever. His forefinger was against the trigger guard.

Hovey was looking from side to side as though trying to decide in which direction to begin running. "I've got to go there. Where is she?"

Talley moved his finger away from the trigger. "Upstate New Hampshire."

"I've got to go there. I mean, is there any other way?"

"I don't see it. That's why I told you. The guys in there—the agency—they won't let you go."

"I've got to! You'll help me?"

"I put saving her above whatever good keeping you here might do for the agency."

"What are we going to do?"

"First, we would have to find some reason for your leaving."

"Why can't we just drive away?"

"They'll come after us."

"You could shoot out the tires of the other cars."

"They're in direct contact with Langley."

"You could shoot out the phone connection."

"That's only for local calls. I'm sure they have a buried, secure line."

Hovey stopped again. "I don't believe this. You're telling me I'm back in prison."

"Well, I guess so."

"I do believe it! Fucking CIA!"

"Yeah! Larry, maybe that's it: if you . . ."

•

"Well, what are you going to do, Walt? Put electrodes on him? I mean, he isn't somebody from the KGB you've kidnapped. He is an American citizen."

"Not by much." McCluskie leaned against one side of a doorway. His hand was up on the opposite jamb, which he seemed to be studying as though he might either have been admiring it or considering breaking it apart with his bare hand. "He confessed for them, he taught in that Czech intelligence school—that's aid and comfort to the enemy. Now he refuses to cooperate in a matter of national security."

"He's only refusing to stay here and do it your way now."

"What's the matter with him, Tom?" Simson shook his head in bewilderment. "He was fine this morning."

"He was fine when I came up to talk to him outside just now. Perfectly good-humored. He just said he didn't like feeling he was still in prison, and he'd thought it over and decided to continue talking to us from his own home. I told him I didn't think you'd allow that, and that's when he started to blow his stack."

"About three days in one of the white rooms in the cellar'll cool him down."

"I don't think so, Steve. That's not how the Czechs got him, and I don't think you will, either. Now, I don't pretend to know much about this business, but I think you'd do better to play him. He is very anti-CIA. Because of what I told him about myself, he is seeing me as a kindred spirit and an ally. Let me drive him up to Boston. If he thinks I helped get him away from here, he'll keep talking to me."

"That would put him in danger. And you too, Tom."

"Come on, Walt. In the first place, we both know Steve was just putting that on heavy for effect. And secondly, you don't tell anyone we've left here."

"If you're not worried, Tom, then how come you're so strung out?"

"It shows? Can't get by you, Steve. Yeah, well, I think I'm going to get the answers. I've been on this for nearly three months now. I got hooked. I want to know. And I think I'm going to get the answers just by myself, when all you high-priced talents can't. I'm not worried about the bad guys gunning us down on the interstate, Steve. I'm worried that you're going to try to strong-arm Hovey and blow it."

"I don't know, Tom. On the one hand, you're right about how we can't really coerce . . ."

Talley felt a thrill of hope. When Simson began by setting out antitheses, he ended by looking for compromise.

". . . might be danger, especially at his home, where he would be expected to turn up. And a debriefing should be concentrated, and done in a place without distractions."

"How about this, Walt? We'll start for his place. After he cools down, if we're still getting along well, I'll put that to him and try to get him off someplace else. I'll keep calling in to you, so wherever we do end up you can provide security— but you'll have to hold back so he doesn't feel pushed."

"I don't know . . . possibly . . . Steve?"

Before McCluskie could respond, Talley added, "Look, as long as you don't report that we're doing this, nobody will know. But if you still think there might be some risk—or you want Hovey to think there is—okay, go by the book and give me one of your submachine guns to carry along. Do what you want to make yourselves feel all right about this, but I'm telling you—if you want to get anything out of Hovey, you'd better do it whether you like it or not."

•

"Where is it we're going in New Hampshire?"
"My house."
"Your house . . . !"
By then Talley had thought out what he could say. "Yes. I run my business from my home. Obviously, when they found out I was working for the agency on this they checked on me and knew about it. They must have figured that I'd be calling in for messages. It's out in the country, isolated—the guy made a point of that. They wouldn't have to give me directions, and I guess it saved him having to find another place to take her."
Hovey seemed to accept it. "I've been trying to figure what to do when we get there. You know, if there's any way . . ."
"Absolutely. We're going there to save Jane, but that doesn't mean you just have to walk in there and . . . I've been thinking."
"Tell me you've got a plan."
"Maybe. First of all, we've got one joker. This gun. He won't be expecting that.

"Now, my house is set back a couple hundred yards from the road—up a long driveway. What I was thinking is this: we'll back in—you driving. You'll be on the side toward the house, so you can be seen. But we'll stop well before we get there. I'll go in. I'll tell him you're willing to exchange yourself for Jane, but she has to be released to walk away from the house. I'll stay there myself, anything he wants, in exchange for her.

"Assuming he agrees—I think he will, even if he plans to trick us—I'll signal you: I'll wave to you to come. When she's clear, you drive up toward the house. But you don't get too close, and you don't get out until you see him. When you do see him . . . you'll have the machine gun."

Hovey shook his head. "I don't think it'll work. Why should he come out of the house—reveal himself? We could have people hidden on the floor of the car."

"If he won't show himself, then you don't get out. You drive away."

"That leaves you."

Talley shrugged. "I don't see any way that one of us isn't going to have to be there. And there really isn't any reason for him to harm me. If we can get that far, it'll be because he'll think he's bluffed us, and we'll have bluffed him."

Hovey was silent for a moment. "That's fine of you, Tom. It really is. But I couldn't do that."

"What?"

"I couldn't leave you in my place. He might not be bluffing. He might kill you just to make the point his side is serious. You're not really involved in this. If you were in the CIA, okay. You'd have chosen this kind of life—these risks. But you're not. However much I was deceived, or let myself be deceived, I did make a choice back at the beginning to be

involved. Whatever happens to me . . . it just has to be part
of working out my karma.''

Talley stared ahead and concentrated for a moment on
driving. "I did choose, Larry. I agreed to take the job.'' He
fought the urge to tell the truth. Perhaps he would have if
he'd loved Jane from afar, and hoped to win her after his
rival returned. But the truth, he believed, could only release
Hovey from his high-mindedness.

"You seem to be pretty firm about your principles," he
said, keeping his eyes on the road.

"I try to be. I think you have to do what's right.''

"How do you know what's right?''

"You know. We—people—have been around for a long
time now. You read all of the major philosophers, you look
at all the major religions, you look at folk wisdom, myths,
fairy tales. You boil them down and they all say essentially
the same things. Sure, there are aberrations, and cults, and
crazies—even whole countries seem to go crazy sometimes.
And the people involved in them believe that they're right.
But they are aberrations. Over the whole of human experience, we can see that.''

Talley realized he had asked a question that Professor
Hovey was prepared to answer. He suspected that the answer
might take exactly forty-five minutes, end in a peroration,
and then Hovey would ask if there were any questions. That
the response seemed practiced, though, did not diminish the
sense of Hovey's commitment to it.

"What happens when there are conflicts? When there's
more than one right?''

"There are hierarchies. Look, most people believe that
there are cases when war is justified. So killing the enemy
warriors makes you a hero. But in no civilized society are
you a hero for committing an atrocity; killing prisoners, or

unarmed civilians. Sure it's done. But we don't give medals for it.

"And this thing with me, deceiving me. I mean, when I believed the CIA had deceived me I assumed that they would say the end justified it. That stuff about missile emplacements that Janos Czerny was trying to get out—I can see that it can be considered a good thing for us to get that. But . . ." This occasion seemed the only chance Hovey would have to present the case he had prepared and rehearsed. ". . . deceiving me was *wrong*. The end does not justify the means. They should have—I mean, if it really had been the CIA—they should have told me exactly what they wanted and let me make an informed choice."

Talley didn't bother to remind Hovey that the CIA had not deceived him, nor that they had fully prepared their true agent. "If they had told you, would you have done it?"

"Of course not."

"Well . . ."

"They'd have had to get someone else. But I wouldn't have told anyone. I wouldn't have denounced them. It was the fact that they had deceived me—that is, if they had—that made me want to get them."

"I see."

•

"I don't understand," Hovey said. He was driving. They had exchanged places after passing Philadelphia. "How could they know about Jane? How could they know to leave a message for you?"

Talley was glad Hovey was having to keep his eyes on the

road. "You've been writing to each other. Their man came to your house, back in March. Obviously they know about you. Your relationship. I don't know how they learned about me—that I've been working on this. I . . ." He decided to reveal more than Hovey had so far been told so that he might continue to hide his relationship with Jane. "How they found out about me is a major question. It's part of the major question about this whole thing. You see, there are two hypotheses . . ."

Talley went through the entire story. Doing so blurred the focus of Hovey's question, and then, as he outlined the evidence on one side and the other, and as Hovey questioned details and speculated, the problem began to absorb them both simply as a problem.

"What sort of thing did you think I could tell you?"

"I don't know. If we knew exactly, we could've just asked. I guess, though, that we would have been interested in anything that indicated what they knew or how they knew it."

"Well, Benda said that they knew about 'the Moldau' for recognition, and the striped tie."

"And, obviously, the electronic coding device. You want to go through it all again? We've got the time."

"Sure. Where?"

"Start right with the first time you met Benda. Do every session you had with him."

They stopped long enough to get coffee and a bag of hamburgers to go, and for Talley to call Simson. Talley drove again so that Hovey could give his full attention to remembering.

Hovey again reached the meeting in which Benda had confronted him with the Czech's knowledge of the recognition protocol.

"Now, there's something I don't understand. If they knew what the recognition signals were going to be, why didn't they just arrest the real contact—that MacDonald? Why did they set me up at all?"

"I guess because MacDonald wouldn't have confessed. He's a former air force flyer, and he'd accepted the mission knowing the risks. I think he'd just have denied it and stonewalled. You know—Czerny gave him these innocent-looking papers; how was he to know?

"But by tricking you, by giving you a grievance—and you didn't have much love for the agency to begin with—well, it was easy to get a really good, damaging confession out of you."

"Yeah. It was very easy."

"It's understandable, Larry. You were tricked."

"Yeah. Very neatly. One of the really neat parts was that Benda kept warning me against confessing."

"How?"

"By telling me that the CIA would have it in for me if I did."

"What did he say, exactly?"

"Oh, he warned me. I don't remember exactly. The first time was after he'd confronted me about the recognition, and told me I was going to get thirty years. And then, when I started to give my statement, he said something . . . 'In fairness, I must tell you that . . .' And so forth.

"And then at the end—I mean a week or two later, after the meetings where we'd worked down into exactly what I was going to say at the trials—he said again, 'Lawrence, I wish to warn you once more'—let's see—'that although this confession will result in leniency here, it will be regarded with severity when you return to America again.'

"And I said something like, 'Just let them try! When I tell

the newspapers about how the CIA used me, those people won't dare touch me.'

"And he said that the implications of my story would damage the credibility of the CIA more than I could imagine. And for that reason, everyone in the agency would have a common interest in trying to prevent me from telling it.''

Talley grunted.

"What?''

"I don't know. Did he ever say anything like that again?''

"No. Not exactly. When he offered me the job lecturing at the institute, he said that it would probably count against me when I got back.''

"Nothing else about discrediting the agency?''

"No. What's the point?''

"I don't know. I mean, 'what's the point?' is the point. Doing the 'fair-minded' routine was one thing. From your record he must have assumed that you wouldn't let yourself be pressured, so he was pretending to let it all come from you. So being 'fair-minded' and warning you was part of that. But why underline the agency's credibility thing? And he really said *everyone* in the agency would have a *common* interest?''

"He didn't stress *everyone* that way.''

"But I can't help stressing it. Having to defend against your story—the only way they could do that would be by telling the truth about your being set up, which suggests the possibility of a penetration of the agency. Concealing that there is a penetration is the one thing that *everyone* in the agency—including their own agent—would be completely agreed on. You see?''

"So you think his saying what he did means there is an agent? No. He was playing me. He was planting that.''

"It would seem to be a strong possibility. Saying what he

did seems unnecessary, except that he would know that when the agency debriefed you, you'd remember, and it would seem to confirm that there is a penetration.''

"But right now it's really suggesting to us that it was a trick, and so there isn't.''

"Well, it would be a gamble on his part. Right now you're believing the agency's story on this. You stopped fighting this morning, when I talked to you. Why? Did the fact the agency got you out help convince you?''

"Yes. Probably so. When I realized the risks that people took, I guess I realized they wouldn't do that just to keep me quiet.''

"So, you're cooperating, and you accept that Benda was tricking you. But if you'd just gotten home after being released by them, after serving your time, and you were still hostile to the agency and believing in him, then when what he said came out you'd be giving it a different coloration. It might seem more like a slip on his part. Like I say, it would be a gamble; it might not work. But what has he got to lose? Our hypothesis is that the penetration ploy is only icing on the cake anyway.''

"But then why do they want to kill me? I mean, we are assuming the point of holding Jane is to get me where they can kill me.''

They were on the Jersey Turnpike now, but not north far enough to see the lights on the refineries and chemical plants. A little band of blue-green translucency still showed above the western horizon; otherwise all was dark over and across the featureless landscape. The conclusion of Hovey's question distracted both men from the question itself. For some time each of them looked ahead: Talley, because he was driving, reading the meaning of rear lights of the cars ahead automatically; Hovey not seeming really to see them at all.

"Why would they want to do that," Hovey said, coming back first, "if he'd planted something he wanted me to carry back."

"I don't know. If I'm wrong about Benda planting that 'everyone,' then there are things like that they're afraid you might tell us. Or—I now suspect more strongly—they could believe that having us think there's something they're worried about, without our ever finding what it is, would serve their purpose better than any plants.

"It's like a game: the escaped prisoner and the posse. The posse has to decide which trail the prisoner really took, and which one he left some false tracks on. If one set of tracks is almost rubbed out, does that mean he really went that way and tried to hide it, or that he's trying to trick them?"

"A game," Hovey said.

•

"Tom?"

Talley came awake with a jerk. "I was asleep. I'm sorry."

"It's okay. I'm going to need directions. Didn't you say we get off on Three-oh-two? It's coming up."

"Yeah. Bear right. You want me to drive?"

"I'm okay. I'd rather."

"I'm sorry I fell asleep. I didn't mean to."

"No reason you shouldn't have. But . . . now that you're back again . . . I've been thinking. I don't think your plan is going to work."

"Why not?"

"He won't come out of your house. That's not how exchanges are made—at least not in any of the spy novels I've read. The two people who are going to be exchanged start from opposite ends of a bridge, meet in the middle, and keep going toward the people who are waiting for them. That way neither side can keep the guy they've got and get the other one, too. He won't come out, or let Jane go until he sees me coming in.''

They swung up and around the exit ramp.

''Well, then . . .'' Talley began, and faltered.

''Yes?''

''I'm thinking.''

''I've *been* thinking. I don't see us pulling any kind of trick. I'm going to have to—''

''I'll think of something.''

''Okay! You think of something. If you think of something that's not as half-assed as your first idea, you be sure to let me know! In the meantime, here's *my* plan. You go in, like you said, to check that Jane is all right, and to arrange the exchange like I said. And you tell this guy not to shoot me right off when I get to him, because I've got a message for him.

''Now, what I'm going to tell him is this: I'm going to tell him the truth about how we got to come here, and that you are in touch with the CIA, who are shadowing us, by radio, and that you are armed. I'm going to tell him how impressed we all are with the things the Czechs have done to keep me from being interviewed, so if impressing us is his mission, he's accomplished it. But now his personal survival depends on not going all the way—on keeping me alive as his ticket out.

''I'm going to ask you—after you're sure Jane is out of range—to drive up close enough so he can't get away without your being able to shoot him or run him down or something.

And if he comes out without me, I'm going to ask you at least to get the son of a bitch for me.''

"What if he comes out with you?"

"You follow him until he leaves me—unharmed—and goes for it alone. If he does that, you surely let him. Which is what I'll tell him you'll do.''

They came to a narrow bridge, and crossed into New Hampshire. No other vehicles were on the roads; no lights showed in the windows of houses in the town on the other side.

Talley nodded to acknowledge his agreement. "It's a good plan, Larry. It's better than mine. You're right.''

Hovey nodded, but his acknowledgment seemed to be to himself.

CHAPTER 14

When the black of night had faded enough so that he could see at least to the far woods, beyond the river, Chip Bolander climbed back up near the top of his tree and looked around with his binoculars. He took fifteen minutes to do it: a scan all around, then holding on one sector, then a scan, then another sector. He satisfied himself that no one had moved up on him during the night in those directions. They hadn't come through the woods behind him, either, at least not as far as his perimeter.

Talley's white clapboard house sat on a gentle hump looking over fields cleared nearly 360 degrees around it. To the south and west the meadows and pastures of the neighboring farm spread on both sides of the road, open for at least a mile. There were woods half a mile away to the north—from which Bolander had watched Talley and Jane go down to their picnic by the river—and around and all along to the east, solid woods, with no road in them, continuing up to the mountains that blocked that side. Only one fingerlike patch of trees pointed from the forest to the house along either side of the brook.

From high in a huge pine tree just back beyond the edge of Talley's lawn, Bolander could see anyone who might come toward him along the road or over the fields, or who might merely lurk at the edge of the woods anywhere around. He had secured the narrow stretch of perimeter behind him that he couldn't see into by running a long line of black button thread from tree to tree, through staples hammered into the trees, just at shin level above the ground. If the line were run into—broken, or even pulled—it would sound a little signal near him.

Bolander had left the house for his position in the tree almost as soon as he had talked to Talley the afternoon before. Giving Talley the idea he would be inside the house had been just one more way of giving himself the advantage.

He didn't really try to figure which possibilities were more likely: that Talley would come by himself; that he'd come bringing Hovey; that he or they would come with the troops behind them; or whether it would be just the troops. It didn't really matter. Someone would come, and then he'd play it for what it was worth: kill Hovey, do a scene with Talley, or just fade away. Best, better, or still okay—the point made.

Bolander did have rough plans formed for each of the contingencies, of course. In the event that Talley did show up with the professor, he imagined that they would stop a little distance from the house, and Talley would come in to check on the woman and try to negotiate. Plan A would be to pick off the professor outside, while he was still in the car, or when he got out to go to the house after they discovered that the coast seemed to be clear. Should that not work, and Hovey get inside, Plan B would be to go in after him. There were similar strategies to deal with the other possibilities.

Whatever happened, he would fade at the end anyway: back through the trees and underbrush along the brook, then into the forest. They'd have to get an entire company back there to keep him from slipping through. They couldn't begin to do that without him knowing. So he'd get by. After he'd gone a mile he'd bury the Beretta and the webbing holster that held it just under his left armpit. He had gear, a pack, food; he was prepared to walk for a couple of days, using whatever logging roads he could find, bushwhacking, until he reached the Appalachian Trail at a point far from Talley's house. There he would bury the suit of cammies he'd bought in a surplus store, and emerge as a hiker in trail pants and sweatshirt. The trail, he'd read, ran from Maine to Georgia; and at this season it would be heavily trafficked with hikers. He'd just walk away.

At about four forty-five he climbed down and went into the house. He had done so at irregular intervals throughout the preceding evening and night to check on Jane.

"Now, honey, you've got your choice," he'd told her. He had secured her with makeshift handcuffs—a bicycle chain and a small padlock—to the headboard of the bed upstairs. "We'll try it that way, just around one hand. But I'm going to be coming back up to check on you, and if I see you've tried *anything* to get yourself loose, then it's going to be a spread-eagle four-points tie-down. Now, you wouldn't want that, especially since—I'm behaving myself now—but I get you flat on your back with your legs spread, why I just might not be able to control myself anymore."

That was only a threat, to give her something to think about, scare her—as he'd done with Talley. She was a nice piece, but Chip Bolander didn't have to tie them down to get his. When he was screwing he believed in letting them know who was in charge, but he wasn't a pervert or a psycho. But it wouldn't hurt to let her think he might be. He had given her a good X-ray-vision look and a leer whenever he came in.

He unlocked her and let her go to the john again, and brought up some milk and apples from the kitchen after he'd secured her once more. Bolander considered that he was in a rough line of work, but that he was a reasonably decent guy about it.

He was back in the tree by five. By five-fifteen the sky was fully light, a fine, pale blue. Because of the mountains, direct sunlight wouldn't reach even the far side of the valley for another half hour. Blueness reflected down over the landscape, tinting the farther hills a medium tone. Evergreens across the fields stood indigo against them, and a layer of mist, baby-blanket blue, lay lightly above the line of the river and over low places in the meadows. Birds had begun singing at first light. Over near the farm a cow bawled for her calf. One pickup sped along the road from south to north, and ten minutes later another. Except for those early risers, the countryside seemed still to be asleep.

At a little past five-thirty, Bolander heard a vehicle approaching from the north. So quiet was the morning that he could hear it for almost half a minute before it came into sight out of the trees. It was a sedan, and it began slowing as it approached the turnoff for Talley's house.

Bolander checked quickly around again with the glasses, then climbed down.

Hovey stopped on the road, backed in, and drove in reverse about halfway to the house, as Talley had proposed. He left the motor running. For several moments he and Talley sat silently, straining around in their seats, looking at the house. Then Talley got out. He started walking slowly toward it.

Hunkered down behind a bush at the edge of the trees, Bolander recognized him. Then he began crawling toward the car in the way he'd planned.

Beyond the drive, paralleling it, an old stone fence ran all the way down to the road. Along the section near the house Talley had let bushes grow: lilacs for their flowers, choke-cherries to bring birds. In his first reconnoitering, Bolander had seen it as a screened route he could use in getting close to the house or car.

The front door was held back by its fieldstone stop; only the screen was closed. Talley stood for a moment before opening it. He had come home, yet he felt like a stranger at the threshold of someone else's house. He went in.

"Hello," he said. Except for the hum of his freezer, which he could faintly hear from the cellar below, all was still. He was in his own house, everything familiar—the kitchen ahead of him, the shelves holding jars of vegetables from his own garden that he'd canned himself—yet everything threatened. The old floorboards betrayed his movement; the kitchen island blocked his view, might conceal his enemy.

"Hello."

"Tom?"

"Jane! Where are you?"

"In the bedroom! Tom!"

Expecting the man to dart out from behind a door and suddenly confront him gun in hand, yet unable to be cautious, Talley bounded up the stairs, raced down the short hallway and into the bedroom. "Jane! Are you all right?"

"Tom! Oh, Tom! Oh, Tom!" She was up on her knees on the bed, her whole body angled, straining toward him from her hand held behind her at the headboard, reaching with her free arm for him.

He grabbed her hand, starting to clasp her to him. Then

he realized that she was bound to the headboard. "My God!" For an instant he almost tore at the chain to rip it from around the headboard bar, to rend the links by the force of his anger and fear. Then rationality took hold again. "Where is he?"

"I don't know. Outside somewhere. He was in here just a few minutes ago."

"I'll be right back."

He leaped down the stairs again, ran to the door. He waved frantically, shouting, "Larry! Come on! Hurry! Hurry!"

Hovey had already pushed off the submachine gun's safety switch and cocked the weapon. He touched it again, where it lay on the seat beside him, then shifted into reverse and floored the pedal. He actually shot past Bolander, who was crawling, flat, behind a low place in the wall beyond the cover of the bushes.

Bolander shoved himself up to his knees. Hands locked together around the pistol butt, arms out full-length, he aimed at Hovey's head as he raced by.

The windshield suddenly went opaque before Hovey's eyes in a crazy lacework of white lines. In one instant he hit the brake and the door handle, grabbed the gun, and fell sideways out of the car. Twisting, he looked under the car and brought the submachine gun to point in that direction. He never actually saw Bolander, but he squeezed off a short burst anyway. The bullets ricocheted and shattered chips from along the top of the wall.

Scrambling to his knees, then to his feet, crouching, he sprinted toward the house, crablike, firing bursts back and forth in a short arc. Most of the bullets hit the car. None hit Bolander, who was flat on his face up against the base of the wall, but the firing kept him there long enough for Hovey to reach the door.

Just before he reached it, he realized the gun was not firing any longer, and he flung it away as he leaped over the threshold.

Talley had been standing by the doorway, holding open the screen door. He bolted through after Hovey, slamming the paneled door and snapping home the lock.

"Quick! Upstairs!" he shouted, shoving Hovey along ahead of him. "Wait!" Talley dashed across to the back room off the kitchen, where he kept tools, and came out again with his bolt cutter. "Here! Jane's chained to the bed! Cut her loose!"

As Hovey ran up the stairs, Talley slammed shut and locked the kitchen door, too. He had no illusion that doing it would lock out danger. The man could break in through a window, but they would hear that and know he was coming.

Then he raced upstairs. There was a telephone in his office.

As soon as the firing had stopped, Bolander had raised himself just enough to see over the wall, ready to drop again, shoot, or sprint if—as he expected—men who had lain on the floor of the car were piling out looking for him.

There were no men. He listened. There were no sirens, no vehicles roaring down the road, no helicopter suddenly speeding in from behind the mountains.

The submachine gun had been an unexpected wild card, but not one from a stacked deck. With growing confidence he lifted his head farther and scanned the area more fully. He saw the gun where Hovey had thrown it away. He grinned. Obviously, however they had gotten the weapon, they had not been supplied with reloads.

They might have gotten other weapons too, though. He would be cautious. However, despite the excitement, everything was really under control: it was simply time to move to Plan B.

When Hovey reached the top of the stairs, he could see into a room on his left that he identified at once as an office. He spun around to look down the short hallway. At its end were two doorways, one on either side. In three quick steps he was close enough to see they were bedrooms.

"Jane?" he called.

"Larry?" Her voice came from the room on his left.

He rushed in. He saw her on the bed, saw her arm outstretched behind her, the chain around her wrist.

"I'll get you loose." The chain cut easily. Freed, her arm dropped of its own weight. She sat back on her heels, hands in her lap, unconsciously clasping and squeezing the numb hand with the other. He smiled at her for one moment, then whirled to race out into the hall again.

Creeping on hands and knees Bolander made his way along behind the wall. He continued to be careful even when he reached the place where the bulk of the woodshed put him in a sector blind from the house.

He listened again. The birds were singing, twittering, cheeping. One sounded like it was laughing. After a moment he realized he could even hear the brook rippling. But there were no sounds to suggest danger.

He got onto his haunches, then rose slowly until he was standing behind the bushes. The camouflage fabric broke his shape. When he moved, the motion seemed no more than a bough stirred by a breeze. With his pistol held close to his body so that he could turn and fire quickly in any direction through the foliage, he pushed between two branches, and smoothly, like something still more plant than human, angled himself over the wall.

Back in a crouch from which he could spring any way, he ran for the corner of the woodshed.

Talley stood with the phone to his ear for several seconds

before realizing he heard no sound, before realizing he had dialed the emergency number without actually hearing a dial tone. He slammed the receiver down, spun away from the desk, grabbed up his swivel chair, carried it out into the hall in two quick strides, and hurled it down the stairs. He saw Hovey. "Throw stuff down the stairs! Barricade!"

As Talley ran back to his office, Hovey dashed into the bedroom again. He seized the small table that stood beside the head of the bed. "We're barricading the stairs! Help!"

Jane sprang from the bed, carried out the straight-backed chair, and threw it over the banister as Hovey had done with the table. Talley heaved the foam pad from his couch down on the growing pile. "More!" he shouted as he turned back toward the office. Hovey was already heading for the bedroom again. Jane ran into the guest room.

Hovey scanned around the bedroom to see what he might take next. Suddenly he focused on the wall beyond the bed and saw, hanging from one of a row of Shaker pegs there, Jane's wine-colored robe. Next to it was a lavender sweat shirt he knew. His eyes swept farther along the wall to a dresser. On it were her jewelry box, a bottle he recognized as her perfume, the photograph of her parents.

Up against the woodshed Bolander shifted to the proper grip on his pistol—one hand clasping the other over the butt, the weapon held pointing upward beside the top of his head. He went around the corner and along close to the back side. At the next corner he dropped to one knee, then duck walked beyond the woodshed, up against the house itself, under the windows on that side.

Something crashed inside the house, like a packing case tumbling down a flight of stairs. Sure, Bolander thought, instantly understanding Talley's device. Another crash followed. Nice, he thought. Let them block themselves in, right where I'll know where they are.

At the far corner of the house, steps led down to the cellar door—which he had made certain was not locked.

Hovey understood at once, yet disbelieving, rejecting, he turned to look at the wall to his left, at the man's robe hanging there, and then to the other dresser that stood opposite the doorway, at the masculine accessories on it.

He swept the pillows and down comforter together in his arms, wheeled back into the hall. Talley was turning after throwing down a small table. Jane stood in the other bedroom doorway, holding a chair.

"You bastard! You bitch!" Hovey shouted and dumped the bedding into the stairwell. He ran into the bedroom again and began pulling at the mattress. He got it off the bed, started to drag it toward the door. It buckled and jammed in the opening.

Talley had been frozen for one moment. Then he forced himself into action again. He had carried everything he could from his office. He started for the guest room. He saw Hovey's predicament, grabbed the end of the mattress.

"You son of a bitch! You brought me here to get me killed!"

"No, I—"

"Pull!"

Together they dragged and heaved the mattress over the railing.

"I think that's enough," Talley said. "Get back into the bedroom." He caught Jane's arm, pushed her ahead of him. Hovey came in behind them.

"What's happening?" Jane asked.

"He was outside. He may come in after us." Talley kept his mind only on the danger, but he couldn't look at Hovey as he explained. "If he comes in, he'll have to climb over that barricade. Maybe we can hit him with something. Or go out the window. He can't stay around here. We'll be all right. We just have to wait.''

Bolander went down the cellar steps, fast, and sidestepped to be out of the frame of the doorway. He was sure they'd all be upstairs, but a trained man does the drill. Then he paused to let his eyes adjust to the gloom. That took only a moment: light came through the doorway and the high narrow windows from a sky brightening almost white just ahead of the sun about to appear over the ridge.

He crossed the cellar to the stairs that led up to the back room off the kitchen. His steps made a slight crackling on the gritty concrete floor—Talley, he thought, should sweep his cellar more often—but nothing that might have been heard except by someone ear-to-door at the top of the stairs.

There was no one listening at the top of the stairs to hear Bolander's weight come carefully onto each tread, to hear the one that always squeaked when stepped upon.

Bolander squatted near the top to look through the keyhole of the lock that Talley never locked, or would have thought to lock even if he had a key for it. Seeing no one in the pantry-storage-tool room, Bolander went into it and toward the kitchen door.

That door was half ajar, as Talley had left it after getting the bolt cutter. Bolander couldn't hear any sound now from the floor above. Swaying back and forth he looked to be sure no one was in sight in the kitchen. He came up to the doorway, checked again, then stepped quickly into the room, his arms swinging down to point the pistol straight out in front.

For several moments Talley, Jane, and Hovey stood just inside the bedroom doorway, listening. There was no sound of danger from below.

"Well," Hovey said finally, softly. "Isn't this cozy."

"I'm sorry, Larry," Jane said. "I wanted to write to you, but we thought it was better, while you were . . . there."

"Thank you. That was very thoughtful . . . considerate . . . of you. I mean, I've been gone for nearly five months. God knows, you couldn't be expected to go all that time without screwing, but it was really considerate of you to do it without letting me know."

"Larry . . ."

"It was really nice of you, while I was rotting away in prison, to let me go on thinking I had somebody to come back to."

"Larry, you know—before you left we—"

Hovey had taken a step backward, away from her. He wheeled on Talley. "And it was really great of you, Tom, to help me get away and get up here. You're a true-blue pal."

"I couldn't— Later. We'll talk about it later. Listen, see if you hear anything downstairs."

Bolander saw the stairs were barricaded, as he had expected. He heard the voices. He smiled to himself, backed silently to the pantry and then crept down to the cellar again, and to the outer door.

For several minutes the three upstairs stood silent, tense. Still they heard nothing.

"You could have written," Hovey whispered. "You could have told me. You weren't doing it for *me*. You had to deceive me because you *never* have the guts to stand up—"

"That's not—"

"I don't want to hear—"

"You *never* want to hear anything—"

"Shut up! Just shut up!"

"Both of you shut up!"

"Don't you tell me— You goddamned fucking hypocrite! You lied to me, and used me—"

Three muffled shots shocked them all.

"What was that!"

"Gunshots."

Talley stepped cautiously into the hallway.

"Tom—"

"It must have been in the cellar. I'm going to check the windows. Larry, look out from the guest room."

Keeping well away from the stairwell, Talley went down the hall, looked from the hall window and then from the ones in his office. He returned to the hall. Hovey was coming from the guest room. "Nothing," he said.

Bolander stood just outside the cellar door, ready to spring up the steps, and watched the fuel oil, spouting from the three holes he had made in the tank, spread across the cement floor. He took out his Zippo lighter. He had quit smoking ten years before, but a well-prepared man always has a reliable source of fire.

Precisely because the quiet explosion and continuous distant roar sounded so much like his oil burner firing, Talley didn't realize at once what the sound was. Hovey did. "He's blown up something! He's started a fire!"

For an instant the three of them stood frozen.

"We'll have to go out the window," Talley said.

"That must be what he wants," Jane said.

"He's going to get it," said Hovey. "See if we can see where he is. He can't watch all sides." He went to the bedroom window.

"Look from the guest room, Jane," Talley said as he started down the hall again. "But try not to show yourself."

Bolander was back behind the screen of shrubs again. He now strongly doubted they had other weapons inside, but he wasn't taking unnecessary chances. By keeping low and trotting from one end of a fifty-foot stretch to the other, he could keep reasonable cover while watching three sides of the house and enough of the area beyond the fourth to spot them before they had gone far if they came out there.

Talley saw him. "He's back behind the wall."

Hovey started to raise the bedroom window screen. "Then out here and run like hell," he called back.

"No. He's moving. He can see around the house."

"We'll have to chance it. We can't stay."

"No. Wait. He can't see the side of the house right behind the woodshed. If we drop down there we can hide behind it."

"It's going to burn too."

"Not for a while. The whole house won't be in flames for a while. He can't wait out there forever. People will come."

Smoke now poured from the downstairs windows. It must be rising up the stairwell, too. Even though flames might not have burned through the ground-floor floorboards yet, the people couldn't stay inside much longer. Bolander tried to figure how much longer he could wait. He gave it another three minutes.

Still they hadn't appeared, running across the field, trying to keep the house between them and him until they were out of range. The smoke now rose in a black column straight up into the clear air. Even way out here in the sticks somebody would see. Somebody would come. He had made his thirty-five thousand bucks by what he'd done already. He shouldn't be greedy.

On the other hand, a few more minutes could mean another forty. They had to come out. Suddenly he got a picture.

Again he came over the wall and scuttled across to the woodshed. In his imagination he saw the three of them huddled, either behind the woodshed or against the fourth side of the house he hadn't been able to watch. Them and him trying to outwait each other. He prowled along the side of the woodshed, the pistol again gripped in both hands, pointing up beside his head.

Talley stood nearest the corner, then Jane, and Hovey on the other side of her, their backs against the clapboards. The fire roared and crackled; they heard no sound above it.

Bolander reached the corner. He put his back to the wall, set his feet, then suddenly pivoted, bringing the gun down.

Talley was right there. In shocked reflex he hit at the weapon and threw himself at Bolander, clasping one arm around him, trying with the other and with his body to force the gun away.

"Run!" Hovey shouted, grabbing Jane's hand, trying to drag her after him.

Talley and Bolander wrestled for a moment. Bolander twisted, forced the muzzle of the pistol toward Talley, and fired.

Jane whirled, her hand breaking loose from Hovey's grip.

"No!" he shouted as she took a step away from him. He tried to seize her hand again, but without looking at him she flung it away.

Talley's knees had buckled. For another instant he clung with his arms around Bolander, until Bolander kneed him away.

Hovey spun and sprinted. He rounded the corner of the house even as Bolander swung the pistol and fired after him.

Jane stood, hands over mouth, staring at Talley who seemed to stare back at her sightlessly.

At once, Bolander leaped to grab her. He spun her around and jammed the pistol muzzle into her back. "Hovey! Come back! I'll kill her!" He pulled her back along the woodshed to the driveway. He didn't see Hovey running toward the road, assumed he must have kept going around the other side of the house and jumped the wall. "Hovey!" he shouted. "You can hear me. You're not out of it. I'll kill her! Come back here!"

Talley tried to raise himself from where he had fallen sitting against the wall. One little part of his mind seemed detached somehow, as though observing from outside and taking notes. While the instant pain and the knowledge of being shot had momentarily stunned him, now his only sensation around the wound in his abdomen was wetness. He had read that soldiers wounded in battle went on fighting and didn't even know they'd been hit until later. The front of his shirt, the top of his trousers, were soaked with blood, but it wasn't spurting.

He considered all that as he brought his legs up, rolled on the pivot of his stiffened right arm, and got up onto his knees. He swayed there and almost toppled sideways, but touched the wall and kept himself fixed. Then he got a foot under him and pushed, sliding up the wall until he was standing.

The corner of the woodshed, the lawn, everything he saw dissolved into red, darkened to black. He kept his cheek pressed to the wall and didn't fall. Gradually the blackness thinned, and the house materialized again.

Bolander scanned left and right. "Hovey, it's you or her!"

Talley heard. He staggered forward, turning himself around, and shambled toward the driveway.

"Come back here, Hovey, or I'll kill her!"

Jane twisted suddenly so that although Bolander still held her upper arm and still pointed the pistol at her head, she faced him. "He won't do it," she said. Her tone was not of pleading. She seemed to be correcting a misguided student. "He knows about Tom and me. He won't come back."

"Shut up!"

Jane looked at Bolander squarely. He recognized her expression as one of contempt. He shouted again, "Hovey, it'll be on your head. I'll kill her, and it's on your head! Come back here!"

"Don't do it, Larry!" Jane shouted.

For the first time wild emotion overmastered Bolander's calculation. "You bitch!" he yelled, striking down on Jane's head with the pistol barrel. She sank to the ground at his feet.

He took a step back and pointed the gun at her head once more. "Your last chance, Hovey! I'm going to count—" He heard the last two running footfalls on the soft lawn just too late to turn completely. He was wheeling when Hovey, sprinting out from the woodshed, cannonaded into him.

Bolander was hurled forward, falling facedown. He got his left arm under him to break his fall, but Hovey crashed down full length on top.

Bolander's right arm was outstretched; the forearm struck the ground hard, breaking his grip on his pistol. And Hovey smashed down again and again with the heel of his fist on the back of Bolander's hand. But as he raised his arm for the third blow, Bolander tried to fling his own arm up and roll. Hovey struck again, and the gun was knocked from the loosened grip.

Again Bolander flung up his arm and twisted. He half rolled Hovey backward, half pulled himself from underneath. He got free enough to strike with his own fist down on Hovey's ribs, then elbowed him sharply in the chest. Then he rolled forward again, reaching out for the pistol.

Hovey flung himself across Bolander, his own hand just beyond the other man's. He touched the gun, grabbed the barrel between thumb and fingertips, pulled it toward him, then flung it spinning away.

Bolander caught Hovey's outstretched arm, rolled, and

was free. He scrambled to his feet to face Hovey, who had done the same.

Talley stopped for an instant before stepping away from the woodshed. He heard grunts and gasps.

Bolander got his hands up and moving, and was surprised when Hovey did the same. He was amazed to see that the egghead not only would fight, but that he could. He was not worried, though; if he hadn't written the book himself, he knew it backward and forward.

Talley stepped out from the woodshed.

Bolander feinted, struck, parried, took a blow, got in another. Hovey had had some lessons, Bolander could tell, but he was strictly amateur night. It wasn't necessary to go grab-ass scrambling in the grass for the gun. Bolander faked a kick, got in close, took a jab on his shoulder to open Hovey's guard, and got him full under the ear with the flattened side of his hand.

Talley saw the two men first, because they were upright, moving. The sun had risen above the mountain ridge, lighting them from behind while they swayed and backed and side-stepped as though performing some ritual dance. Against the brightness of sunlit dew sparkling on the grass, the figures seemed almost as two-dimensional as their long shadows that swept and thrust, joined and parted over the lawn.

For an instant the shadows overlapped, making a shape that pointed. Talley saw Jane sprawled where she had fallen. He nearly ran to her. But the fury that suddenly raged more fiercely than grief raised his eyes to the men again and sent him lurching toward them.

Hovey staggered from the blow to his head. He kept himself together just enough to weave and hold up his guard. Bolander came in, swung a kick, and caught Hovey hard in the ribs. The blow doubled him. Bolander hit him twice in the head, and he sank to his knees.

Bolander waited for a second, watching to make sure there was no faking. Then he stepped in for the kill.

And then Talley, stumble-running, swung his arms out to the side, letting the handle slip through his hands to its length, clutching it again at its end. In continuous motion he swung back and up full over his head and brought the splitting maul down with all his strength.

•

When Hovey got back from running to the nearby farm for help, flames were pouring from the house's windows. Talley was still sitting with his back to it, by Jane, where they had moved her. He was shielding her eyes from the sun with his hand.

"How is she?"

"I think she's all right," Talley said softly.

Hovey moved so that he could look into her eyes. She saw him, focused on him, half smiled. She seemed fuzzy, but her eyes appeared normal. "Is she . . . Are you nauseous?"

She seemed a little confused but made her lips form "no."

"No skull fracture, then," Hovey said. He straightened, looked off across the now sunny meadow toward the road. "They had already called in the fire alarm. I told them to send an ambulance, too. They should be here soon."

"You didn't run away," Talley said weakly. He was becoming light-headed, and there was a ringing in his ears. "Thank you."

"I didn't run away. I hid in the woodshed. I figured I'd catch him off guard."

"When you ran, he was going to kill her."

"Not right away. Not if he thought he could use her to get me back."

"He might have."

"I knew he wouldn't."

"You might have been wrong."

"I wasn't."

"Then why did you stay?"

"I thought he might kill her later."

Talley was silent for a moment. "Why did you care?" he asked.

"You have to ask that, don't you? Why did you bring me up here without telling me the truth? You thought if I knew I wouldn't come, because I wouldn't care about her anymore. That must be the system you operate on. Well, it's not the system I operate on."

"I'm sorry. I didn't know. I couldn't risk . . ."

"You deceived me for her. Not because it was *right* to save her, but just for what she means to *you*. That's how it was, isn't it?"

"Yes."

"All for the love of Jane. And you'd do it all again, wouldn't you."

"Yes. Oh, oh, yes."

"Yes. Anything for love, for *my* love, for *me*. That's why the world is as rotten as it is. And it's going to be that way until people start doing what they *know* is *right*! Until they . . ." But he realized Talley wasn't listening.

AFTERWORD

Chip Bolander was identified as a former agent who had been discharged after repeatedly exceeding agency guidelines while working with government forces in Honduras. He could have been contacted by anyone who learned of his anger toward the agency. However, there was no direct or circumstantial connection between him and any of the agency officials under suspicion.

Investigation established that there was an official named Dr. Benda who might appropriately have had administrative charge of the Czerny–Hovey trials without participating in the courtroom proceedings. A photograph, however, showed him to be a short, plump, balding man probably in his mid-forties. Further investigation revealed that the man who had prepared Professor Hovey was Jan Suk, a colonel in the counterintelligence section.

Given the nature of Czerny's activities and the device of securing Professor Hovey's confession by gaining his confidence, the role-playing by Colonel Suk might not have been

seen as especially significant. However, that such a man
would inadvertently have let slip to Hovey anything suggesting a penetration was beyond belief. Uncovering this aspect
of the affair seemed to justify abducting Hovey from prison.

For these reasons, along with the complete lack of any
positive evidence, the investigating committee gave as their
formal opinion that the affair was a stratagem by the Czechs,
and that there was no penetration within the CIA. The report
was accepted, although afterward some members of the Defense Intelligence Agency seemed even more reluctant than
usual to share their information, and two CIA officials believed privately that they were later denied assignments and
promotions for which they were qualified.

Talley's further assistance was not invited by the committee in reaching its decision, and Walter Simson did not reveal
that he had had a private discussion with Talley before the
final meeting. Talley received no official thanks for the work
he had done, but neither were any charges brought.

In the period following his arrest, it had been made clear to
Janos Czerny that since he had been caught red-handed, and
since Professor Hovey was going to confess, there would be
no suspense about the outcome of his trial. Because he would
not be permitted to rise and—speaking with righteousness
and power—justify his actions on the basis of higher law (as
he had so often imagined himself doing), there would be little
drama of any kind. Therefore, he allowed his friends and
professional colleagues to persuade him to accept his fate in
dignified meekness.

In recognition of that docility, and in deference to the
concern of the world about such a great, old artist, Czerny's
sentence to life at hard labor was commuted to incarceration
in an institution like the one where Professor Hovey had been
held. Furthermore, after a while the authorities suggested to

him that good behavior and an attitude of contrition on his part might lead them to permit him to pay his debt by producing works of dramatic art that would demonstrate the glory of Czech culture. Czerny could see that such work would be a greater service to humanity than sterile defiance.

Although an occasional monitoring of the activities of Monsieur D'Avignon was kept in effect, the surveillance on him was dropped. In the spring of the year after Janos Czerny's trial, he made his debut as a director with the production in Lyon of a new play. It was a great success, and was brought to Paris for a limited run to great critical acclaim. When interviewed, D'Avignon was modest about his accomplishment. He pointed out that he had been a theater artist for nearly thirty years, and should have been expected to have knowledge beyond his specialty. And, he added self-effacingly, he had always felt that the mystique of the director was overexaggerated.

Although Professor Hovey's return and his story were not as dramatic as he had imagined, he still had a good tale to tell. He was interviewed by the newspapers and television, and so gave a synopsis of it while working on his book. With the help of an associate writer, the book was ready in eight weeks, and its appearance in paperback and in the *Reader's Digest* had been contracted before its publication.

The book brought him talk show appearances in which he was as articulate and witty as he had known he would be. These led to a lecture tour. Since his experience had proved to be of the duplicity of the Czechs rather than of the CIA, he found himself speaking more often to conservative groups and at bible colleges than to the audiences he had expected. As a result of acquaintances he made while lecturing, though, when he was approached about a film of his adventure, he was able himself to identify possible backers, which helped secure him an even more satisfactory financial arrangement. (In the film, with Talley's wholehearted agreement, Talley appears as a very minor figure; there is no suggestion that he had become Jane's lover, and it is Professor Hovey who—at the last moment—escapes Bolander long enough to grab the splitting maul.)

This one thing leading to another led Professor Hovey to develop another set of popular lectures on the subject of brainwashing, a book from these, a TV documentary from the book, a "dark, compelling, Kafkaesque" novel, a filmscript from the novel, and a method and manual for theater directors to use in working with actors. While he accepted residencies and guest appearances at various universities, it seemed unlikely to him that he would ever return to full-time teaching.

Throughout the next year, Jane and Talley found trying to live and work in and between her apartment and his new house far more difficult than they had imagined. Everything each needed was always in the other place. As time passed they discussed most of the alternatives: becoming suburbanites; having Jane work as a free-lance scholar from his house; finding a new college position for her somewhere where they could live in the country. The one logical possibility that did not occur to them was living apart.